MY
SISTER'S
BOYFRIEND

BOOKS BY NICOLA MARSH

MY SISTER'S BOYFRIEND

NICOLA MARSH

Bookouture

Published by Bookouture in 2024

An imprint of Storyfire Ltd.
Carmelite House
50 Victoria Embankment
London EC4Y 0DZ

www.bookouture.com

ISBN: 978-1-83618-228-3
eBook ISBN: 978-1-83618-227-6

For Sandy Barker. Thanks for the quick-fire brainstorm that resulted in this book.

PROLOGUE

I don't believe in déjà vu, but here I am again.

At the house I grew up in, a house that once made me feel safe, a house that hides too many secrets.

Home.

With another corpse.

Trembles wrack my body. I'm terrified I can't pull this off.

Protect the family I made over the family I'm born with.

But I must try.

This has to be the start for us, not the end.

So, as I see the red and blue flashing lights of the police pulling into the driveway, I make a snap decision.

I'll lie. I'll deflect. I'll cover up.

I'll do whatever it takes to protect what's mine.

ONE

BROOKE

The briny ocean breeze and the roar of the ocean crashing on the rocks below evoke pleasure and pain as I take my daily stroll along the clifftop behind our house.

Pleasure, because I have vivid memories of growing up in Martino Bay, the picture-perfect town along California's coastline with its legendary towering cliffs. Fun days at the local fair with my friends, beach parties with the high school crew, coming home to hearty meals. The crimson roadside mailbox of our house always made me smile and I loved riding my bike up the twisty driveway, the sight of our single-story stucco in terracotta signaling home. Safety.

Until it didn't.

Life was simpler then. The biggest decisions I had to make revolved around fashion, and whether I'd sneak beer or wine at the beach parties the local kids held regularly. I adored my Aunt Alice, who cooked the best buffalo wings, smoked brisket, and key lime pie, and I good-naturedly bickered over who'd have the last s'more with Freya and Lizzie, my siblings regardless of genetics. We had a curfew but could roam freely, pretending to be daredevils and joking about who'd get a speeding ticket first.

We had bonfires every week, camped beneath the stars, and teased each other relentlessly over who the new boy working behind the counter at the ice cream shop liked most. The Shomack girls were inseparable.

Until our lives fell apart.

So I have painful memories of this place too.

Of these jagged, treacherous clifftops in particular.

"Brooke, come on, we're going to be late."

Hope has snuck up behind me while I've been lost in my musings, and I turn to see a scowling twelve-year-old wearing too much makeup and a skirt that's way too short for the crisp fall chill.

I glance at my watch, relieved we've got loads of time to get to her friend Sasha's birthday party and my grumpy tween is just overeager.

"You ready to go?"

She rolls her eyes. "The gift is wrapped, so yeah, I'm ready."

I want to tell her to take off the eyeshadow, lose the lip gloss, and change into something more suitable for a backyard bonfire, but I don't. Our relationship has deteriorated lately, and I want to mend fences, not tear them down.

"You're staring at me funny," she says, patting her shoulder-length auburn hair self-consciously. "Stop it, because you're freaking me out."

"Just thinking how fast you're growing up."

Sadness swamps me at the thought because I've already missed out on so much with Hope. I missed her first tooth, her first steps, her first day at school. The first time she tied her shoelaces, the first time she won an academic prize, the first time she drew a picture of our family. So many firsts I'll never get back and I wish I could make time stand still to enjoy the upcoming years.

I've said the right thing for once, because like any preteen,

Hope wants to be twelve going on twenty, and the corners of her mouth lift.

"I'll be thirteen in four months, and I can't wait."

Like I need a reminder. She's been talking about becoming a teenager since she turned twelve.

"I'm getting old," I mutter, feeling like the most ancient thirty-year-old on the planet.

I've lived too hard, seen too much. I guess that's what living in a family full of betrayal gets you.

She chuckles and it's the sweetest sound I've ever heard. "You're still pretty cool."

"Thanks, honey," I say with a smile, and we share one of those moments I treasure when we're in total sync.

It won't last, because since Hope discovered the truth about her parentage, our relationship is fragile. Her moods change daily, and sometimes she's nothing like the sweet, loving child who welcomed me into her life two years ago.

Before she learned I'm her biological mother and blamed me for everything.

The sad thing is, Hope doesn't know the worst of it.

I've shielded her as best I can, but I'm all too aware that the more time passes, the more she may resent me when she discovers the truth.

So for now, I live a lie.

TWO

NOEL

I believe in second chances. I have to after what I've seen behind bars. Otherwise, there's no hope, and I'd be bitter and resentful like most of the inmates I did my best to avoid the last four years.

Even now, almost three months since my release from jail, I can't shake the feeling of being watched. Which is crazy, because I don't need to look over my shoulder anymore like I did in there, fearful that I'd cop a beating—or worse—for merely looking at another prisoner the wrong way.

I'd kept my head down, been civil to everyone, but that fear of being surrounded by criminals capable of anything never left me. It ate away at me for the entirety of my incarceration, leaving me watchful and jumpy even now.

And I was cold. All the time. The entire prison had been kept at frigid temperatures, as if the guards thought we'd be more compliant if we semi-froze. I spent a lot of time in my cell wrapped in a blanket, and reading, because books were my only escape from the horror of my surroundings.

Reading helped with the loneliness too. I avoided the other inmates, so I didn't make friends, and I refused visitors. I didn't need people from my past seeing me at my lowest. A reminder of the life I'd lost when I'd done the unthinkable and killed my brother.

"Noel Harwood?"

I startle and focus, finding a statuesque blonde staring at me with all-seeing eyes at the door of the annex where I attend rehabilitation classes. Her unblinking gaze makes me uncomfortable, but I hide it well. I'm used to hiding my innermost thoughts from my time in prison, where the slightest hint of vulnerability makes you a target.

"Yes, that's me."

The blonde nods and ticks my name off a list. "You're here for the art therapy class?"

I nod, stifling a groan. I would've preferred more practical classes after my release from prison, like carpentry, a useful skill to supplement my income working at the grocer stocking shelves. But while these art therapy classes aren't mandatory upon release, I'd chosen to attend because I wanted to ease back into life as a free man. I wanted to keep busy. I wanted some semblance of normality after being treated like a subhuman.

The blonde is new. I haven't seen her here before. Thankfully, this is my last session, so I don't have to tolerate the way she's staring at me through slightly narrowed eyes, judgmental and assessing. I'm used to it, being treated like a criminal. After all, that's what I am.

"I'm Lizzie and I'm teaching this class today. Annie is sick, but she should be back next week." She glances at her clipboard before looking at me again, a forced smile curving her mouth upward in the corners. "The medium we're using in class today is clay, which should be fun."

Nothing about art therapy is fun. I don't believe in the psychologist mantra that expressing feelings through art can decrease depression and increase self-worth. But I've attended this class not far from the correctional center every week since I got out, and I want to complete the program, to prove to myself —and those who run the classes—that I'm capable of seeing it through. That I am a man of my word. That I'm worthy of respect. Plus, it'll look good on my record.

"Noel? Is everything okay?"

I've been daydreaming again, something I do way too often these days, wishing I could change the past, and Lizzie is staring at me with a frown grooving her brows.

"I'm fine. Just need something to eat."

Somehow, I've said the wrong thing because her frown deepens, so I try a smile, the one that Mom used to say transformed me from sweet to angelic. It doesn't work on Lizzie.

"Head on through and help yourself to coffee and donuts, class will start in another five minutes."

"Great. Thanks."

I smile again but Lizzie glares at me like she knows something I don't. It shouldn't bother me, but it does, because since I've been released I've made it a point to show people I'm not a bad guy. That I can assimilate. That I can be trusted. That I deserve a fresh start.

That's why I've returned to Martino Bay. Because some people there might have long memories and won't question my version of the truth.

THREE

LIZZIE

People often ask me if I'm scared working with felons and I always reply, "Everyone deserves a second chance."

Being a psychologist consulting one-on-one with patients never interested me, but using my degree in art therapy is a calling I never knew I had.

Eighteen months ago, a friend from college reached out, saying the Wilks Inlet Correctional Facility was looking for a psychologist to start an art therapy program, and because of its proximity to Martino Bay, the friend had thought of me.

I'd never taught art therapy before but after doing a short course and loads of research, here I am. It's a wonderful tool to help ex-cons interpret, express, and resolve their emotions and thoughts. Art therapy fosters healing and mental well-being and I love what I do. I've used so many mediums—painting, coloring, doodling, collaging, finger painting, photography, drawing, sculpting—and each is wonderful in its own way for my students to develop self-awareness, cope with stress, boost self-esteem, and explore emotions.

I've had several hundred ex-cons come through my class over the last eighteen months and I think I've become adept at

reading people. Some are forced to be here as part of their rehabilitation and they're angry and resentful. Some are desperate
for a second chance at a normal life and they're eager to learn.
Some are curious, others exhausted by a system that robs them
of control.

Then there's Noel Harwood.

I don't know what it is about him that has me on edge.

It's nothing overt. For the duration of this class, he's been
nothing but polite. And Annie, who usually teaches this class,
would've warned me about potential troublemakers or if there
was anything off about him.

But it's a feeling, something nebulous I can't put my finger
on, that has me watching him more than the others.

He's incredibly handsome, with impeccable bone structure,
his dark hair and tan making his blue eyes pop. He appears
mild-mannered, sharing a laugh with the men either side of him
as they use clay to sculpt what they'd like to change about their
past.

But I see his eyes darting around when he thinks no one is
watching and I wonder if his affability is forced.

He catches me staring and raises an eyebrow in a silent
taunt, so I force a smile and walk to his table.

"Is there something wrong with my creation, Lizzie?"

Even his voice is well-modulated and calming, and I'm
annoyed anew that I don't know what it is about him that has
me on guard.

"Not at all, Noel." I glance at the surprisingly good SUV
he's crafted from clay. "Tell me about this car."

And there it is, a flicker of angst in his eyes before he blinks
and assumes a bland expression.

"You asked us to make what we'd like to change about our
past and this is it for me." His mouth downturns at the corners
as he points to the car, a detailed rendition of an SUV, complete
with spare tire clipped on the back, and a roof rack. "I acciden-

tally ran over my brother and killed him, and that's why I was incarcerated."

"I'm sorry for what you went through," I say, a small part of me wondering if I misjudged him.

But an accidental vehicular death would be classed as manslaughter and a misdemeanour, so why was he jailed?

"How does recreating the car make you feel?"

His lips compress in a thin line before he says, "Angry. Bitter. Filled with self-loathing."

My sympathy ratchets up. "That's why we do this. Expressing ourselves through art makes us examine how we feel and, in turn, work through conflicts that affect our thoughts, behaviors, and emotions."

He nods, his expression remorseful. "It reminds me how sorry I am for what I did to my brother," he mutters. "How I wish I could take it all back."

He sounds contrite, but he casts a sideways glance at the door, like he can't wait to get out of here. It makes me wonder if his penitence is just for show, and my sympathy wavers.

"Well, it sounds like you've got something out of these classes."

His nod is almost too eager. "Yeah. Being here every week for the last three months has grounded me. Made me feel more normal."

"Glad to hear it. Means we're doing something right."

His gaze is guileless as he locks eyes with me. "Annie's been a great teacher, but I think I've got more out of your class today than the last eleven weeks."

His stare is too intense and the skin along the nape of my neck prickles, like ants marching across it, and I resist the urge to rub it.

"Class is almost done, so you can leave your creation on the window ledge and collect it in a few days when it's dry."

"Okay, thanks."

When he carefully picks up the SUV he made and walks away, my shoulders slump in relief. I had no idea I'd been holding them rigid, an unconscious reaction to a man who makes me uncomfortable, yet I don't know why.

The next fifteen minutes are uneventful as the class winds up and the participants filter out. Thankfully, Noel leaves without interacting further and I'm cleaning up when Max, my boss and the chief psychologist who runs the program, strolls in.

"Thanks for filling in for Annie today." He grimaces. "There's a nasty flu going around."

"Yeah, I was missing a few in my class yesterday." I dry my hands on a towel and hang it on a rack near the supply closet. "There are a few interesting characters in this class."

"Yeah? How so?"

"Noel Harwood. What's his story?"

"Why do you ask? Did he do or say something?"

I shake my head. "More a gut reaction. I can usually get a read on my ex-prisoners but there's something about him that feels off."

"That's interesting." Max's mouth is grim as he perches on the edge of a desk. "Annie sings his praises, but one of the guards says Noel gave him the creeps."

"Why?"

Max shrugs. "Like you, nothing he could put a finger on. Said Noel was the model prisoner. Kept to himself. Kept out of trouble. Polite to prison officials. Appeared remorseful for his actions."

"But?"

"The guard thinks it's an act. That Noel was playing the part of a perfect prisoner, while biding his time."

An inexplicable shiver shimmies down my spine. "Biding his time for what?"

"To do whatever he wants to do when he got out."

My boss is a serious, no-nonsense kind of guy, so he

wouldn't make his proclamation lightly, and I resist the urge to rub the goose bumps off my arms.

"Have you met Noel? What do you think?"

Max's eyes screw up slightly, as if he's mulling a problem. "You know I vet all participants in the program personally, and like you, I couldn't get a read on Noel Harwood, which makes me suspicious. What's he hiding?"

Max pauses, before chuckling. "Or maybe the son of a bitch is too good-looking for his own good and makes me feel like an ugly blob next to him."

I join in Max's laughter but can't shake the feeling that something's off about Noel Harwood and I'm glad that's the last I'll see of him.

FOUR

NOEL

My earliest memories of being a twin are good. I remember Ned's and my fifth birthday party, our first day of school, our first bikes.

But I also remember my brother's first quirk: scaring people. I didn't think much of it at the time because that was Ned's thing. He loved hiding behind doors or in cupboards and leaping out, scaring Mom and me. He delighted in our screams. He laughed the time I peed my pants a little.

So when Ned's best friend, a boy named Cal, came to me in third grade and said he didn't like Ned scaring him, I defended my twin. I told Cal my brother always did silly stuff to scare me and Mom at home, and he shouldn't be worried. He should tell Ned to back off if it bothered him. And I gave him half my peanut butter sandwich and a brownie to placate him. Cal had the same lunch every day—a cheese sandwich and an apple—so he thought what I'd shared with him was the greatest thing ever. We were eating and laughing over the chocolate smudges around our mouths when Ned arrived.

I'll never forget the look on his face. An eerie stillness, like Cal had betrayed him, before he turned red from rage. He barely glanced at me, because I could still do no wrong in my twin's eyes at that stage, but the way he stared at Cal... I inadvertently leaned toward him to protect him.

But in the next second, Ned smiled and ran toward us, shoving his way between me and Cal and grabbing my half-eaten sandwich, turning his back on me so he had Cal's full attention. Another thing my brother loved, having all eyes on him: being the class clown, the one girls giggled over, the one teachers scolded. Yeah, Ned even craved negative attention.

I forgot about Cal telling me he feared Ned until two days later, when I find Cal slumped against the wall of the boys' toilets sobbing.

"Cal, what's wrong?"

He's crying so hard he can't speak, and snot mingles with tears streaking his face. Helpless, I pat his back. "Want me to get a teacher?"

He shakes his head and dashes a hand across his eyes. "He killed Ana."

I suppress a shiver. Some of the kids brought pets to school today and Cal's anaconda had been a hit. Every classmate had wanted to touch or hold Ana, making Cal the center of attention for once.

I ignore the tiny voice inside that says *And taking the attention off Ned.*

I don't want to ask who killed Ana because deep down I know. I know it with the conviction of our twin bond.

"Ned killed Ana," Cal says, tears filling his eyes again. "I saw him do it."

Sick to my stomach, I say, "Are you sure?" A stupid question because what reason would Cal have for lying?

He nods, tears trickling down his cheeks again. "Mr. Barbory put Ana's glass cage near the basketball court so my dad could pick her up after lunch." He sniffles. "I went to check on her after music and saw Ned crouched next to the cage. He'd trapped her head between a forked stick and was stabbing her with another stick..." Cal hiccups and his tears fall faster. "I thought he was my friend..."

I'm speechless. I thought Ned was envious of the attention Cal got for Ana, but to kill his best friend's pet?

So I reach for the first lie I'll tell on Ned's behalf, the first of many to come. "I'm sorry, Cal, but there's something wrong with Ned. Mom knows, and if you say anything to anyone, he'll get sent away and we'll be separated."

The tears pooling in my eyes at the thought of losing Ned are real, even if what I'm telling Cal isn't true. "He's always been petrified of snakes, and maybe he tried to pick Ana up and she struck out and he got scared so he retaliated. I'm begging you not to say anything. Just let your dad take Ana home and do a burial there. Please."

I don't like the way Cal's staring at me, as if he's scared of me too, but he eventually nods. "I won't tell anyone I saw Ned kill Ana. But my dad's going to be mad someone killed her and he'll make a fuss here at school."

"That's okay, as long as you don't say Ned's responsible." I hold out my pinkie. "It'll be our secret."

I want to vomit as Cal links his pinkie finger with mine because I'm not sure if I've done the right thing in protecting Ned.

If my twin is capable of killing his best friend's pet, what else will he do?

That night at home, I ask Ned what happened to Ana and he laughs, a chilling sound that will give me nightmares.

"That stupid snake. Cal's always trying to get me to hold it when I'm at his place, even though I've told him I hate it. So when I saw the tank by the basketball court, I wanted to see if I could do it, without having anyone witness if I chickened out."

He makes clucking noises. "Even that scaredy-cat Sally picked her up in class, so I reckoned I could do it. But when I lifted the glass flap on top of the tank, the dumb snake attacked me."

A smug smile I don't like tugs at the corner of Ned's mouth. "So I got two sticks and tried again." His snicker is unnerving. "This time, when she struck again, I was ready."

"You didn't have to kill her," I mutter, frowning at Ned's callousness.

"It was an accident." He's blasé, and shrugs. "Oh well."

He returns to reading a book, ironically about snakes in the jungle, and I'm dying to tell Mom what happened. But I already see her watching Ned closely, like she suspects something's not quite right with him, and I don't want to make things worse for my brother. Despite his quirks, I love him. And because he's different to me, it's my job to protect him.

Besides, maybe this incident is a one-off.

FIVE

BROOKE

Because of my new job and the hours it will keep me away from home, I've hired someone so Hope isn't on her own. Hazel is a godsend. She's young enough that Hope doesn't think of her as a nanny and old enough to have experience as a housekeeper. I found her via the manager at the supermarket, and her references from a family in Wilks Inlet are impeccable. She's two years younger than me and in the week that she's worked for us, she's become indispensable.

I don't trust easily, so I don't have many friends. Since my sister Freya died two years ago, I've been so focused on raising Hope and establishing a good relationship with her that I've sacrificed a lot of myself. She's my world.

I know that's a major reason why my relationship with Hope's father didn't work out. Riker wanted more from me than I was willing to give. I neglected him, and like any male, he looked elsewhere.

I just didn't expect it to be with Lizzie. Another betrayal by another sister.

Discovering Lizzie's treachery gutted me. She moved into the main house after Freya died, and we had a ball reconnecting. We cooked dinners together, streamed countless trashy series that contained more drama than our crazy lives, drank wine and chatted into the early morning on weekends, went hiking, and grew so close I thought nothing would ever tear us apart.

I was wrong.

She adores Hope and that's the only reason I let her anywhere near the house when I'm not around. I haven't seen or spoken to her in the month since I learned the truth after seeing Lizzie making a move on Riker with my own eyes, but I don't want Hope to suffer. Lizzie practically raised her alongside Freya and Aunt Alice when I wasn't around for the first decade of her life, and my daughter's happiness is all that counts.

"I'm done for the day, Brooke. Is there anything else you need before I leave?"

I glance up at Hazel and smile. "No, we're all good. Thanks, Hazel."

"Then I'll see you tomorrow." She hoists her handbag higher on her shoulder but hesitates. "Please tell me if this is out of line, but you've barely left this den all week after work and I was wondering if you'd like to come out tonight? I'm meeting a friend for a drink at that new bar in town."

Her invitation surprises me because we're not friends. I'm her employer and I barely know her. But she's made an overture and, considering I was just thinking about my lack of friends, maybe it can't hurt to meet up for a drink.

Besides, she's right. I haven't left this room much over the last seven days, other than to work, eat with Hope and hang out with her for a few hours after school. Hazel has picked up the slack, thank goodness, but I'm bleary-eyed from staring at the computer too long and a night out will do me good.

It also gives me the perfect excuse not to be around when Lizzie comes over. Hope dropped that little bombshell on me earlier and I'd been livid but hid it well. How dare Lizzie organize to catch up with Hope, knowing I'd be around?

"That sounds great. What time?"

"About eight." Hazel glances at her watch. "Is that enough time? Hope has had her dinner and is doing homework and she said your sister is popping around at seven-thirty."

It's thoughtful of Hazel to know I wouldn't normally leave Hope alone, so she's timed her invitation well.

"Eight is perfect. Thanks for the invite."

Hazel smiles. "You're welcome. See you then."

I wait until she leaves before knuckling my eyes, which are gritty from too much screen time. This new job is a godsend—doing marketing for a chain of high-end grocery stores in this pocket of California—and I know I wouldn't have it if it wasn't for Aunt Alice. My lack of qualifications didn't deter the owner, Toby, who said he's known Alice since I was little. Aunt Alice put in a good word for me and that's why I got the job. It reminds me that I haven't visited her in a while. But it's hard for me to be in the same room with her since I discovered what she did.

"Hey, Brooke, got a minute?"

I paste a smile on my face and swivel my chair to face Hope. "Sure, sweetie. Come in."

She doesn't. She leans in the doorway, gnawing on her bottom lip. "Did you and Lizzie have a fight? She's hardly round here anymore."

My heart sinks. I've done my best to shield her from so much but my twelve-year-old is intuitive.

"I've just been super busy with this new job. And Hazel said she's coming over tonight to hang out with you, right?"

She's wary but nods, her stare accusatory. "Yeah, but the three of us haven't hung out together for ages. I miss our game nights."

So much for thinking she was past those fun nights the three of us spent bickering over Monopoly and rummy.

"Once I get the hang of this job, I'll try to make more time for game nights. How does that sound?"

She shrugs. "Okay, I guess."

Maybe I shouldn't go out tonight? Then again, facing Lizzie so soon after discovering her betrayal, having to fake pleasantries, will be difficult. I need more time. Though she's broken my trust and I doubt I'll ever get it back.

"You'll have fun with Lizzie tonight," I say. "I'm going out for a drink with Hazel."

Hope visibly brightens. "I like Hazel. She's cool. But if she works for us, how come you're hanging out with her?"

Good question, but I can't tell my daughter the truth: I'm lonely because I don't trust anyone and have no friends.

"She noticed I've been working hard and probably felt sorry for me." I laugh. "How much of a sad case am I?"

Hope snickers. "Really sad, Brooke."

Her face falls and I know in an instant she's thinking about Freya. This happens occasionally, though less frequently over the last few months, thank goodness, when we'll be bantering and she'll suddenly appear sad. The first time it happened she blurted how much she missed her mom, and it gutted me. Freya had taken her obsessive jealousy of me to extremes, making me believe Hope was her child, when in reality, Hope was the baby I'd been told died at birth when I was a teenager. Freya and Aunt Alice had hidden the truth from me for a decade. They'd robbed me of so much. My sister didn't deserve Hope. And I still haven't mustered the courage to tell Hope the truth about what they did.

Instead, I'm shouldering the blame like a martyr, to make it easier on Hope. She thinks I gave her up willingly when nothing is further from the truth.

"Are you okay?" I ask, and she nods, biting her bottom lip.

"I miss Mom, I mean Freya, sometimes," she murmurs, sadness clouding her eyes. "Even though she was crazy erratic at times and could get really grumpy."

"It's okay to miss her." I stand and cross the den, relieved when she doesn't shrug off my hug. "But I'm here for you. Always."

She leans into my embrace and as I rest my cheek on the top of her head, I know the time is fast approaching when I'll tell her everything and I hope she understands.

SIX

LIZZIE

As per our agreement, I wait until I see Brooke get into her car before I cross the yard to the main house. Hope's waiting for me at the front door and I wave to Brooke as she drives away, getting a terse nod in response. It's better than nothing.

"How's my favorite girl?" I ask Hope as I envelop her in a hug.

She squirms a little and I know she'll be too old for hugs all too soon. "I'm good. Want to make sundaes and watch reality TV?"

I hate reality TV. Real life is tough and nothing like the overdramatized lives of rich people bickering for no reason. But I'll do anything for Hope.

"How about we make the sundaes, then stream a vampire flick?"

Her eyes light up. She loves paranormal stuff as much as I do. "Sounds good."

I follow her into the kitchen, and she gets the vanilla ice cream out of the freezer while I assemble our favorite toppings from the pantry: crushed hazelnuts, chocolate topping, cherries, marshmallows, and chewy caramel.

As she scoops the ice cream into two parfait glasses, she says, "Why did you move out?"

The first time she asked me this, a month ago, I made a half-hearted excuse about meeting someone on a dating app and needing my own space. But there's a shrewdness in her eyes that suggests I won't get away with a lame excuse this time.

"Because the bungalow is bigger than the other cottage I used to live in before I moved into the main house." I gesture around the kitchen. "I liked living here, but after getting back from college I needed my space, and I was lucky enough to be close by."

I hate bringing up Freya, but I want to be honest as possible because Hope is increasingly astute these days. "I only moved back into this main house temporarily after Freya died because you, Brooke, and I were grieving. But don't you think it's about time I moved out again?"

"I guess." She eyeballs me and I glimpse suspicion. "I asked Brooke if you two had a fight and she didn't answer me. Did you?"

My heart sinks. "What makes you say that?"

"Because you're only ever here when she isn't."

"We're both busy with work. Our schedules don't always match up."

She continues to stare at me for a few moments before lifting her shoulder in a dismissive shrug. "Grown-ups are weird."

I laugh and the tension holding my back rigid eases. "And precocious twelve-year-olds shouldn't ask so many questions."

"I'm going to be thirteen in a few months."

I mock shudder. "A teenager. Yikes."

She rolls her eyes but she's grinning as she pushes the lid on the ice cream tub to reseal it before sliding it back into the freezer. "How's Aunt Alice? I haven't seen her in ages."

And just like that, my relief dissipates. The last person I

want to talk about is Alice, but I know Hope is advanced for her age and this is only the start of her inquisitive questions. The older she gets, the more she'll pick up on, so I need to be careful not to lie to her, just dance around the truth.

"She's good."

Hope frowns and crosses her arms. "Brooke's new job is keeping her way too busy. Maybe you can take me to see Aunt Alice?"

I know what Brooke's response to that will be: hell no. So I reach for an excuse too. "I'm happy to, sweetie, but I've just taken on extra classes at the correctional facility, so it might be a little while."

Her resigned expression, like she's used to adults letting her down, makes my heart ache. "Okay," she says, but it's not, and I silently curse Brooke for driving a wedge between us.

I apologized for what I did. And in the grand scheme of things, my embarrassing slip-up with Riker was nothing. It wasn't like we slept together. She needs to forgive me so our little family can reunite.

We haven't spoken in a month, and if Brooke knew the truth, she'd understand. I know it's my fault, after what I did that drunken night, and considering Brooke doesn't trust easily, she feels my betrayal is unforgivable.

I would never intentionally hurt her, and I wanted to explain at the time: the bad day at work with Grant Litt, a prisoner who'd almost assaulted me, the fear that affected me more than it should have so I drank that night to forget, how the vulnerability exacerbated my loneliness, the kindness in Riker's eyes as he listened to me offload.

I don't scare easily but what Grant had done—waiting until the class emptied before pinning me into a corner of the classroom when I'd been putting tools away in a cupboard, bracing his arms over me so I could smell his pungent body odor, leering at me as his creepy gaze stripped me naked—I haven't been the same since.

I relied on alcohol that night to wash away the memory of feeling helpless, of realizing that no matter how brave I am there may come a time when one of the ex-cons I rehabilitate might turn on me.

Making a move on Riker had been foolish but I'd been craving protection from a strong man who's inherently good. A man far removed from those I deal with daily.

I'm hoping there'll come a time one day soon that Brooke will let me explain.

We've been through enough trauma to last a lifetime.

It's times like this I miss Alice. Our estrangement is necessary after what she did, but I wish I could confide in her like I used to. She'd been a good mom. Supportive. Nurturing. Affectionate.

Until I discovered it was all a lie.

But without Brooke talking to me, I'm more alone than ever and I yearn to pick up the phone and call Alice. I want to tell her about my estrangement from Brooke. How I've moved into one of the bungalows on the property, so I don't bump into Brooke in the main house, even though Alice left her home to Brooke and me.

I can't reach out to Alice though. Her lies are too raw. And I'm still hurting two years later since I discovered the truth. She's reached out many times, but I can't stomach the deception, so I respond with terse texts because hearing her voice makes me want to bawl.

We haven't celebrated birthdays, Thanksgivings, or Christmases like we used to. Lavish affairs where Alice would insist Hope and I help her prepare for weeks in advance: soaking dried fruit in rum for the plum puddings, stringing popcorn to decorate the tree, transforming the interior of the house with plush toy snowmen, reindeers, and Santa. We'd hang angels from the lights and drape tinsel over everything, singing along to carols while we did it.

Or the days before Thanksgiving when our kitchen would be filled with warmth and laughter as we baked pumpkin pies, prepared green bean and sweet potato casseroles, roasted brussels sprouts, prepped the stuffing for the turkey, and competed to see who made the best cranberry sauce.

Instead, for the last two years since I discovered the truth, Brooke, Alice, and I have faked it for Hope. We've tried to maintain normality for her, particularly as she grieved for the loss of her mother, Freya, but we've had a snatched Christmas and Thanksgiving brunch at Alice's, so we eat quickly and leave as soon as possible.

Brooke and I know Hope's not a fool, but we framed it in terms she'd understand: that Alice wants us to celebrate with her at her new place, and we still have Christmas and Thanksgiving dinner at ours, so she gets to have two celebrations rather than one. And Alice takes Hope out for a treat on her birthday, while Brooke and I do something special for her at home.

I've coped seeing Alice on these rare occasions, maintaining a brittle civility while wanting to scream at her, *Why didn't you tell me the truth earlier?* But it's times like this I miss her acutely and wish we could go back to the way it was.

The irony isn't lost on me. I want Brooke to forgive me when I can't forgive Alice, the woman who raised me. But what she did is far worse than my aborted kiss with Riker. She deceived me for years. She deceived all of us and the ramifications of her lies are still reverberating through our family.

What's left of it.

I hate the helplessness that gnaws at me, but for now, there's little I can do to convince Brooke to hear me out, no matter how much I wish our fractured family could reunite.

SEVEN

NOEL

"You look nice," I say, holding the passenger door open for Hazel. "New dress?"

A faint blush stains her cheeks. "Yeah. Having a regular wage is better than casual waitressing at the catering company."

"That's great. So, it's working out?"

She nods as she buckles up. "Brooke is nice, and Hope is sweet. It almost feels like I'm taking advantage of them, getting paid for keeping the house tidy, cooking meals, and hanging out with Hope after school."

"They're lucky to have you." I close the passenger door and jog around the car, sliding behind the wheel. After I got released from prison it took me three weeks to be able to sit in the driver's seat, let alone fire up the engine. Not that I didn't try. I sat behind the wheel every day, willing myself to reverse out of the drive, put the car in gear, and cruise the block. But every time I tried, I saw Ned's stricken expression in my rearview mirror, the panic on his face, before the scream and thud that haunt me.

If Hazel hadn't sliced her thumb open while cooking and needed to be driven to the ER, I probably still wouldn't be driving three months later. She's done a lot for me, letting me move into the spare room in her tiny cottage, helping me get a job at the local grocer, treating me like I haven't been incarcerated for killing the man she loved.

Hazel's faith in me has been amazing. She adored Ned yet forgave me for killing him. I think she's the only person who ever believed what I did was an accident. She wanted to visit me in prison, but I couldn't face her. Not after what happened. I sometimes think Ned didn't deserve her loyalty. My twin had a dark side he hid well from many.

"I'm really grateful you told me about the job at Brooke's after you overheard your manager talking about it at the grocer." Hazel touches my arm. It's an impersonal brief squeeze but I inwardly flinch. It's been a long time since I've felt the touch of a woman. "You're a good guy."

Her praise makes my chest tighten with emotion and to my horror, tears burn the back of my eyes. I never used to be this emotional. I'm tough. Clever. Invincible. Everyone used to think so and I used it to my advantage.

Until I made a catastrophic mistake that changed the course of my life, and while I pretend like it doesn't bother me most days, the resentment is locked deep inside, festering despite every attempt I make with my fresh start.

"You're the good one. Letting me stay with you, accepting minimal rent, helping me get a job." I clear my throat. "I know you're probably doing all this because of your past feelings, but you don't owe me anything, Hazel."

She turns to face me, her expression solemn. "Everyone deserves a second chance."

"I'm glad you think so."

"His death wasn't your fault," she murmurs, her eyes soft with understanding. "I know how close you two were and you'd never hurt him deliberately." Her mouth hardens. "Despite what that jury and judge sentenced you to."

I quell the spark of fury that inevitably ignites when I think of my unjust sentencing. I'd pleaded my case. I'd had a great defender. But the judge had been a righteous prick and had sent me away with a resounding pounding of his gavel.

I'd hated his holier-than-thou condescension, when he'd looked down on me in the dock and said I should be thankful he'd taken my stellar reputation into account. Otherwise, my sentence would've been longer. I'd gritted my teeth in response, the epitome of subservient, when I wanted to yell, *What would you know? I'll be serving a life sentence in my head every damn day for killing my brother.*

"I didn't mean to upset you by bringing up your sentencing."

I wipe the resentment from my face and force a smile. "I'm not upset, Hazel. And thanks, your support means a lot."

We smile at each other and my gratitude for this sweet woman knows no bounds. Her loyalty is heartwarming and I value her friendship, the way she's stood by me.

"By the way, I've invited Brooke to join us for a drink tonight. Hope you don't mind?"

"Fine by me."

I intend on staying in Martino Bay for the foreseeable future, even though it's tiresome having to fake it all the time, especially for those who remember me. I hate their overt pity, their prying questions about Ned. I don't want to talk about a past I can't change; I want to embrace a future I can.

The more people who believe I'm a changed man, the better.

EIGHT

BROOKE

I haven't been out since my sister died, so entering the trendy bar with its neon lighting, chrome backsplash, and hipster crowd makes me feel gauche. Soft jazz pulses through state-of-the-art speakers as I fight my way through the youngsters to reach the bar, where I pick up a cocktail menu and pretend to find it infinitely interesting so I don't look out of place.

But the cocktails I've never heard of intimidate me as much as the young crowd. Horse with No Name, Yuzu Sour, Bijou, Le Fatigues, and Clover Club have me bamboozled. What happened to an old-fashioned Cosmopolitan or Martini?

I order a champagne and drink half of it in a few gulps, second-guessing the wisdom of coming here when Hazel enters the bar with a guy I assume is her boyfriend, and I do a double take.

He's seriously gorgeous. Brown wavy hair so dark it's almost ebony, cerulean blue eyes, chiseled jaw, and the hint of dimples when the corners of his mouth curve upward in reaction to something Hazel says. He's wearing faded denim and a navy polo that accentuate the hardness of the muscles beneath. Impressive. I hope I'm not drooling as they approach.

"Hey, Brooke, I'm so glad you came." Hazel waves at the guy standing a foot behind her. "This is my housemate, Noel."

Relief fizzes through my veins better than the glass of champagne I've half drunk. He's her roommate not her boyfriend. Though why I should care is beyond me. I don't have the time or the inclination to date. Getting a handle on my new job and spending time with Hope is my priority. But I'm human and a girl can look, right?

"Pleased to meet you, Brooke."

Noel holds out his hand and I shake it, trying not to register how warm and comforting his grip is. Then he smiles and damned if those dimples don't make my breath catch a little.

"Nice to meet you." My smile is genuine, and I belatedly realize I'm still squeezing his hand.

I give an awkward laugh and he does the same, endearing him to me. There's something strangely vulnerable about him, at complete odds with a guy so good-looking.

"Would you like a drink?" He glances at my half-empty glass and I shake my head.

"No, thanks. I'm good."

"What about you, Haze?"

"I'll have a cola, thanks."

"Coming right up."

As he wends his way to the bar, my gaze follows him, and I don't realize I'm staring until Hazel barks out a laugh.

"Are you okay?"

I tear my gaze away from checking out Noel's butt to find Hazel staring at me in amusement. "Yes, why?"

"Do you drool over every guy you meet?" She chuckles.

"I'm not drooling." My rebuttal is swift, but when Hazel's eyebrows rise so high they almost reach her hairline, I burst out laughing. "Okay, I may be drooling a little. What's Noel's story? Are you two just housemates or is there something more going on?"

She screws up her nose. "Absolutely not. I used to have a thing for his brother, so we're just friends."

"How long have you known each other?"

"Years. We were neighbors on the outskirts of LA."

"You had a thing for the boy next door?"

She blushes, but I don't understand the sadness in her eyes. "Yeah, I had a huge crush on Ned."

I want to ask more but Noel returns, and she thanks him for the cola. I'm surprised to see he's having the same. He must see me staring at his drink because he raises it.

"To new friends," he says, those dimples on full display again, and as I clink my glass against his, I find myself wanting just that. For us to be friends.

"I'll be back in a sec," Hazel says. "I've just spotted my old boss at the catering company over there and she's waving me over."

"No problem," Noel says, and I'm glad to be left alone with him.

But he doesn't look so happy as he glances over his shoulder toward the bar.

"What's wrong?" I ask.

"There's a woman at the bar. I overheard her talking to the bartender about how this is the first date she's been on in a long time, and she hopes her daughter is okay on her own at home." A frown grooves his brow. "I don't think her date has arrived yet but the guy next to her looks shady and I saw his hand snaking toward her drink, so I'm afraid he might slip something into it."

Before I can say anything, he shakes his head. "I'm sorry to ditch you, Brooke, but do you mind if I check she's okay?"

"Go." I shoo him away with my free hand, beyond impressed that he's already making his way toward the bar, where a petite brunette in a plain black dress appears terrified as she slides off a stool and backs away from the guy next to her.

Noel's right, the guy must have nefarious intentions because he isn't looking happy at Noel's intervention. But Noel says something to him, and fear crosses the guy's face before he backs off and disappears into the crowd, leaving Noel to guide her out the door.

Not many men are that chivalrous, and for someone like me who doesn't trust easily, I'm beyond impressed by Noel's concern for a woman he doesn't know.

I can't see Hazel in the crowd and I'm contemplating finishing my drink and leaving when I see Noel re-enter the bar. His eyes search me out and when our gazes meet across the crowd, a jolt of pure lust shoots through me, the likes of which I haven't experienced in a long time.

I wait, my pulse pounding in anticipation as he walks toward me. Who knew chivalry could be such a turn-on?

"Did the woman get into a taxi?"

He nods. "The driver's a local and he knew her, so she'll be fine getting home."

"I'm glad. That's a good thing you did."

His smile is bashful. "It was nothing."

"Would you like another drink?"

He shakes his head. "Actually, I was wondering if you'd like to have a coffee with me. Hazel slipped out while I was outside and said to tell you she'll see you tomorrow." He points to his temple. "She's got the beginnings of a migraine but refused to let me drive her home because she didn't want to leave you alone."

"She's lovely," I say, even more grateful for my new house-keeper. Not only has she streamlined my home life, she has introduced me to a lovely man who has her stamp of approval. I would never have coffee with a stranger I just met, but Hazel has known Noel for years and she vouched for him. I need to let down my barriers a bit. "And I'd love to have a coffee with you."

"Great, let's go."

I hesitate when he holds out his hand to me, but I quell my insistent mistrust of everything and everyone and place my hand in his.

NINE

NOEL

"When Hazel convinced me to come out for a drink tonight, I never expected... this." I wave my hand between Brooke and me, genuinely surprised by how fast we've clicked. Maybe it's because I haven't been attracted to a woman in a long time, or maybe it's the way she's looking at me—part wonder, part doubt, like she can't quite believe this is true either—but whatever the reason, I'm grateful she came out tonight too.

"And what's this exactly?" Brooke asks, her lips curved in a teasing grin.

"To connect with someone so quickly." Her eyes widen a little, as if surprised by my blunt response, so I add, "I hope my honesty doesn't scare you."

She shakes her head, her silky brown hair tumbling over her shoulders, and my fingers itch to touch the strands. "Not at all. I'm just as shocked by our swift connection as you are."

"In a good way, I hope."

This time, her smile is coy. "Of course."

I struggle to hide my elation. During the last forty minutes, we've bonded over our mutual love of desserts, our loathing of historical dramas, and our taste for thrillers. She listened intently as I gave her snippets of my past growing up on the outskirts of LA. She shared that she doesn't miss her transient lifestyle and is relishing living in the hometown she grew up in. Our conversation has flowed easily, and I can't believe my luck. Brooke is exactly the woman I need in more ways than she knows.

"In that case, shall we have another coffee to celebrate our newfound friendship?"

"No thanks. I'll be up all night if I have another."

I refrain from saying—*Would that be a bad thing?*—knowing it would be too much too soon. Our flirting so far has been gentle, unobtrusive, and I don't want to scare her off. Brooke is the first woman in a long time who's looked at me devoid of judgment and I like it. Of course, that will change when I tell her the truth, something I know I have to do before the end of our unofficial date, and I'm dreading it.

"This has been nice," she says, her gaze lowering to the table where our hands are interlocked. "I'm not usually so impulsive but being with you tonight has been a pleasant surprise I hadn't anticipated."

"Same." I squeeze her hand, her touch anchoring me to broach the subject of my recent past. "And I'd really like to see you again, Brooke, but there's something I have to tell you first."

Her smile slips. "That sounds ominous."

"Just hear me out, okay?"

Her expression has closed off, and my heart sinks. She'll probably walk out of this café without looking back when I tell her everything, but I can't help but hope she's more open-minded than most. From what she's told me, about being on the move for ten years before returning to Martino Bay two years ago, she might know a thing or two about life not always following the path you assume it will.

"So, what's this big secret?"

"Not a secret, as such, which is why I want to tell you now rather than after our tenth date."

"Tenth?" Her eyebrow arches. "Wow, you are planning ahead." She smiles.

"I can't help it. That's how I feel about our unexpected connection." I squeeze her hand again and release it because I know it'll break my heart when I tell her the truth, and she removes her hand from mine as if she can't bear to touch me.

Her expression softens but she remains silent, waiting for me to continue, so I drag in a deep breath and release it, trying to calm my rampaging nerves and failing.

"I already told you I moved to Martino Bay recently, about three months ago, but I haven't told you where I was before that."

"Uh-huh."

Here goes nothing.

"I spent four years in Wilks Inlet Correctional Facility after accidentally killing my brother."

There's no easy way to say that and she pales from the shock, her mouth hanging open slightly.

"We had a big fight, and I was mad, so I got in my car to drive off and cool down. But he was slamming his fists on my windows trying to stop me and there was all this noise, then he disappeared from view, and I panicked, not sure what he was up to because Ned could be unstable at times. I didn't see him behind my car when I reversed..." I trail off, glancing away in case I see judgment in her eyes. "I was convicted on a felony hit-and-run."

My throat tightens as it always does when I think of that devastating day. "I've been grieving ever since, trying to get a handle on the relentless guilt." I shake my head and press a hand to my chest. "Hazel was Ned's girlfriend at the time. She's been supportive of me. She's my only friend, really." I pause and look her in the eye. "Until now."

Thankfully, I glimpse pity in Brooke's eyes rather than revulsion, and when she reaches out to reclaim my hand again, my heart expands.

"I appreciate you telling me and I'm sorry for what you went through."

She's gripping my hand so tight I wriggle my fingers a little and she eases her grasp. "Sorry. It's just that I lost my sister two years ago, so I understand the whole grief and guilt thing."

"What did you have to be guilty about?"

"It's a long story." Her lips twitch and her gaze is evasive. "Maybe I'll save it for our eleventh date?"

"I'll hold you to that."

I lean forward and brush my lips across hers. It's impulsive and rash and too soon, but when she presses her mouth against mine, harder and insistent, I know I've made the right decision.

I've finally found a woman who will trust me.

TEN

LIZZIE

"Hey, Lizzie," Hope yells as she barges into the kitchen, flinging her school bag into the corner and pausing to give me a quick hug. "School was the pits today, so I'm going to have a shower."

She gives me a wide-eyed beseeching look she's honed down pat since she was four years old, the one that makes me want to squeeze her tight and ensures I'll do anything she asks.

"One of your special banana smoothies will make me feel better."

I smile and tug on her ponytail like I used to when she was little. "Coming right up."

"You're the best."

My smile fades as she clomps toward the bathroom, as I wish Brooke thought the same. I hate how fraught our relationship has become, though thankfully she's okay with me helping out with Hope when Hazel isn't around. There's no way I can live without this girl, considering I raised her alongside Freya and Alice.

Freya had been inordinately strict with Hope—not surprising, considering she must've been terrified of anyone discovering the truth, that Hope was Brooke's daughter and not hers—

so I'd got to play the fun aunt. I took Hope out for milkshakes weekly, I picked her up from school when Freya couldn't, I snuck her an extra candy after dinner. I spoiled her rotten because she's the sweetest, and the only niece I have.

And a small part of me, the one that doubts I'll find a guy to settle down with, laments the loss of having children. I'm not even sure I want them, but as the years go by and I'm still single, I feel like the choice is being taken away from me.

In the meantime, Hope fills that void for me. I resent Brooke for robbing me of quality time with my niece and it sucks that Hazel gets to spend more time with her than I do. The new housekeeper seems nice enough, but I'm wary of people these days. Everyone has a motive. At least they do in my experience. Maybe it's jealousy that Hazel has usurped my position in Brooke's household so quickly that has resulted in me not warming to her, but it's more than that. In her first week here, I witnessed her braiding Hope's hair. Absolutely nothing untoward about that, but it's the expression on her face as she did it that set off alarm bells for me. She'd looked... possessive.

Then again, I'd resent anyone who gets too close to Hope. I adore that girl and perhaps my protectiveness made me see things that weren't there.

I hate that I've become a cynic. I never used to be like this. But after what Alice and Freya did to our family, who can blame me?

"Knock, knock." Riker sticks his head around the back door. "Mind if I come in?"

I hesitate. That's all I need, for Brooke to come home early and find me and Riker together. I'm supposed to be minding Hope but if her father picks her up from school and wants to linger after dropping her off, I can't exactly ask him to leave, so I'm torn.

When I take too long to respond, Riker's eyebrow arches

and I feel like an idiot. We're friends, nothing more. And if Brooke gave me a chance to explain, she'd understand that.

"Sure. I'm just about to make Hope a banana smoothie. Want one?"

He pauses, his gaze looking over my shoulder, like he expects Brooke to barge into the kitchen at any moment.

"She's not here," I say, with a grimace. "Because if she were, I wouldn't be."

A frown grooves his brow. "You two still not talking?"

"She keeps communication to a minimum, mainly confined to discussing Hope." I close the door leading to the hallway on the off chance Hope overhears us. "It's been over a month though and I hoped she'd be over it by now."

"Technically, nothing really happened." He winks. "Though if I hadn't held you off..."

I wince. "Don't remind me. I'm mortified I came on to you."

"You tried to kiss me, so what?" He flexes his biceps. "Who can blame you?"

We laugh and I'm relieved that my relationship with him hasn't changed. He has stuck by us, providing Hope with the stability she so desperately needs after losing the only mother she's ever known.

The first year had been the toughest, with Hope alternately clinging to Brooke then having tantrums and pushing her away. But as Hope's grief waned, and she learned the truth about her parentage, she became more reliant on Riker and Brooke, leaving me out. I pretended that it didn't hurt, secretly wishing our lives could go back to the way they were before Alice and Freya's deception tore us apart.

"How is Brooke? I haven't seen her in ages."

"From what I observe during our brief interactions, she's good. Happier over the last two weeks than she's been in a long time. Smiling more. Humming under her breath. And she actually nodded at me once in greeting." I grab the bananas from the fruit bowl, and milk and yogurt from the fridge. "Has she said anything to you about meeting someone?"

His eyebrows rise. "No. Though now that you mention it, when we spoke a few days ago about Hope spending next weekend with me, she did sound upbeat. Wonder who he is?"

"I'm sure we'll meet him when she's ready."

Riker will. Brooke probably won't trust me near any of her boyfriends ever again.

If only she'd let me explain what happened that night I made a move on Riker. It had been a drunken mistake born from loneliness and sorrow. At the time, I'd blamed it on the fright I'd had at work and the copious amounts of alcohol I'd drunk that night to cope.

But it had been more than that. Having that prisoner pin me up against the wall had unleashed something in me: a futility, that if something happened to me at work, would anybody beyond Brooke, Alice, and Hope really care?

I've been single for too long, my last relationship—if you can call a few dates that—sacrificed because my family needed me. I'd met Colby at the supermarket not long after Freya died, our shopping carts colliding in a corny meet-cute. The sparks had been instant and when he asked me out, I said yes. He'd been courteous and sweet and a great listener, but ultimately, I hadn't been able to invest fully because Brooke and Hope were struggling. My sister and niece needed me, so I chose them over Colby, a decision I hadn't regretted at the time.

But that night after being attacked at work and downing one too many bourbons, with Riker being a caring listener as usual, he reminded me of what I'd lost with Colby, and I'd mistaken Riker's compassion for something more. I leaned in for a kiss, he'd stopped me, and I blamed it on my vulnerability and loneliness, never acknowledging that my transgression could've been born from resentment toward Brooke for taking up so much of my time back then that I'd sacrificed a chance at real happiness.

I'd been mortified afterward despite Riker's attempts to laugh it off and attribute my move on alcohol, but at least Brooke didn't know. Turns out, Brooke had seen us and had waited a week for me to tell her, and when I hadn't, she'd chalked up another betrayal from a member of her family, ostracizing me in the process. I'd moved out of the main house a day later so Hope wouldn't pick up on Brooke's animosity toward me.

"Hey, are you okay?" Riker touches me on the shoulder, and I nod, blinking back tears.

"Yeah, I'm fine. Now, do you want a smoothie or not?"

"Sure." He takes the milk from my hand and grabs the blender with the other. "Let me help."

We work in companionable silence, dicing bananas, adding them to the blender along with milk, yogurt, and a pinch of cinnamon, and pouring the smoothies into tall glasses just as Hope opens the door and strides into the kitchen.

"Thanks for picking me up from school, Riker." She sits on a stool at the island bench. "All the girls in my grade have a crush on you because of your motorbike."

Riker's expression is a comical mix of embarrassment and horror. "You're welcome, kiddo."

"I'm getting serious street cred because of those crushes," she says, before taking a giant slurp of her smoothie.

Riker reddens and I laugh. "Hope, I don't think Riker's entirely comfortable with tween girls crushing on him."

Hope rolls her eyes. "What can I do about it?"

Riker's gaze meets mine and I'm sure we're thinking the same thing: here's the start of teen attitude.

"I saw Brooke at lunchtime today. She was cruising past the school with some guy in her car. Who is he?"

I convey a silent message to Riker with my eyes—*Told you so*—and answer Hope. "I don't know, sweetie. Maybe a work colleague?"

"Maybe." Hope shrugs and drinks half her smoothie in a few gulps. "She's so busy with work all the time."

"New jobs are like that, kiddo." Riker sits on a stool next to her. "Want to do anything in particular when you sleep over this weekend?"

"There's a new chick flick I wouldn't mind seeing at the cinema."

Hope's sideways glance is pure cheek. She knows how much Riker hates chick flicks. But I also know how much he loves Hope.

He groans but slings an arm across Hope's shoulders. "You're killing me, kid, but sure, I'm always up for gallons of popcorn, candy, and soda."

"Good. Want to help me with my homework?"

"As long as it's not algebra."

They stand and move to the dining room, their gait similar. When Freya had been pretending to be Hope's mother all those years, she'd never discussed Hope's paternity. But now I know the truth, that Riker is Hope's biological father, I wonder why I hadn't seen their similarities sooner.

We're lucky to have Riker in our lives. And for the briefest moment, I resent Brooke and Freya for having relationships with him, because if my sisters hadn't been involved with him, he's exactly the type of guy I'd want to be with.

ELEVEN

NOEL

THEN

A few years later, Ned escalates from tormenting pets to torturing humans.

I have an inkling Ned likes Sonya, a girl in our fifth-grade class, when he starts leaving her notes. An oddity, because most of us have phones and we text to communicate, but I figure Ned's trying to emulate the hero in an eighties movie we watched with Mom.

I want to ask him about the notes, but I know my brother. He'll get defensive or tell me to butt the hell out, so I watch.

Sonya smiles when she gets the first note, slipped between the pages of a science text. And at lunch, I hear her giggling with her friends about having a secret admirer. I'm around when she finds the next note too, in the outer pocket of her backpack, and her smile is smug. The next time, when it falls out of her jacket pocket and she picks it up and reads it, a tiny frown appears between her brows and my heart sinks. After that, I'm on guard, wondering what Ned's writing in those notes.

Two days after Sonya receives that third note, I see her crumple a piece of paper and stuff it in her pocket toward the end of gym class. She asks the teacher to be excused, grabs her bag, and heads out. A minute later, Ned fakes a stomach-ache. I know he's faking because he's grinning as he leaves the gym.

In a flash, I know what he's doing.

He's following Sonya.

I clamp down on the urge to run after them because I might be jumping to conclusions. Besides, Mrs. Ameretti, our gym teacher, is strict, and if I make up a flimsy excuse to leave, she won't buy it. So I wait an appropriate ten minutes before asking if I can check on Ned, because I'm getting "odd twin cramps" in my stomach too. She rolls her eyes but lets me go.

I sprint out of the gym, unsure where to look. The rest of the kids are in class, so Ned won't be strolling around the corridors. Which leaves three hiding places where kids sneak to if they're cutting class: the equipment storage facility near the tennis courts, the row of benches behind a wall at the end of the teachers' car park, and the gardener's shed.

I head for the tennis courts first, but there's a class playing a tournament, so Ned won't be here. I run to the car park but there's no movement in the trees either, which leaves the gardener's shed.

It's situated at the back of the school, hidden from the main buildings by a row of trees. There's no sign of life as I near the shed, its weathered wooden walls overrun by a flowering vine, shading the walls in a pretty pink. Mr. Abbott, the gardener, is part-time and works on Monday and Friday, meaning kids sneak down here the other days.

I creep forward and peer in the first window. I see nothing but rakes, a hoe, trowels, a spade, coils of hoses hanging from gigantic hooks, and a dividing bamboo wall, cutting off my view from the rest of the shed. Sunlight dapples the workbench, where Mr. Abbott has a row of pots, with packets of seeds lined up next to each one.

I scuttle around a wheelbarrow resting against a wall covered in moss and lichen and look in the second window. At first, I think the shadows cast by the sun must be playing tricks on my eyes because I swear I see Sonya tied to a chair in the middle of the shed.

I inhale sharply, the dankness of the moss tickling my nose, and I stifle a sneeze. Taking a deep breath, I peek through the window again, and this time, Ned comes into view, rubbing his hands together as he advances toward Sonya, who's saying something I can't hear. But I see her terror and the tears in her eyes as she pleads with Ned, while her hands are in constant motion behind her back trying to loosen the rope knot binding her.

I turn away and dry-wretch, unable to comprehend why my funny, smart brother would do something like this. I saved his ass when he killed Cal's snake but there's no way to spin this.

He's restrained one of our classmates, a girl, with the intention of doing goodness knows what. The thought spurs me into action. I have to stop Ned before he does something irreversible.

I pound on the window and Ned's head snaps toward me. He can't see who's out here, not with the sun at my back, but it's enough to distract him and draw him outside.

When he flings open the door, he's brandishing a sharp, hooked hoe, and I hold up my hands in surrender. Ned laughs when he sees it's me and lowers the hoe.

"What are you doing here, Noel?"

"Stopping you from making a terrible mistake."

He rolls his eyes. "Stop being so dramatic. Sonya likes me. We're just having fun."

"It doesn't look like she's having fun," I say, keeping my voice calm, when I want to yell at him to stop being a psychopath. "Let her go, Ned."

He pouts like an annoyed tween, but I see the calculated gleam in his eyes. "But we haven't done anything yet."

I dare not ask what he had planned because tying up a girl against her will means Sonya doesn't consent, something we learned about in health ed last week.

"What do you think is going to happen when you untie her?" I tap my temple. "Did you even stop to think what restraining her means for you?"

"Who said I was going to let her go?"

My stomach churns with dread as I process his meaning and try not to think of Cal telling me how Ned stabbed Ana repeatedly.

"Ned, let her go. Now."

I'm the only person who holds sway over my brother, apart from Mom, and I silently pray he'll listen to me because I know there will come a day soon when Ned won't give a damn what I say.

"You're no fun," he mutters, flinging the hoe aside as he trudges back inside.

I hear Sonya's muffled sobs a second before she comes barreling out the door and almost knocks me over in the process.

"Are you okay?" I reach for her and she shies away, staring at me in wide-eyed horror, like I've been a part of this. "I followed Ned when he left gym and saw him come down here. Then I looked in the window and saw you..."

I trail off, hoping she'll believe me, because no way do I want to be implicated in my lunatic twin's crimes.

"Thank you," she whispers, starting to shake. "He's been leaving me notes, from a secret admirer. Said he had a surprise for me down here. I didn't know it was Ned, otherwise I wouldn't have come..." She shakes her head. "I know he's your twin but he's creepy. All the girls think so." Her lips thin. "And now, he's going to be expelled when I tell everyone what happened."

I nod, knowing this would be the outcome from the moment I peered through the window and saw Sonya tied up. It's annoying, because if Ned gets kicked out of school, I'll have to leave too. Mom says we're a package deal and we need to look out for each other.

"You better go," I say. "And I'm sorry for what Ned did to you."

Her lower lip wobbles before she says, "I think I'm lucky, thanks to you. I hate to think what he would've done if you hadn't shown up."

With that, she sprints away, leaving me wondering the same thing.

TWELVE

BROOKE

It's an indictment that I'm thirty and have never had a real relationship.

And after only dating Noel for two weeks, I'm reluctant to label what we have. But he's kind, considerate, and content to take things slow, so I'm almost at the point of having the conversation with him about the momentous monogamous relationship status.

The thought alone makes me incredibly nervous because telling people that we're exclusive—particularly Hope and Riker—means I'm serious about Noel, and it seems too soon for that. Then again, I've been cautious my entire life because I've been robbed of so much, and when it feels right, I know it in my gut.

Our dates have been low-key but memorable. A picnic at the moonlight cinema, where we watched a black-and-white double feature under the stars with other nostalgic couples. A six-course degustation dinner at a new Asian fusion restaurant in town that enabled us to talk about anything and everything between courses. Early morning walks along the beach on the weekends, holding hands and laughing as we kicked at the waves skimming our feet.

I'm comfortable with Noel in a way I never anticipated. For someone who's been betrayed and hurt by those closest to me, it's a big deal to admit I trust him.

Though I haven't told anyone about Noel yet. I want to introduce him to Hope, and Riker won't mind who I date, so I know the real reason I'm keeping him to myself a tad longer is because of Lizzie.

What I saw that day in our house devastated me. I knew something was wrong when Lizzie got home from work but she didn't say much because Hope had been around. Riker had come over for dinner and Lizzie had drunk half a bottle of wine before suggesting we do tequila shots. I'd refused because Hope wanted to be dropped off at a friend's house after we ate, and Riker had one shot because he had to ride home.

I'd asked Riker to keep an eye on Lizzie before I gave Hope a lift because I was concerned about her. I hadn't expected to come home and find Riker sitting close to Lizzie on the couch, with Lizzie leaning in to kiss him. Even now, I remember the overwhelming sense of betrayal as I stood outside that window, the icy gusts off the ocean chilling me almost as much as watching my sister make a move on my daughter's father.

I thought I could trust her.

I was wrong.

It's not about Riker. That's what Lizzie doesn't understand. Riker and I never worked as a couple. We conceived Hope as virtual strangers during a one-night stand at a party as teens. When we met a decade later and reconnected as co-parents, Hope had been our priority and that hasn't changed. We care about each other. That's it.

But it's Lizzie targeting Riker when she knows we share a child that has me equal parts shattered, disbelieving, and mistrustful.

I know she isn't directly responsible for robbing me of the first decade of my daughter's life, but she got to be a part of raising Hope in those ten years when I couldn't, and a small part of me resents her for it. She got to be a mother to Hope when I didn't, so to have her make a move on Riker, Hope's father, made me panic that I'd be cut out of the family dynamics yet again.

An irrational fear because Riker would never allow that now he knows the truth, but in the heat of the moment when I saw Lizzie come on to him, I'd been catapulted back to the moment I discovered Hope was mine and I'd been duped by those I trusted most.

As dusk descends, I watch Noel standing in line at the take-out coffee cart that is stationed on the edge of this park daily. It does a roaring trade from joggers who want to take a break, evening strollers, and couples like us who are time poor and want to catch up at the end of a busy day without going through the rigmarole of dinner.

Noel's a head taller than anyone in the line, so handsome and striking silhouetted against the pastel pink and purple hues streaking the sky. He's impressive and I hope he's as into me as I'm into him.

I close my eyes for a moment, wondering when's the last time I was this happy, content to sit on a park bench, listening to the chirping of crickets and the occasional dog bark, waiting for my man.

My man. I like the sound of that.

The excited squeal of a toddler who's spotted a duck gliding across the surface of a nearby pond disrupts my peaceful intro-spection and I open my eyes, smiling as the little girl crouches down at the edge of the pond, her hand firmly held by her mom. Their heads are bent close and they laugh when the duck dives, and my smile fades.

Did Freya, Lizzie, or Alice do this very thing with Hope?

Did they point out the fireflies flickering between the branches of the tall sycamore trees edging the park? Did they push her on the swings and bounce a ball on the basketball court? Did they share picnics on a rug?

I've missed out on so much with my daughter and while I treasure every moment we now have together, it's times like this that my resentment against those closest to me rises to the surface and I feel like screaming at the injustice of it all.

"Looks like you could use this." Noel hands me a coffee in a take-out cup and sits next to me on the park bench. "It's a double shot."

"Thanks." He has no idea how glad I am to see him, considering the grim turn my thoughts had taken, so I gently bump him with my shoulder and he smiles, making my heart lighter in an instant. "Did you know today is two weeks since our first coffee date, the night we met?"

"Best night of my life." He taps his coffee cup against mine. "Or is that too much too soon?"

"Honesty is never a bad thing." My chest is warm, whether from his proximity, his thoughtfulness, or the coffee I'm not sure. "I'm really glad we met too."

His expression is pensive as he sips his coffee. "Tell me if this is none of my business, but have you had many relationships in the past?"

I don't say *None* because that makes me sound pathetic. "Nothing too meaningful, because as I mentioned on the night we met, I traveled a fair bit. My parents died when I was a toddler, so my aunt who raised me moved to this town and I grew up here, before leaving at eighteen. I moved around a lot after that, doing odd jobs here and there, spent five years in South America working for a peace organization, then returned two years ago for my sister's wedding."

He's staring at me so intently I wonder if I have milk foam on my top lip. "That must've been special."

"Sadly, she died before the wedding, so it didn't go ahead."

"I'm so sorry." He reaches out with his free hand and squeezes mine. "If anyone can empathize, I can. Losing Ned gutted me."

He looks so sad I want to hug him, but he raises his coffee cup to his lips and stares into the distance.

"He was the only family I had left," he murmurs, his voice thick with emotion, and this time I place my cup on the bench next to me so I can slide my arms around him.

It had been horrific for me witnessing Freya's death. I can't imagine how much worse it must've been for Noel, being responsible for killing his brother. He must be an incredible man for Hazel to trust him after he was responsible for the death of the man she loved, and I see glimpses of his emotional depth, like now, that I can't help but fall for.

Besides, if anyone knows what it's like to have a complicated family, I do, and when he looks into my eyes, I know he's a good person. A man worthy of my trust. A man I can develop real feelings for if I let my guard down completely.

He rests his head against mine and we sit that way for ages, silently absorbing each other's strength, and I know in my gut I've made the right decision in letting this man who's almost as broken as me into my life.

THIRTEEN

NOEL

THEN

It's hard being the good twin.

The honest one. The dependable one. The responsible one.

Because even Mom expects me to be amenable to every decision she makes, which is not the case when she uproots us from Reseda and moves us to Martino Bay, two hours south of LA on the California coast, when we're seventeen.

I know why she had to do it. Ned forced her hand. Again.

If I didn't love my brother so much, I'd kill him.

I've been protecting him—mostly from himself—for as long as I can remember. Not that I think he's a psychopath, despite his penchant for pulling wings off bugs and torturing cats from a young age, but Ned has a nasty streak that manifests at random times, and if he's lucky, I'm around to temper him.

I hate to think what happens when I'm not around to take the edge off.

Unfortunately, "the incident" with Candy at our high school was one of the times I wasn't around—I have a newfound infatuation with the guitar and didn't want to miss a lesson to hang out with Ned and two senior girls—so I'm not entirely sure what happened that resulted in Ned being expelled.

He won't tell me either, despite how much I've badgered him, and Mom has been tight-lipped since the day three weeks ago when she was called to the school to pick us up after we'd cleared out our lockers. Because of course I had to leave too. There was no question of me staying, because kids had already started to look sideways at me ever since our junior year, like they expected me to morph into Ned's clone.

Bad enough we look the same. I often cop anger or abuse from someone Ned has mistreated, until I grew my hair longer, at complete odds with Ned's crewcut, so nobody can confuse us. But I know my brother. He gets a kick out of sullying my good reputation and he's growing his hair too.

"Boys, the bus will be here soon. Don't forget your lunch," Mom yells, as if we're not already trudging toward the kitchen because we'd rather miss the bus on our first day at our new high school.

"This is your fault," I hiss at Ned, who elbows me in the ribs, before pasting a beaming smile on his face when we enter the kitchen.

"Thanks, Mom." He grabs the lunch bag she has prepared for us—I'm guessing the usual tuna salad sandwich, an apple, and a banana because she doesn't want us eating what she deems to be unhealthy cafeteria food—and presses a kiss to her cheek. "You're the best."

"Don't try to sweet-talk me, young man." But there's no bite to her words as she waggles a finger at Ned. "And please be on your best behavior."

"Always." Ned hugs Mom, towering over her, and winks at me. I flip him the finger behind her back. "You coming, bro?"

"Yeah," I mutter, waiting until he's out the front door before turning to Mom. "Let me guess. You want me to keep an eye on him."

"Yes please, sweetheart." She frames my face in her hands like she used to when we were twelve. "I know this is hard on you, always being the grown-up around your brother, but he needs you."

I want to say, "What about what I need?" but I don't because I've seen Mom's harried expression too many times when confronted with one of Ned's "misdemeanors" and I want to make it easier for her. She's amazing, never playing favorites despite what Ned thinks or doling out harsh punishments no matter how badly Ned deserves it. Our dad died before we were born but she's never been resentful or self-pitying. She works two jobs and gives us everything we need. I know that's why I try extra hard to be good, because Mom doesn't deserve two kids who make trouble.

"I'll look out for him, Mom, you don't have to worry."

But after she releases me from a hug, I see the concern in her eyes and know that all the promises in the world to keep Ned out of trouble may prove fruitless.

"See you after school." I pause at the front door to wave and she blows me a kiss.

"Have a great first day, honey."

I flash her a smile that fades swiftly as I see Ned already charming two girls waiting for the bus at the stop next door. I should be glad he's already making friends and he's so charismatic that he often paves the way for me to make friends too, because I'm the dorky one. But Ned's friendship has conditions and if he tires of you too quickly... watch out.

He's done some horrible things to other kids over the years. Killing his bestie's pet snake, tying up Sonya in the gardener's shed, and putting laxatives in the class cupcakes he took to school on our twelfth birthday. And his pranks only escalated in high school, with some awful online bullying, distributing a disgusting naked pic in the class chat, and whatever he did to that girl Candy that resulted in expulsion.

I know our teachers used to marvel at how different identical twins can be and I hate that sometimes in the dead of night, when Ned's snoring softly beside me and I'm reading under the bedcovers, I wish I didn't have a twin.

The bus arrives as I'm sauntering over and predictably Ned doesn't wait. He boards with the two girls, and I'm left to sprint to catch it. The only vacant seat is the one behind the driver, while Ned is cozily ensconced with the girls toward the rear.

No one speaks to me, but I feel curious stares boring into my back and hear Ned's raucous guffaws, as if he's the life of the party. Popular Ned. Cheeky Ned. Irresistible Ned.

When a part of me in the deepest, darkest recesses of my soul wishes he was Dead Ned.

FOURTEEN

BROOKE

Riker moved out of one of the bungalows on our property about six months ago because we tried to deepen our relationship and it didn't happen. Not that things got awkward between us, but we both agreed it was time. He wanted to expand his studio and that's the reason we gave Hope for his move. I'd worried about how she'd take the news at the time, but our daughter has learned to be stoic with the losses in her life.

His new studio is within walking distance of Main Street and he gets loads of tourists wandering in, drawn to the massive tin shed because of his metal sculptures in the front yard. He's constructed animals—a bear, raccoon, squirrel, wolf, cougar, alligator, moose, coyote, deer, and bobcat—from metal scraps he scours the country for, and they are spectacular.

Hope is fascinated by her father's talent, and for a tween who can happily spend hours scrolling on her phone, she puts it away when she enters Riker's studio because the inside is as interesting as the outside. He does commissions, so there can be anything in his workspace from a ten-foot sign for a surf shop to an intricate iron bracelet. And she told me she loves the smell of

heated metal, whereas the times I've visited I don't like the
scent of oil and grease.

She's intrigued by his equipment too, the scarred anvil from
repetitive hammer blows, the forge with its intense heat, the
chisels, power tools, and tongs used to shape molten metal,
whereas I'm concerned about my daughter being around them.
Though I trust Riker and he's assured me that if she ever wants
to try metal sculpting, it will be under his strict supervision,
using small scraps of steel and copper, and nowhere near the
forge.

As I pull up outside Riker's studio to drop Hope off for her
weekend sleepover, she turns to me.

"Do you have a boyfriend?"

I gape a little because her question is from left field, and I've
deemed it too early to tell her about Noel. He may be the most
amazing guy, but we've only been dating a few weeks and I
don't want to introduce him to Hope unless I'm absolutely sure
our relationship is heading somewhere.

Before I can answer, she says, "I saw you drive past school
one lunchtime with some guy in your car, then I heard Lizzie
tell Riker you might have one."

I hate the irrational flash of jealousy at the thought of Lizzie
and Riker together, let alone talking about me. I have no right to
be jealous, but I'm still hurting from her betrayal.

Hope's staring at me quizzically, so I have to respond. I
don't want to lie, especially if things develop with Noel as I
hope, so I say, "I have met someone and I like him."

"When can I meet him?"

The old me would've already introduced them but I need to
protect this precious girl at all costs. "Soon, sweetie."

I've never been more relieved to see Riker exit his studio,
shoving his welding visor up and shucking of his gloves. "Looks
like someone's waiting for you."

Thankfully, my distraction technique works and Hope

waves at Riker. "He has the coolest job," she says, flinging the passenger door open. "I can't wait until I can try to sculpt metal."

My throat clogs with emotion at the thought of Hope inheriting some of her father's talent. "Have a great time, sweetie."

She barely gives me a backward glance. "I will." She raises her hand in a half-hearted wave. "See you Sunday, Brooke."

She's so excited about this sleepover she's left her backpack behind, so I cut the engine and grab it from the trunk. Hope hugs Riker and heads inside, while I walk toward him holding out the backpack.

"Who knew sorting through hubcap scraps would be remotely interesting to a twelve-year-old," he says, with a grin. "She couldn't get in there fast enough to help."

"She thinks your job is the coolest." I do too and our house is dotted with Riker's creations. A hat stand made from a light post, a vertical garden made from a bed frame, and ornamental birds made from various car scraps. "Puts my sales rep gig into perspective."

He takes the backpack and slings it over his shoulder. "How's that going?"

"Good. I like being on the road and talking to various grocery chains about changing the way they order and who they order from, but a lot of them still order online and stick to the tried and true."

"I'm sure you'll be able to talk them around." His head tilts to the right in the exact way Hope's does. "A little birdie told me you're seeing someone?"

Of course he'd ask. He's Hope's father and if a stranger is hanging around his daughter he wants to know. I'll be the same if he enters a serious relationship with a woman.

"Your little birdie has good intel." I nod. "I am seeing someone. Noel Harwood. He's a good guy, but you know me, I'm taking it slow."

"That's great, Brooke. I'm happy for you." He folds his arms and mock frowns. "And if he doesn't treat you right, he'll have me to deal with."

I laugh, but I'm secretly grateful to have someone looking out for me. I know he'll do whatever it takes to protect Hope and that means he cares about me too.

We've been through a lot together and sharing a child bonds us like nothing else.

"What does Noel do?"

This is another reason why I wanted to keep Noel to myself for a bit longer. I expected questions would arise once Riker knew about him. Questions he's perfectly entitled to ask as Hope's father, but I know Riker. Like me, he's overprotective when it comes to our daughter, and the moment I mention Noel's an ex-con, he'll freak. I know if Noel hadn't revealed the truth to me the night we met, I wouldn't trust him like I do, but it's different for me because I've spent time with him and seen his caring side in action.

Do I worry that I've fallen for him too quickly, and allowing any man into my life means letting him close to Hope? Yeah, a little, but I'm not some naïve woman who's never been hurt. I've seen the worst of people, been betrayed by those closest to me, and at some point, I need to start trusting my judgment again.

Whereas I've had the chance to get to know Noel—his gentleness shines through—and understand how guilt-ridden and remorseful he is about accidentally killing his brother by the way his face falls when he talks about it and the guilt in his eyes, Riker will focus on the "ex-con" label and see little else.

For now, I'm keeping Noel's past to myself.

"He's recently moved to town so he's working at that boutique grocery store for now."

"Uh-huh."

There's judgment behind those two syllables, as if Riker

doesn't think a guy working at a supermarket is good enough for me, and I try not to bristle.

"Anyway, if our relationship progresses, I'll introduce you, so you can see for yourself he's a good guy." I glance at my watch. "I have to be somewhere, so have a good weekend with Hope and call me if you need anything."

It's the wrong thing to say, as if he can't be trusted with our daughter, and his expression tightens.

"We'll be fine."

Riker turns and walks away, only pausing when I say, "Bye."

He glances over his shoulder and at this distance, I see he's worried about something. "Just be careful, Brooke, okay?"

His protectiveness is endearing but unwarranted. I'm not rushing into anything with Noel. I know what I'm doing. I empathize with Noel because I know better than anyone that a dark family history doesn't mean you're a bad person. Noel made a terrible mistake, but he's paid his dues. We all deserve a second chance. I've got mine, and a small part of me feels privileged to be alongside Noel for his.

I raise my hand in farewell and try not to let the spring in my step show how eager I am to meet my new man for another date shortly.

FIFTEEN

NOEL

THEN

Ned can be obsessive. With things and people, so the minute he introduces me to Freya, I know he's in trouble.

He has a look in his eyes, almost manically possessive, that indicates she's his new obsession, whether she likes it or not.

But that's the thing. I swear Freya's looking at Ned the same way.

And that terrifies me.

"Wow, it's hard to tell you two apart." Freya's gaze swings between us. "I bet you prank people all the time."

"Yeah," Ned says, at the same time I say, "No," and he glares at me.

Freya laughs and even that grates on me, like she's forcing it. "Why did you move here?"

I freeze, trying to come up with a plausible excuse, but Ned, smooth as ever, doesn't hesitate. "Our old school was a drag. Poor curriculum, average teachers, and Mom had an old friend whose kids used to go here, so she moved us to Martino Bay."

"Lucky for me." Freya's practically simpering all over Ned

and I inwardly groan. "If you want someone to show you around, I'm your girl."

"Sounds good to me." Ned winks and Freya's eyeing him like a prize she won at a fair. "Meet you in the cafeteria at lunch?"

Freya glances over my shoulder and whatever she sees makes her pale a little. "Actually, I prefer eating outside. There's a shady spot under an oak tree near the football field. Meet you there?"

Ned nods like an eager puppy. "Sure. See you then." He glances at the printed timetable we were given ten minutes ago at the principal's office. "I've got English first up in Room 5A. Can you show me where that is?"

"Of course."

They completely ignore me as they join the throngs milling the main corridor. Rather than feeling left out, I'm relieved. The itch on the inside of my elbows, the one that starts up whenever I get a bad feeling about Ned, is prickling like crazy. I think Ned has met his match in Freya, and if she's half as bad as my brother, they'll be notorious.

"Stay away from Freya Shomack," a deep voice says from behind me. "She's a whacko."

I turn to find a nerdy guy with slicked-back brown hair and steel-rimmed spectacles staring at Freya's back with concern.

"You're new here, right?" The guy points to Ned and Freya. "And that guy's your twin?"

"Yeah."

"I'm Damian." He pushes his spectacles up to the bridge of his nose. "You wouldn't think Freya's sister's boyfriend just committed suicide, the way she's swanning around here."

Before I can comment, Damian continues. "Brooke still hasn't made it back to school, and it's been two weeks, but Freya's here and is pretending like nothing happened."

While my first impression of Freya isn't favorable, I don't

like talking about others behind their backs, especially when I
don't really know her.

"Everyone grieves in different ways."

Damian's eyebrows shoot up. "Freya's not grieving, she's
celebrating."

Unease lodges in my gut. "What do you mean?"

"Brooke's the popular one. She's a year older and everyone
loves her. She and Eli were prom queen and king. And a lot of
us saw how Freya fawned over Eli and was jealous of her sister.
So when Brooke breaks up with Eli and he kills himself, it's
weird that Freya isn't more cut up about it, don't you think?"

I don't know what to think, other than my gut instinct on
meeting Freya is right.

She's no good for Ned and he should stay away.

But I know my brother. If I tell him not to do something,
he'll go out of his way to do just that.

"Anyway, just a bit of friendly advice. Be careful of that
one." Damian makes loopy circles at his temple. "She's batshit
crazy."

I nod in response, and as Damian lopes away, juggling a
stack of books, I wonder what he'd think if he knew I often label
my twin the same way.

SIXTEEN

LIZZIE

I glimpse Hazel through the kitchen window as I take a bucket of tools into the garden to do some weeding. We rarely cross paths because I'm usually at work when Hazel's at the house, but I wish I could get to know her better because that would mean I'd get to spend more time with Hope. But from what I see, Hazel always appears frantically busy, and I'm still unsure how much Brooke has told her about me.

Besides, I know Brooke. If I establish any kind of friendship with Hazel, she'll take it as a sign I'm interfering, or weaseling my way back into the main house. Of course, there's a sliver of truth to that, but I don't want her accusing me of anything underhanded. I want us to be family again and I'll have to continue biding my time.

Though I can't forget my initial misgivings about Hazel and what I saw while she did that French braid, so I've been subtle when grilling Hope about her. But my niece doesn't say much other than "she's cool" and it irks that a stranger is spending more time with Hope these days than me.

Brooke and I need to get past this because I miss my family. Can't Brooke see how lonely I am now that she's shut me out? I used to love our nightly family dinners, where Hope, Brooke, and I would take turns choosing our favorite meals on alternate evenings—mac 'n' cheese for Hope, fish tacos for Brooke, barbecue ribs for me—and help each other cook before giving a rating out of ten. We'd turned those dinners into a fun competition, but we could've been eating sawdust for all I cared because it had been the affection I valued.

Having Brooke back in our lives made everything better. We'd been close growing up and I missed her when she'd been away for a decade. I'd marveled at how she'd held up after learning the horrifying truth about what Alice had done and been all too happy to be her main support. I loved the nights we'd curl up on the sofa with a glass of wine and talk about anything and everything. She shared her travel adventures with me; I told her about life at college: the parties, the late nights, the frat boys.

Getting to know my sister over the last two years has been a privilege and the permanent ache in my chest signals how much I miss her.

If it wasn't for my limited interactions with Hope, I'd be going stir-crazy.

I'm nothing like Freya, but a small part of me now understands why she went to extreme lengths to gain Brooke's attention. The world's a brighter place when Brooke's around and she makes everyone in her sphere feel special. It makes me sad that she thinks so little of me she's cut me out of her life without a second thought.

I pick up a trowel and stab at the soil, trying to loosen it. An excellent way to vent frustration. I enjoy gardening but haven't done much of it lately due to my manic schedule of art therapy classes. On the upside, I'm building a healthy nest egg for the future, whatever that entails. If Brooke and I remain estranged, who knows what may happen? Though I doubt she'll have the money to buy me out and make the house hers exclusively.

"Hey, Lizzie. Nice day for it." Hazel has to pass me to get to her car, so she stops. It's the first time she's said anything to me beyond "hello" when we first met, which makes me think Brooke has mentioned our estrangement to her.

"Sure is." I stand, press my hands into the small of my back, and stretch. "You heading off?"

"Yeah. I've made a chicken pie for dinner, Hope's doing her homework, and I saw you out here, so I'm sure Brooke won't mind if I leave a little early today." She glances at her watch. "My housemate needs my help with a rental application."

"That's fine. I'll keep an eye on Hope."

More than fine. Any extra time I get to spend with my niece is a bonus.

"You used to live in the main house?" Hazel hesitates, like she wants to say more. "Hope mentioned it. She said you used to look after her..."

I know what she's asking. Why would Brooke hire her if I used to do free babysitting?

But I don't know this woman and I'm not saying a word in case she runs back to Brooke and blabs. She appears nice enough, with a ready smile and clear eyes, but she's also nondescript, the kind of person who could blend into any surroundings, and that makes me a tad wary. She's assimilated into Brooke's household very quickly and my sister isn't the only one who's reluctant to trust.

"You're right, I used to spend a lot of time with Hope, but my job hours have escalated, so I'm unreliable for regular childminding." I choose my words carefully, wanting to know more about Hazel, but not in a way that will alert her. "I think it's great how seamlessly you've blended into our family. Have you always been a housekeeper?"

I watch for the slightest tell, a change in her expression or a glance away that would indicate evasiveness, but she meets my gaze head on. "I didn't go to college, so I've worked a lot of odd jobs over the years. Mostly retail in the early days, before doing some nanny work the last few years and working for a catering company more recently." She shrugs, endearingly bashful. "I love being a nanny though. Kids are blunt and I prefer that than the game-playing many adults indulge in."

My respect for her increases. "Me too."

"What do you do?"

So Brooke hasn't mentioned me much and I'm not sure whether to be offended or relieved.

"I'm a psychologist, but I run art therapy sessions for prisoners once they've been released."

"That's admirable." She glances over my shoulder toward her car, like she can't wait to get away, and I wonder what's made her edgy. "Everyone deserves a second chance, like my housemate."

Before I can ask who her housemate is, Hazel rushes on. "Anyway, it's been nice talking to you, Lizzie, but I have to meet my housemate."

She takes a few steps before pausing. "He's a good guy who definitely deserves a second chance. You might know him."

Unlikely. Martino Bay isn't a small town anymore and I work in Wilks Inlet, but Hazel's been nothing but pleasant and I don't want to appear rude, so I say, "What's his name?"

"Noel Harwood."

SEVENTEEN

BROOKE

The last three weeks have passed in a blur. My days are filled with road trips to nearby towns, trying to get a handle on my new sales job for the grocery chain that's taken a chance on me, and my evenings are spent with Hope.

Or Noel.

I'm exhausted, but our relationship is so new that I want to invest time in seeing if we're as compatible as I think we are. If Noel had his way, we'd spend every spare second together, but I have Hope to consider and she needs me more than a fledgling boyfriend.

"Hey, what are you thinking about?" Noel tightens his arm around my shoulders as we sit in front of the fire at a new cigar bar in town. Neither of us smokes but we love the vibe of the front room of the bar, filled with low-slung leather sofas, dark wood paneling, huge armchairs, bookcases, and an extensive cocktail list.

I can't stand the smell of cigarette smoke, but here the richness of aged tobacco mingles with the scent of leather, creating a warmth that's inviting. And I feel like I've stepped back in time, surrounded by framed photos of old Havana and people in cocktail wear as I watch a bartender in black tie mixing drinks behind the gleaming mahogany bar.

Soft jazz mingles with muted conversations and the clink of glasses, adding to the nostalgic vibe. I love it, and I'm glad Noel shares my taste. But my life has become a constant whirlwind of juggling work, Hope, and Noel, and as much as I enjoy spending time with him, I'm exhausted.

"I'm just thinking about how fast the last few weeks have flown and how tired I am."

His eyebrows arch. "Not tired of me, I hope?"

I gently nudge him with my shoulder. "Of course not."

"Good." He presses a kiss to the top of my head. "Never in a million years did I expect this to happen after the worst four years of my life."

Shadows cloud his eyes, and I can't imagine this kind, gentle man spending a single day in prison, let alone four years.

"Good things happen when we least expect it," I say, sounding like a corny greeting card and inwardly wincing.

But he smiles and my heart gives a predictable thump. "Moving to Martino Bay again is the best thing I ever did."

"Again?"

He stiffens and the oddest expression—fear—flickers across his face before it's gone so fast I wonder if I imagined it.

"Mom, Ned, and I moved here for a few months way back in my teens. We didn't stay long." He rolls his eyes. "Ned got into so much trouble back then that it felt like we moved constantly."

It sounds plausible enough, but he can't look me in the eyes and a sliver of doubt worms its way into my suspicious soul. Why hasn't he mentioned living here with his family before? "What kind of trouble?"

"You don't want to know." He shakes his head. "I miss Ned, but at the same time he made my life hell, and a small part of me resents him for that. For wasting what time we had together by being an idiot and getting into trouble that I had to get him out of."

I can empathize. I feel the same way about Freya. I miss the sister I once had, but I hate her for what she did to me and to Hope.

"Anyway, enough about my sordid past." He brushes a strand of hair off my face and tucks it behind my ear, his fingertips skating across the tender skin below my ear and sending a quiver of longing through me. We haven't done anything beyond kiss at this stage and I'm happy to take it slow, but Noel's an attractive man and I'm looking forward to consummating our relationship when the time is right. "Are you ready to introduce me to your niece?"

"Not yet."

There's that flicker of something in his eyes again before he blinks, and it's gone. "Still not sure about me, huh?"

He sounds disappointed and I take his free hand in mine, intertwining our fingers. "It's not that. I'm overprotective where Hope's concerned. I'm all she has since she lost her mother and I'll do anything to make life easier for her."

I hate having to pretend to the outside world that Hope is my niece but the three of us—Riker, Hope, and I—agreed it would be less complicated for her if only the family knew the truth. She's been through enough with everyone pitying her following Freya's death, the last thing she needs is schoolmates and townsfolk pointing fingers at her for her freaky family.

"I'm not here to complicate your life or hers, Brooke. But I care about you, and I want to be a part of your life."

He's so somber my chest aches and I know he's right. We've been dating long enough for me to get a read on Noel and gut instinct tells me he's one of the good guys. Hope should meet him. It's time.

I squeeze his hand. "I'll talk to her this weekend and set up a time for her to meet you."

He beams like I've given him the greatest gift. "Your trust in me means everything."

He lifts our joined hands to his lips and presses a kiss to the back of mine. "Thanks Brooke. For believing in me. For taking a chance on me."

Tears sting the back of my eyes as he lowers his mouth to mine, and I'm glad I'm dating this wonderful man.

EIGHTEEN

LIZZIE

A day later, I'm still kicking myself for not interrogating Hazel further when she mentioned Noel Harwood is her housemate. But I'd been too stunned when I'd first heard the name, and by the time I'd reassembled my wits, Hazel had been in her car and waving goodbye.

Not that it's any of my business, but it's strange that the one ex-con I got a bad feeling about happens to be living with our new housekeeper.

It has to be a coincidence because neither Hazel nor Noel has ties to my family, but I still have an icky feeling that Noel is too close for comfort.

At work, I read through the file of any new members of my class because I like to get a heads-up on any potential triggers. It makes me a better facilitator to know the background of my class. But in Noel's case, I didn't know anything about him because I'd taken Annie's class as a one-off favor, and if there'd been anything to know, Max would've briefed me beforehand.

Having my boss reinforce my bad feeling about Noel after that class had vindicated my gut instinct, which hasn't steered me wrong to date. I'm good at reading people, which makes me excellent at my job. I can coax the most hardened heart into opening up a little and the ex-prisoners I've taught appreciate my input.

What is it about Noel Harwood that makes me uneasy?

By Hazel's proclamation about second chances, she doesn't share my concerns. Then again, was she rushing home to help Noel with his rental application because she can't wait for him to move out? If so, why have him move in with her in the first place? Did he answer an ad for a roommate? Did he know Hazel beforehand? Did he call in a favor?

I have way too many questions regarding a guy who has nothing to do with me and I won't see again, but I'm curious, so during my lunch break I grab a tuna on rye from the vending machine and eat at my desk so I can peruse the database.

Does Brooke know that Hazel's housemate is an ex-con? Probably not, so I can justify my snooping as a way to protect our family. Considering how protective Brooke is of Hope, she'll freak if she thinks an ex-con is remotely connected to her daughter, and if I can forewarn her, maybe she'll see how genuine my remorse is.

I take a bite of my sandwich and type with my other hand, entering my password to access our client files. With one finger, I enter "Noel Harwood" into the search bar and within five seconds I'm perusing his file.

Thirty years old, resided in Reseda until he moved to Martino Bay with his mother and twin when he turned seventeen. Attended Martino Bay High, and that gives me pause. Considering his age, he could've been in some of Freya's classes. Not that I can ask her, but Alice might know, and I make a mental note to quiz her.

He attended college and worked for a finance company in LA before his twin Ned's death four years ago, when Noel was tried and convicted of a felony hit-and-run. Served his sentence at Wilks Inlet Correctional Facility and was a model prisoner. Spent his days in the library, with a particular interest in law books. Zero altercations with other prisoners. Followed rules. Maintained a high level of fitness. Helped out in the kitchen.

The model prisoner indeed.

And considering Wilks Inlet Correctional is a low-level security prison for lesser crimes like fraud and manslaughter, he wouldn't have mixed with hardened criminals. It's why I enjoy my art therapy classes, because I know most of my students are open to rehabilitation.

Nothing I've learned about Noel screams "red flag," so I delve a little deeper into his conviction and discover something that makes me sit up and peer closer at the screen.

Noel told me in class that he killed his brother. But he didn't mention that he reversed over him then drove away, leaving him to die.

How could he have left his own brother to bleed out?

I try to imagine what I would do if I ever hurt Brooke by accident, and the thought alone is gut-wrenching. One thing's for certain, I would never be able to leave her in pain. The lack of empathy that would require, to leave a sibling to die... it's horrifying.

But my experience with prisoners has taught me that not everything is black-and-white. Maybe Noel had been in shock, torn apart by grief for accidentally killing his twin, and unable to cope, which is what the judge said in his sentencing.

But I can't help but think Noel's glaring omission reinforces I'm right about him having a darker side he likes to keep hidden.

When I click on the link for Ned Harwood, I'm stunned by the list of charges to his name. Several instances of sexual assault against girls at his high school in Reseda, including one that got him expelled, a few counts of trespassing, stalking, two

counts of breaking and entering, and numerous other misdemeanors.

It makes me wonder. Was Ned's death entirely accidental
or did his twin do something so terrible that Noel felt compelled
to do the world a favor?

I finish my sandwich and read through Noel's file again. I
should be relieved I didn't find anything sinister about his time
in prison, but I can't ignore the sliver of doubt about his fleeing
the scene of the crime—and my gut instinct is rarely wrong.

I'm about to close the file when I spot a recent attachment
dated yesterday that I missed. I click on it, surprised when
PRISON LIAISON OFFICER CANDIDATE pops up as the
heading.

I know Rod, who's currently serving in the role, is leaving,
so it makes sense Max wants to replace him. Rod served a
twelve-month sentence for defrauding his in-laws and is the
nicest prisoner to ever enter our program, to the point Max
created the liaison officer role especially for him—to act as a go-
between the prisoners and us—and it's worked well. The liaison
officer has already been in prison, then done our program, and is
trusted by the ex-cons we strongly encourage to do our art
therapy.

But I'm surprised Max in considering Noel as Rod's
replacement, especially after our chat several weeks ago. Then
again, from what I've just read in Noel's file, I'm not surprised
he's the perfect candidate. He presents well. I guess others don't
share my misgivings.

"Knock, knock. Got a minute?" Annie sticks her head
around the door, and I beckon her in. Perfect timing. I'd been
about to reach out to get the lowdown on Noel, so her arrival is
fortuitous.

"Sorry to disturb your lunch, but I want to run something
by you." She takes a seat opposite my desk. "Has Max
mentioned appointing a new prison liaison officer?"

I shake my head. "No, but I assumed it would happen soon, with Rod moving to San Fran."

"Do you have any candidates you'd like to put forward?" She asks.

"Not really. Though it looks like you have."

She shrugs, sheepish. "You've seen Noel Harwood's file? I think he'd be perfect."

I stiffen and try to cover my reaction by faking a cough. But Annie's eyes narrow and she says, "You would've met him in my class. You didn't like him?"

"It's not that..." I trail off, choosing my words carefully. I trust Annie's instincts and if she's singing Noel's praises, it means mine are way off. "I just had a bit of a gut reaction, that's all. But he was perfectly polite and completed the clay task I set."

Annie's expression is somber. "Your gut reactions haven't steered you wrong in the past though. So what is it about Noel that has you doubting him?"

"That's just it, I don't know. I can't explain it. It's nothing more than a feeling."

Annie gnaws on her bottom lip before saying, "I'm not trying to undermine your feeling, but I had him in my class for three months and he was a standout. Unfailingly enthusiastic, friendly with everyone, went out of his way to make new students feel welcome."

I bite back my first response, *He sounds too good to be true*, and force a smile. "Annie, I trust your judgment and you definitely know him better than me, so if you think he's a good fit for the prison liaison officer role, and Max agrees, he should definitely interview."

"You sure you're okay with it?"

"I'm okay with whatever you decide."

Besides, if Noel accepts the job, we'll be working in close proximity during the transition period when newly released prisoners join my classes, and I'll be able to keep an eye on him.

Maybe I've misjudged Noel and he's as nice as Annie says. But on the off chance I'm right, guys like Noel—perfect on the outside, dark on the inside—need to be watched.

NINETEEN

NOEL

I have a surprising homework load for my first day at a new school and I want to get it all done to make a good impression on my teachers, who seem chill, but Ned has other ideas.

His obsession with Freya is worse than I thought and she's all he can talk about until I slip headphones on and crank up my study playlist. Thankfully, he gets the hint and goes out for a walk. Mom's working late tonight—she has a new job at the local cinema complex—so I immerse myself in the complexities of algebra until my stomach rumbles. Only then do I realize it's dark out and Ned hasn't come home.

A sick feeling in the pit of my stomach replaces the hunger of a moment ago and I push back from the table, grab a flashlight, and head outside. Our rental is small but the land surrounding the cottage is large, and I have a fair idea where Ned will be. The first day we arrived we explored extensively and found a small treehouse near a creek that runs at the back of the property. The previous tenants must've had kids who loved it, because the rungs of the ladder are worn and the treehouse looks well-occupied, with gouged notches on the posts, pocked floorboards, and a threadbare beanbag.

Wherever we've lived, Ned's always had a hiding spot. A go-to place where he can chill whenever he needs to, which is often. I'm not sure if Mom loves us so much that she's oblivious to Ned's problems or she's too terrified to get him diagnosed because then she'll have to deal with labeling her son, but whatever the reason, I'm tasked with keeping my brother level-headed. Easier said than done.

I follow the trail toward the treehouse and as I near it, I hear voices. Ned and a girl, talking in low tones.

My heart sinks. I think I recognize the voice.

It's Freya.

"So how bad is it at home?" Ned asks, and I hate that I'm eavesdropping, but I need to see if I'm right about Freya and she could spell trouble for my brother. "Is your sister coming back to school?"

"Who knows? She's still moping over her boyfriend's death and taking it out on everyone around her. Like me." She pauses and I imagine her rolling her eyes. "I'm sick and tired of being second best when it comes to Brooke. She's the perfect one, the pretty one, the clever one, and I'm over it."

"I know what you mean. Noel's the perfect one and I have no hope of living up to the high expectations of Mom and teachers. I hate it." Ned pauses. "I sometimes think I hate him."

Shock makes me lean against a nearby tree. I love my brother, despite his numerous faults. I defend him. I even cover for him sometimes. And despite the many times he's got us into trouble, I've never remotely disliked him, let alone hated him.

"I hate Brooke sometimes too." Freya's laugh has a maniacal edge and a chill sweeps over me. "I've done some bad stuff to her, and she doesn't even know."

"Bad stuff, huh? Tell me more."

I want to interrupt them. I should. Because the last thing

Ned needs is to become besties with a freak like Freya. My first impression of her was right. She harbors the same darkness Ned does and the two of them together could spell trouble.

She laughs again. "Maybe I'll tell you when I know you better."

"Well then, let's start getting to know each other," Ned murmurs, a moment before I hear smooching noises.

Ugh. And when Freya moans, I know it's time to leave.

I head back to the house to figure out how I'm going to drive these two apart.

TWENTY

BROOKE

"It's been too long since we've done this," I say, handing Hope a charcoal nub. "Remember how we used to sketch all the time when I first came home?"

"I remember," Hope says, her mouth turning down at the corners as I belatedly realize bringing up my arrival in town coincided with Freya's death not long after.

"You've moved on from unicorns," I say, pointing to the bungalow she's sketched. It's Riker's old place, the bungalow Lizzie now resides in, and Hope's depiction is so accurate I can almost see the front door opening and my sister stepping out. "It's brilliant, sweetie. You're very talented."

"I like art." She shrugs, like my praise means little, but I see the gleam of pride in her eyes.

"Is that something you'd like to pursue after you finish school?"

She rolls her eyes, reverting to a recalcitrant tween in an instant. "I've got plenty of time to figure that out."

"Yeah, you do." I drop a kiss on the top of her head and, thankfully, she leans into me rather than wriggling away. "How are things with Hazel?"

"Good. I like having her around when you're not here." She wrinkles her nose. "Though I prefer Lizzie, but she's at work a lot." She eyeballs me. "Like you."

Her tone is clipped, her stare accusatory, and I wish I could tell her why I'm driven to save money. That I'm working hard to save a healthy nest egg so if something happens to me and I'm not around to look after her, she won't want for anything. I know Riker will take care of her if the unthinkable happens, but I want my daughter to feel secure in a way I never did when I left home at eighteen, stumbling my way through life.

"I know this new job is taking a lot of my time, sweetie, but it won't be this way for long. Once I establish myself, I won't be on the road so much and we'll get to spend more time together."

"Whatever," she mutters, her pout so reminiscent of Riker my breath catches.

The thing is, I have an ulterior motive for introducing Hazel into the conversation. With Hope liking Hazel, I'm hoping she'll like Hazel's housemate too, and it's a gentle lead-in to bringing up Noel.

I know he still doubts if I'm fully invested in us and introducing him to Hope will prove how committed I am. I want our relationship to work, but I intend to be careful so as not to confuse Hope. She's been through enough.

"Hazel has a housemate," I say, aiming for casual. "Has she mentioned him?"

"Nope." Interest sparks her eyes. "Is he cute?"

I laugh. I've seen her checking out boys at the supermarket or at the beach. I'm not looking forward to her teen years.

Though in a way, she's given me the perfect opening to introduce my relationship with Noel.

"I think so."

Her eyes widen at my admission. "Do you like him?"

I nod, feeling heat surge into my cheeks. "Hazel introduced us and I really like him."

"Is he your boyfriend?" She sounds accusatory, like I've deliberately kept this from her, and I brace.

"We enjoy hanging out together, so yeah, I guess that makes him my boyfriend. And I want you to—"

"When do I get to meet him?"

She folds her arms, defensive, but I see the fear in her eyes, like she thinks Noel will take me away from her. The last thing I want is for her to feel like she's losing me, so I rush to reassure her.

"You can meet him this weekend if you like, but I want you to know something." I take her hands in mine and, thankfully, she doesn't pull away. "You're my world, Hope. I'm here for you, always, and nobody, not even a boyfriend, will interfere with that."

Her bottom lip wobbles and my heart implodes. "But what if you marry him and have kids? I'll always just be the daughter you never knew for years who's in the way."

Grief blossoms in my chest for all I've lost with this precious girl. She needs to know that nobody will ever supersede her in my affections, and I yearn to tell her the truth. That I didn't choose to give her away. That my options had been taken away by my conniving aunt and sister. That the moment I discovered her existence I vowed to love and protect her.

But now isn't the time, though I hope our relationship will change when I reveal everything to my daughter. In Hope's eyes, I'm the bad guy in all this. She thinks I couldn't cope with being a teen mom and gave her away, and that's why Freya raised her as her own. The lie paints me in a bad light, but after Freya died it was better than the alternative: telling a grieving ten-year-old that her pseudo mother and aunt were crazy and robbed me of my daughter.

"Brooke?" Hope lays a hand on my arm, worry furrowing her brow. "It's okay if you have other kids. I won't be a bother."

My heart breaks at her earnestness and I hope she heeds my

reassurance. "Marriage is the furthest thing from my mind, sweetie, and you'll never be in the way. Ever. I love you, and nothing or nobody is going to change that."

I tug on her hands and pull her close, wrapping my arms around her, relieved when she embraces me back.

Hope is my everything. I'll do whatever it takes to protect her.

TWENTY-ONE

NOEL

THEN

Our first six weeks in Martino Bay are blissfully uneventful.

Mom's job at the cinema is going well, I'm enjoying my classes, I've made friends, Ned's behaving, and while he's hanging out with Freya a lot after hours, she seems to be having a calming influence on him.

I should've known it wouldn't last.

I'm making a peanut butter and jelly sandwich when Ned barges through the back door, banging it so hard the hinges rattle.

"I don't believe this."

"What's happened?" I screw the lid back on the peanut butter and slip the knife into the dishwasher.

"Freya's leaving." He kicks at a chair and sends it flying. "Fuck!"

It's news to me and I struggle to hide my elation. I've seen Ned in these kinds of relationships before: intense, short, usually explosive at the end. I have no doubt things will end with Freya in the same way, and when they do, I'll be left to pick up the pieces yet again.

If she's leaving, an ugly ending will be prevented and I'm hugely relieved.

"Where's she going?"

"LA."

"How long?"

"Fucked if I know." Ned scowls and starts pacing the kitchen. "Freya really got me, you know? And now she's leaving. I thought…" He trails off, anger twisting his mouth. "We could've been anything together."

The only thing Ned and Freya would've been together is trouble, but I wisely keep that to myself.

"There are plenty of other girls, Ned—"

"I don't want any other girls!" He yells so loudly I wince. "Don't you get it? I'm different than you, and Freya is the only one who understands the real me." He thumps his chest. "Nobody gets how I feel but her."

I want to placate him, but I know he'll rail against anything I say right now, so I remain silent, hoping he'll get his angst out of his system and calm down before Mom gets home. She's been happier lately, lighter, and I know it's because there have been no incidents with Ned. His behavior takes a toll on her, and I hate him for that.

My selfish, insufferable twin is a narcissist, and I often marvel how we can be twins.

Besides, after what I overheard during their conversation in the treehouse six weeks ago, what binds Ned and Freya is their mutual antipathy to their siblings, and after all we've been through, after all I've done for him, the fact that he hates me for being perfect really hurts.

If he thinks Freya is the only one who understands him and his out-of-control emotions that often result in hurting others, I can't wait to see the back of her.

"What's wrong with you?"

He stops in front of me, his question so far out of left field I'm confused.

"What do you mean?"

"What do you mean?" He mimics in a high-pitched voice. "What I mean is, you look like me, yet you never have a girlfriend. I'm the one they want. So, I'll say it again, bro, what's wrong with you?"

I've learned to be calm around my twin because losing my temper is pointless; it only spurs him on to be more of an asshole. But the fact he's staring at me like I'm the freak out of the two of us really irks.

"You know I'm focused on grades because I want to get into a good college."

And considering our finances, a scholarship is the only way to do it, hence my obsession with studying.

"But what about girls, man?" He slugs me on the arm, too hard to be playful. "I bet you're still a virgin."

I redden and, predictably, he pounces. "Bro, you have to live a little. Freya's my sixth in the past year."

Six? I didn't know he'd been close enough to other girls to have sex with them. Unless... I push the ugly thought that it may not have been consensual with those other girls to the back of my mind.

Is that what happened with Candy at our old school in Reseda? Had he forced himself on her and she'd been brave enough to report it?

"Hey." He snaps his fingers in front of my face. "You better get with the program, bro, or you'll give us a bad name."

He squares his shoulders, the crazy glint in his eyes making me grit my teeth. "The Harwood brothers can do anything they want."

He winks. "At least, one of us can. Just watch me."

TWENTY-TWO

LIZZIE

Martino Bay has an amazing farmers market on the last Sunday of every month. It's become so famous for its artisan produce that people flock from nearby towns and some even make the two-hour trek from LA for it. The stalls sit under sunny yellow awnings and the vendors offer a wide variety of goods, from homemade preserves and jellies to locally sourced honey, from freshly baked bread to fragrant herbs, and huge bouquets of flowers that perfume the air. The handmade wares, like jewelry and pottery, are almost as tempting as the food produce, and I never leave empty-handed.

I haven't been in ages and want to stock up on the handmade fig and goat milk soap that I've been using forever. Plus it's a good opportunity to scout for gifts for Hope's thirteenth birthday. She loves the market almost as much as I do but she's out with Brooke today.

Brooke has been busy the last few nights and I haven't had a chance to tell her about Hazel's housemate being an ex-con. Not that she'll appreciate the advice—she'll think I'm interfering—but I'm hoping it's one step closer to the two of us reconciling.

I saw Max at work on Friday and he's going with Annie's suggestion to interview Noel for the prison liaison officer job. Max is a fair man and, while he's heard doubts about Noel from a guard, and my gut reaction, he prefers to judge people on performance, so he's giving Noel a chance.

If Noel gets the job, we'll be spending a lot of time together and the thought makes me uncomfortable. I can't forget the way he looked at me that day in class—the kind of stare that makes me want to take a hot shower to slough off the day. But there's an upside. If we're working together, I can keep an eye on him, and see for myself if his nice-guy persona is an act.

Annoyed that I'm thinking about work on the weekend, I slip my earbuds in and choose a relaxation playlist featuring soothing pan flutes and harps as I stroll through the market. Tempting aromas of frying onions and hot dogs war with popcorn and cotton candy, and I pass countless stalls stacked high with fresh produce, relishes, fudges, and cakes.

I turn down the music when I reach my soap supplier, who is doing a bustling trade. Unfortunately, my favorite soap is out of stock, so I choose a new blend, lavender and rosehip, which smells divine.

"Have you seen these, Lizzie? They just came in." Felicia, the vendor, thrusts a long rectangular box at me, and I smile when I see what's inside.

A set of six multicolored unicorns. Hope will love it. She used to sketch them all the time when she was younger.

"They are gorgeous," I say, handing over twenty-five dollars. "My niece will love them."

"How is Hope? I haven't seen her around much." Felicia's face falls. "Young people hit a certain age and don't find my farmyard animal soaps so cute anymore."

I smile. "Like most tweens, she's twelve going on thirty."

Felicia nods. "It's tough watching them grow up so fast."

Though not as tough as being ostracized from Hope's life.

I'm tired of only spending brief amounts of time with her. I think it's time to have a confronting conversation with Brooke and clear the air so the three of us can be close like we used to. Maybe if I told her about what happened to me at work that day with Grant, she would understand. But the idea of talking about the incident, which could've escalated into an assault, makes my throat close. She hasn't given me a chance to tell her the truth, and I hope that when she does, I'll be able to talk about it.

I'm not deluded enough to believe Brooke will forgive me completely even if she knows, but however long it takes, I'll make sure we're a family again.

Another customer arrives at the stall, so I brandish my bag at Felicia. "Thanks for these."

Felicia beams. "You're welcome. Please say hi to Brooke and Hope for me."

"Shall do."

I place the cute unicorns in the bag with my soap and wave goodbye. Felicia's lovely. but she's nudging eighty, and by her penchant for long chats, I think she's lonely. I know the feeling.

After perusing a few more stalls and choosing a small topaz star on a thin gold chain as another gift for Hope, I make my way along Main Street to my car, which is parked on the opposite end of town thanks to the crowds that flock to the market. It's a lovely day, with a light breeze taking the edge off the sun, and many people are out for a Sunday stroll.

The park behind the main square is packed too, with families picnicking, kids flying kites, and couples lounging on blankets in the shade of trees. It's easier for me to cut through the park to my car and I'm three quarters of the way along the winding path that bisects it when I see something that stops me dead.

Hope and Brooke are sitting on the edge of the fountain, laughing and in animated conversation with a man who has his arm around Brooke's waist. It must be her new boyfriend, a guy who's important enough to her that she's introducing her to Hope, and I can't help but feel hurt.

Over the last two years, I would've been the one she confided in first about a new man. Heck, she'd come to me about trialing a relationship with Riker because she wanted to get my thoughts, and I'd been nothing but supportive.

If this guy is special enough that she's introducing him to Hope, I'm happy for her. Until I get closer, and the guy leans into Brooke so he can say something to Hope, and I catch a glimpse of his profile.

I swear my heart stops as recognition hits.

My sister's boyfriend is Noel Harwood.

TWENTY-THREE

BROOKE

I'm on cloud nine. This afternoon has gone off without a hitch, and while Hope is usually quieter around strangers, she's taken to Noel. They've chatted about music (they both like rap but disagree on what constitutes pop), favorite foods (Hope's obsession with mac 'n' cheese is shared by Noel, who's also partial to a good pot roast), favorite colors (Hope's is purple, Noel favors navy), and school, which Noel loved, much to Hope's amusement—and I can't keep the grin off my face.

With the sound of the fountain tinkling behind our backs, the sun on our faces, and laughter of little kids running through the park, I can't remember the last time I felt so at peace.

"I've had such a great time. Would you ladies like to join me for pizza?" Noel asks, his expression open and friendly as his gaze swings between me and Hope.

It's a sweet invitation, but before Hope can answer I say, "That's kind of you to offer, Noel, but Sunday night is our prep time for the busy week ahead."

"That's too bad." His shoulders slump slightly in disappointment. "Maybe next time?"

"Sure," I say, a rote response to placate him.

Because the truth is, while today has gone better than I could've anticipated, I don't want to rush things. Hope spending more time with Noel and me will build up her expectations too soon and I want to take things slow. Hope hanging out with us screams *family*, and Noel and I aren't in a full-blown relationship yet. I may have let him into our lives but I'm not rushing anything.

"Actually, it's probably time we headed home." I stand, surprised that Hope hasn't said a word since Noel's offer of pizza. I thought she would've jumped at the chance to forego our Sunday night chores.

"Yeah, me too." He gives me a quick hug then extends his hand to Hope. "It's been lovely meeting you, young lady. Let's catch up again soon."

Hope's silent as she stares at Noel's outstretched hand for an uncomfortable few moments before she shakes it quickly and releases it.

As Noel strides away, Hope says, "He has a cute butt for an old guy."

"Hope!" I admonish, but her teasing melts my heart and I tug her ponytail. "So, what did you think?"

"He's okay," she says, with a shrug, and her lack of enthusiasm punctures some of my earlier joy at how well this afternoon went.

"Just okay?"

She nibbles on her bottom lip and can't meet my eyes. "I know you like him, and he seems nice enough, but I kind of got the impression he's trying too hard. Like Bette at school. She's always smiling and saying nice things and sharing her lunch, and she talks to everyone, but I've seen her stare at kids behind their backs and it's a little creepy. Like that handshake. Why couldn't he just say bye without being all stiff and formal?"

The bubble of elation surrounding me from earlier well and truly pops. Hope thinks Noel's creepy?

She must see my crestfallen expression because she adds, "Don't worry, Brooke. It's great you're dating, and if you think he's a good guy, that's all that matters."

"Thanks, sweetie."

But as I sling my arm across her shoulders and hug her, I can't ignore the niggle of worry eating away at my euphoria. Hope is my number one priority and if she doesn't like Noel, there can be no future for us.

I try to reassure myself that it's early days and I'm taking it slow, so maybe I'm foreseeing problems that aren't there and thinking too far ahead. Though considering I just introduced my new boyfriend to my daughter, the speed of our relationship feels like it's moving along faster now. A good thing, I think, but considering my past, I can't let go of all my reservations at once.

"Come on," I say. "Let's head home."

We make aimless small talk on the short drive home—she's excited about a new boy at school and whether he'll be in her English class or not—and I'm almost relieved to be left to my own thoughts when I pull into our drive and she bolts for the house so she can call a friend to discuss the new boy further.

As I get out of the car, I see Lizzie watching me from her bungalow and I raise my hand in a wave. We can't ignore each other forever and deep down I'm starting to feel foolish at over-reacting about what I saw between her and Riker. It's been two months now and maybe I've punished her enough. Though maybe my lenience has more to do with me finding happiness with Noel and I'm softening, wanting to mend fences with the only sister I have left.

I ponder how I'm going to broach the subject with her when I see her marching toward me, her strides long, her expression thunderous.

So much for mending fences.

"Hey, Lizzie—"

"Is Noel Harwood your boyfriend?"

Stunned she knows Noel, I take a step back and lean against the car. "How do you know Noel?"

"How do *you* know Noel?" She shakes her head. "And how could you introduce him to Hope?"

Anger burns in my gut that she presumes to know what I should and shouldn't do with Hope.

"Noel is Hazel's housemate, so she introduced us at a bar almost a month ago, and we've been seeing each other since. Today's the first time he met Hope. And it went very well."

I add that little white lie because the last thing I want is for Lizzie to quiz Hope about Noel and my daughter vocalizing her misgivings like she did with me earlier.

"Noel's not who you think he is," Lizzie mutters, her lips compressed.

I glare at her in disbelief. She doesn't know a thing about Noel, and if she thinks I'll tolerate her interference in my relationship, she's deluded.

But then I glimpse genuine concern in her eyes and I relent a little. Lizzie works at the correctional center in Wilks Inlet, so maybe they've met? Noel has never mentioned taking her classes, so I have no idea if that's it. But I won't give her the satisfaction of thinking I'm completely in the dark.

"I know he's an ex-con. I know he accidentally killed his twin brother, if that's what you mean."

Lizzie gapes for a moment, before saying, "And you're okay with that?"

Annoyed by her judging me when she has no right to, I say, "I'm okay with a guy who's honest with me from the start. He never tried to hide his past and he owned up to his mistakes. I believe we all deserve a second chance, don't you?"

Lizzie's expression is mutinous. "Yes, I do, but I've met a lot of ex-cons at work, so I know when they're truly capable of change, and I don't see that in Noel. There's something off about him, Brooke, and I wish you'd reconsider dating him."

My patience with Lizzie cracks. We haven't spoken in eight weeks and now she's lecturing me about who I can and can't see?

"Why? So you can have him for yourself?" I snap my fingers and she recoils. "Maybe this is Riker all over again, and you want what I have." I scowl.

"Don't be ridiculous." Lizzie's cheeks redden. "Nothing happened between Riker and me. I was drunk and lonely, he was comforting me and saying the sweetest things, and I misread the signals. I leaned in, which is what you saw, but I never would've kissed him. It was a spur of the moment mistake I regretted immediately and felt like an ass, then you saw it and blew it out of all proportion."

There are tears in her eyes, and I see nothing but sincerity. But she said something I've never heard her admit before and considering my lack of relationships over the years, I can identify.

"You're lonely?"

Sadness darkens her eyes before she blinks, but it does little to eradicate the vulnerability I glimpse. "Please don't take this the wrong way, Brooke, but the last two years have been about us reconnecting as sisters and me being there for Hope. I don't resent it, but sometimes I miss dating and..." She glances away, her blush deepening. "Seeing you with Hope, the mother-daughter bond you're developing, shows me how truly alone I am."

Tears burn my eyes as she presses a hand to her chest. "I think I'd like to have a child someday but there are no prospects on the horizon for me. That night you saw me with Riker I'd had a really bad day at work with an intimidating client. He pinned me in the corner and I was paralyzed by fear, until my flight reaction kicked in and I pushed past him and made a run for it. The incident shook me up because it was the first time at work I've felt so vulnerable, so I drank too much that night after it happened and mistook Riker's kindness for something it wasn't."

She eyeballs me and her candor is heart-wrenching. "I truly am sorry, Brooke."

I'm horrified by what Lizzie went through and relieved it hadn't been worse. Now I understand her rationale, I feel awful and emotion clogs my throat. "I'm sorry too, for you going through something so terrifying, for not giving you a chance to explain. For not having this discussion sooner." I grimace. "For not believing in you."

Lizzie's smile is tremulous as she steps into my open arms and we embrace. I hug her tight, unable to stop my tears flowing with hers. I know she's going to have more to say about Noel, but for now, it's enough that we've finally reunited.

I hate that I thought Lizzie was like Freya, a sister capable of lying, of stealing, of betraying. Freya's traitorous behavior in making me believe I was Hope's aunt, not her mother, broke my heart.

Even now, with Freya dead and Aunt Alice cut out of my life, I can't believe they told me my baby had died at birth, enabling Freya to raise my little girl.

Freya had been Hope's mother for too long, been the one to soothe her cries and snuggle with her at night, to teach her to read and get her ready for school. She'd denied me my rights for so many years, and I can never forgive nor forget.

But Lizzie isn't Freya, and in forgiving her this minor indiscretion, I feel like I can have a true family again. I can have my daughter, my sister—and Noel, if our relationship continues its current trajectory.

Freya's terrible choices are in the past.

Lizzie and I will be better in the future.

TWENTY-FOUR

NOEL

With every month after Freya leaves, Ned's bad behavior escalates. He picks fights with guys at school. His truancy rate is sky-high. He hooks up with girls at parties, smokes a lot of weed, and drinks to excess.

And lucky me, I have a ringside seat to it all.

Things come to a head at a bonfire at the base of the cliffs about six months after Freya has left. Ned played way too much beer pong earlier in the evening and he's practically staggering around the fire. But that doesn't stop him coming on to the primmest girl in our grade, Bonnie Mors. Rumor has it she's never kissed a guy, let alone dated one, but kids respect her because she's nice to everyone and is super smart. I have a secret crush on her because her intelligence is next level and I admire her diligence. Plus, it hasn't escaped my attention that her cleavage is falling out of her tee.

Ned has been hanging around Bonnie all night. Running a hand over her hair as he passes. Plying her with beer in red plastic cups that she doesn't drink, thank goodness. Leering at her from across the flames. I know it's only a matter of time before he does something inappropriate and I'll have to step in, but I don't want it to get to that point, so I must pre-empt it.

While Ned's getting a beer refill from a keg, I make my way across the sand to Bonnie, who's choosing a soda from an ice bucket.

"Hey Bonnie, want to go for a walk?"

"No thanks." Her response is instant and my heart plummets before she peers a little closer at me. "You're not Ned."

"I'm Noel."

She smiles and I swear my heart skips a beat. "In that case, I'd love to."

She glances over my shoulder and wrinkles her nose. "I know you might not want to hear this, but your brother's a creep."

I shrug. "He can be a real pain in the ass but he's my twin, so I have to look out for him."

She opens her mouth to say something before thinking better of it and shaking her head instead. "The girls think he's stalkerish, the way he keeps coming on to everyone and moving from one girl to the next, especially when..."

She trails off and looks away, her expression furtive.

"Especially when...?" I prompt, knowing if this has something to do with Ned it won't be good.

Her gaze returns to mine. "Have you heard the rumors about Freya?"

I want to say, *That she's as bad as my brother?* But I shake my head instead. "What rumors?"

She hesitates, before blurting, "A few of the girls think Freya's pregnant, and that's why her aunt moved her to LA. There are whispers that Ned is the father of the child."

I bark out a laugh. "That's ridiculous."

"I guess, but that rumor about Ned and Freya is going

around." She shrugs. "I suppose we'll see soon enough, if Freya comes back to town with a baby."

That's the moment I know Ned has to leave Martino Bay.

Because if what Bonnie says is true, Ned can't know he's fathered a child. He's obsessive enough and I'm afraid of what he might do to Freya, and the child, if he learns she kept it from him.

Ned can never know.

TWENTY-FIVE

LIZZIE

After Hope goes to bed, Brooke and I curl up on the sofa, nursing a glass of shiraz each, like we used to.

We've done this so many times over the past two years, when our world as we knew it had been tipped off its axis. Discovering Alice and Freya's treachery had affected us all in different ways, and after Freya's death, our focus had been entirely on Hope. I've missed this. Missed us.

So I tell her. "I've missed you so much." I raise my glass and she taps hers against it. "To us."

"To us," Brooke echoes, taking a sip of wine and eyeing me over the rim of her glass. "I'm sorry I didn't give you a chance to explain earlier." She grimaces. "I've got some serious trust issues in case you didn't notice."

We laugh in unison, and I gulp half my wine before placing the glass on the coffee table. "You and me both, which is why I freaked out when I saw you with Noel."

Her expression sobers. "You clearly know of Noel from work because you said he's not capable of change, but he's been honest with me from the very beginning."

We've only just resolved our differences, so I don't want to lie to her.

"It's more than just observing him at work." I take a deep breath and let it out. "I've met Noel."

Suspicion clouds her eyes, like she thinks I'm going to pounce on him like I almost did with Riker. "When?"

"About a month ago. I was taking an extra class at work, standing in for Annie, another art therapist, and Noel was in my class. It was his last of the three-month program."

"And?"

I have to tell her all of it. "And I got a bad vibe off him. He didn't do or say anything, but it's just a gut feeling, you know?"

Brooke's smart and she won't let this go. "There's more, right? Otherwise, you wouldn't have freaked when you saw him with Hope and me earlier."

I give a slight shake of my head. "I asked my boss about Noel, and he mentioned one of the guards at the prison felt he was too good to be true. Though Annie, my co-worker, thinks he's great, to the point she's put him forward for a job as prison liaison officer, and Max has agreed, so Noel will probably get the job."

A tiny frown mars her brow. "He hasn't said anything to me about it."

"Probably because he hasn't interviewed yet, though I get the feeling it's just a formality. They want him to take the job."

"I know you're looking out for me," Brooke says, "for us. And I appreciate it. But I'm taking things really slow with Noel, so you don't have to worry." Her glance slides to the closed door leading to the hallway and Hope's bedroom. "I'd never put Hope in danger."

I reach out and clasp her hand. "I know you wouldn't. You love that girl, and she knows it."

Brooke takes a healthy gulp of wine. "Will you see much of Noel at work if he accepts the job?"

"Yes, our paths will cross regularly, because he'll be the go-between for the released prisoners and our art therapy classes. Why?"

"Will it be weird for you if I introduce him to you outside of work? As my boyfriend?"

"A little."

I lie. It's a lot weird. The last thing I want is Noel knowing where I live and being forced to socialize with him. Though he's done nothing untoward, I can't get what he went to prison for out of my head and I would never normally let anyone in my classes anywhere near my private life.

I don't want to push Brooke too much, but I wonder if she knows the full extent of what Noel did. He may have killed his brother accidentally, but he also left him to die. Could she know that and still have feelings for him? Doubtful. But I know if I bring it up now, I risk the tentative re-establishing of our relationship. Not to mention I could get in serious trouble for passing on information about a former client to someone outside of work if Brooke tells him what I've revealed.

With Noel, it feels too much too soon. I don't care how much Brooke trusts him, I don't.

"I know this is a lot to ask, Brooke, but I'd prefer it if you didn't invite him here for a while yet. To the house. It blurs the lines, you know?"

I expect her to protest, but to my relief, she nods. "This is our sanctuary and until I get to know him better, and really invest in us, I'll hold off inviting him to the house. Hope's too precious to me." She smiles. "You are too, sis."

"Right back at you."

I should be relieved as we clink glasses. We've resumed our relationship and she's being cautious with Noel.

But the truth is, I can't deny my gut instinct and I need to keep Noel away from my family. I'm just going to have to be more careful about how I do it.

TWENTY-SIX

BROOKE

I'm relieved I've resolved my differences with Lizzie. She's too important to me to hold a grudge. But I can't get her warnings about Noel out of my head.

Not that she warned me away from him per se, but that "gut feeling" she has about him niggles. And hot on the heels of the amazing day I've had, with him meeting Hope and it going well for the most part, I'm a tad annoyed.

I also hate my inner voice that insists maybe Lizzie is more like Freya than I think, and she covets what I have.

First Riker, now Noel.

Is Lizzie advising me to tread carefully with Noel because she wants him for herself?

It's an outlandish thought. Just because they've already met doesn't mean they hit it off. Heck, by Lizzie's expression earlier, she's definitely not a fan.

But I've trusted those closest to me before and been burned badly so I can't dismiss my doubts completely. That's the real reason I agreed to her not wanting Noel anywhere near our house, and why I asked if they'd see each other at work if he accepts the job offer.

My sliver of jealousy may be irrational, especially now we've made up, but doubt is too ingrained in me to trust anyone completely.

I hope I'm not overthinking things as I get into bed and grab my e-reader to immerse myself in a new thriller. Nothing like a twisted plot to take my mind off my own convoluted life. But I barely swipe the first page when my phone buzzes and Noel's name pops up on the screen.

I answer, unable to keep the smile off my face. He's attentive, calling almost every night, even when we've seen each other during the day.

"Hey, you."

"Hey, yourself. I know I saw you earlier today, but I miss you already." His voice is low, and a ripple of desire runs through me. "So, did I pass the test with Hope? Does she like me? I think she's wonderful. She's a really amazing kid."

And just like that, I'm doused with cold water. Noel almost sounds too eager, and I'm reminded that I need to take our relationship slowly and maybe I've done the wrong thing in introducing him to Hope. We've barely been dating a month. Have I let my euphoria at having my first real adult relationship taint my judgment?

Or maybe Lizzie's got inside my head and her doubts are making me second-guess myself.

"She is wonderful. I think the meeting went well."

If he notices I'm less enthusiastic than him, he doesn't say. "She mentioned she's turning thirteen in a few months. That must be exciting, having a teenager in the house soon."

I have no idea if he's being sarcastic or genuine and my unease increases. Time to change the subject.

"How was work for the rest of the afternoon after we met up in the park?"

I'm steering the conversation toward his job to see if he'll tell me about the offer Lizzie mentioned. Underhanded, maybe, but I may as well use the information Lizzie told me.

"The same." He sounds weary and nothing like the upbeat guy discussing Hope a few moments ago. "Don't get me wrong. I'm grateful they gave me a chance when a lot of employers won't touch an ex-con. But bagging groceries or stocking shelves isn't exactly difficult or brain taxing."

"Have you considered any other possibilities?"

"Not really. I have a few thoughts on potential jobs, but if I'm moving out soon, I need to show steady employment, you know?"

He doesn't mention the prison liaison officer job offer and I'm disappointed. If we're dating, shouldn't we discuss stuff like that? Unless he doesn't want to get his hopes up if it doesn't happen and then he'll have to explain his failure to me. I already get the impression he wonders why I'm dating someone like him, so I understand his reticence to discuss a new job that may never eventuate.

"Yeah, that makes sense."

There's a loud bang in the background, like a door being flung open, followed by raucous female laughter.

"Is Hazel having a party?"

"No." He sounds annoyed. "One too many wines, I think."

I laugh, but he doesn't join in. "I'm not that much of a hard-ass boss that she needs to resort to alcohol, am I?"

"Of course not. You're the best."

I like how he instantly leaps to my defense, but there's an edge to his voice that wasn't there before.

"Anyway, I better go. I've got an early start tomorrow but just wanted to hear your voice."

"Thanks for calling," I say, sounding way too formal and inwardly wincing. "We still on for drinks at the end of the week?"

"Absolutely. And Brooke?"

"Yeah?"

"Thanks for letting me meet Hope. It means a lot because I know you have faith in me."

Before I can respond, he hangs up, and thanks to Lizzie instilling doubts in my head, I'm left wondering if maybe I've shown too much faith too soon.

TWENTY-SEVEN

NOEL

THEN

I don't sleep that night. How can I, when what Bonnie divulged about Freya being pregnant is playing like a horror reel on repeat in my head?

Thankfully, Ned hasn't heard the rumor yet. If he had, he wouldn't be sleeping peacefully in the bedroom next to mine. I've seen him react to things when he's unhappy and it's not pretty. *Ballistic* would be a tame label for what Ned might do if he thinks Freya is pregnant with his child and left town to keep it from him.

He became obsessed with Freya too quickly and I knew it wouldn't end well.

There's only one way to stop this ending badly.

Get Ned away from Martino Bay.

I run through a plethora of scenarios in my head, trying to hash out a solution that's foolproof. Then again, whatever I come up with is risky, but I have to try.

The way to do it comes to me as dawn breaks and the first slivers of gold and mauve streak my ceiling.

It's bad. Something I would never do because I hate deceit. But protecting my brother calls for extreme measures.

Thankfully, he's grown his hair longer to mimic mine, so we look identical. No one will ever guess that good Noel can morph into bad Ned, even for ten minutes, the time it will take to set my plan in motion and get Ned as far away from Martino Bay as possible.

News of Ned's indiscretions must've reached the principal of Martino Bay High because Mom warned us both before we started that if either of us screwed up—meaning if Ned got up to his usual tricks—we'd be forced to leave.

So that's exactly what will happen.

Ned needs to be expelled.

Today.

I know if he's asked to leave school, our mom will move us away—just like last time.

I feel bad involving Bonnie because she was so nice to me on our walk yesterday. She's lovely inside and out—probably why Ned targeted her because there's nothing he loves more than a challenge, and corrupting the good girls is his favorite pastime. But for this to work, I need everyone to believe Ned went too far with Bonnie, and there were enough witnesses yesterday to see Ned harassing her. With what I have in mind, they'll back up Bonnie when she complains to the principal, which is guaranteed once I follow through.

Just before lunch is the perfect time to execute my plan. Ned and I have a study period in the library on a Wednesday, which I always attend, and Ned never does. But I know he'll be there today because I told him Annette, another good girl he has his eye on, needs help with geometry, his favorite subject, and I told him she'd welcome the tutoring. No way in hell he'll pass up that opportunity. And of course I told Annette I'll be helping her, so she won't know the difference. Even if Ned corrects her, she'll think I'm playing a game because I already played the whole twin-swap trick on her this morning and she laughed.

To make sure Ned takes the bait, I wait until Annette sits at a carrel and sure enough, Ned saunters up to her, full of his usual swagger, and within minutes their chairs are pulled close and they're solving geometric problems. Ned's so engrossed he barely gives me a second glance when I walk to their carrel and pause to greet them—and long enough to swap my cell for Ned's.

I don't have long, so once I leave the library I sprint to the gymnasium and arrive just in time for the girls to be filing into the locker room. They don't see me as I wait behind a column. They don't see me when one of the girls leaves the room and the door is ajar. But I make sure they see me when I jam my foot in the door, leaving a gap big enough that I can raise my cell and snap a pic of Bonnie about to tug her jersey over her head.

It's not a risqué photo as such—I don't want to sully her reputation or embarrass her too much—but it shows her bare midriff, and when the girls start yelling at me, calling me "perv" and worse, I know the job is done.

When Bonnie tugs her jersey down and sees me, I give the same cocky salute Ned had given her yesterday. She screams, and that's my cue to make a run for it. I sprint back to the library, where Ned and Annette are still sitting close together, and clap my brother on the back, asking how it's going. I get a scowl for my trouble, and he's oblivious when I switch our phones again.

I take a seat a few carrels away and wait, knowing it won't be long until Ned's hauled to the principal's office. But Ms. Edi must be busy because the bell rings and it's lunchtime before his name is bellowed over the PA to attend her office.

Of course I go along with him, the solicitous brother who always has his back.

"Do you know what this is about?" I ask him, and he shakes his head.

"Who knows what bee Beady Edi has in her bonnet?" Ned rolls his eyes. "She's a troll. But at least I got to get up close and personal with prissy Annette thanks to you."

He elbows me. "I owe you one, bro."

Guilt makes my gut churn with dread and nausea swamps me as we reach Ms. Edi's office and she's standing in the doorway, glowering at us because she can't tell the difference between us and isn't sure which one of us is Ned.

"Ned Harwood, in my office. Now." Her tone is icy, her frown formidable, but in typical Ned fashion he shoots me a wink and says, "Yes, ma'am."

"Can I come in too—"

"You can wait out here, young man." Ms. Edi points to the row of chairs outside her office. "This doesn't concern you."

I feel dreadful as I sit and wait. I half expect to hear yelling because I know Ned has no respect for teachers, let alone Ms. Edi. But it's surprisingly silent and it only takes ten minutes before her office door is flung open and Ned saunters out, looking surprisingly smug and nonchalant for someone who just got expelled. I hope.

Ms. Edi appears startled to see me, as if she forgot I was waiting. "Noel, I'm very sorry, but your mother will be here shortly to collect Ned. Your brother will be leaving our school."

"Which means I'll be leaving too." I sound devastated and keep my gaze downcast, so she doesn't see my plan has worked.

I didn't want our time here to end like this. I like Martino Bay and I've made friends here, but with Ned expelled, Mom will want to leave town for him to have a fresh start elsewhere and that means I'll be going with them. Ned and I are a package deal. I'm the shiny wrapping on the outside; he's the nasty surprise inside the package.

I shouldn't care about leaving Martino Bay because we'll

find another school and I'll still excel and go to college and become the man Ned will never be. But this time I resent him for forcing my hand so I had to do whatever it took to protect another girl potentially getting hurt.

"I'm sorry you've been put in this position, Noel." Ms. Edi sits next to me. "You're a stellar student and will go far. I wish you all the best in your academic endeavors and I'm sorry our school will lose a student of your capabilities." She tut-tuts. "But your brother has committed a grievous violation of privacy against a fellow student, and while he won't be charged because he didn't distribute the photo he took, this school has a no-tolerance policy for indiscretions of this nature."

I don't need the explanation, but I can hear she's genuinely sad to lose me, so I say, "I understand, Ms. Edi."

"Best of luck, young man." She offers a tight smile as she stands. "And a word of advice? Don't let your brother drag you down."

I don't respond. What's the point when I happen to agree with her? But Ned's my twin and as long as I'm around I'll look out for him.

He's waiting for me outside, leaning against the red brick wall, the sole of a foot braced against it, arms crossed, his expression nonchalant. Typical Ned, he doesn't give a crap about being expelled again. It's Mom I feel sorry for, but in the long run she'll thank me if I prevent Ned from doing something unforgivable to Freya. Or worse, his child.

"Well played, bro," Ned says, his grin smug, his eyes filled with admiration. "I didn't know you had it in you."

I've rehearsed this part in my head and I'm hoping Ned buys it.

"You're always telling me to loosen up and I know you like Bonnie, so I thought I'd snap a pic." I grimace. "I had no intention of getting caught though, so I'm sorry you got the blame for me being an idiot."

He shrugs. "Hey, don't sweat it. Though why did you swap phones when you could've taken the pic and texted it to me?"

"Because I'm not that much of a rebel." I roll my eyes. "I didn't want to be the one caught with it on my phone."

He laughs. "Nice."

"You're not mad at me?"

"Mad? I'm rapt you're not the goody-goody nerd I pegged you for." He straightens and slaps me on the back. "About time you lightened up."

"What about Mom? She's going to be livid I screwed up."

He pauses for a moment. "I'll take the blame. She expects the worst of me anyway. Why tarnish your reputation too?"

I counted on this, Ned's sense of loyalty. He may be unstable at times, but I know he takes our twin bond seriously.

"Thanks, Ned." I shake my head. "I don't think I'm cut out to be bad. The first time I try and do something a little rebellious and this happens."

"Relax, bro. Besides, Mom's going to make us move again and I'm glad. Martino Bay sucks without Freya around. I can't wait to leave."

Me too.

The further we get from this town and the ramifications of Ned's relationship with Freya, the better.

TWENTY-EIGHT

LIZZIE

Two days later, I'm in my office, catching up on admin, when Max knocks on my door.

"Are you free for the next thirty minutes?"

He knows I'm not, because I'm neck-deep in writing reports for every participant in my last twelve-week art therapy course. Parole officers want to be kept abreast, and while report-writing can be tedious, I quite enjoy giving mostly positive feedback on those in my classes.

"If it's for a coffee, yes. Anything else, these reports can't wait."

Max chuckles at my droll response. "I want you to sit in on Noel Harwood's interview."

I can't hide my distaste quick enough and Max points a finger at me. "There. That right there is why I want you in his interview. You had a gut feeling about the guy from your one interaction and I want to see if there's something Annie's missing, because she can't sing his praises enough."

"Max, you're the boss. What you say goes. And your judgment hasn't steered you wrong, so whatever Annie thinks, you'll be making the final decision regardless."

"Yeah, but it can't hurt to get different perspectives." He huffs out a breath. "Come on, Lizzie, you and Annie are our best workers and I want to ensure I'm making the right choice in hiring this guy."

Technically, I can't say no. Max could demand me to be at Noel's interview. But he's a good boss and a nice guy, and I guess what he's saying is right. I might give a balanced opinion if Annie's hellbent on singing Noel's praises.

"Okay, give me five minutes."

"Great. See you in the conference room."

I smile, because our "conference room" can barely hold a table and four chairs, but it's where we hold our more official meetings.

After my chat with Brooke a few nights ago, I've wondered how I'll handle running into Noel at work if he gets the job. For the moment, he doesn't know I'm a relation of Brooke's, and it's not my place to tell him. He'll probably think I'm underhanded when he discovers our bond, but I don't care. My loyalty lies with Brooke and when she deems it the right time to introduce him to the rest of her family, I'll be okay with it.

When I reach the conference room, Max is seated in the middle of three chairs, with one placed opposite.

"Annie's bringing Noel in," he says, gesturing to the empty chair on his right. "Why don't you take a seat?"

I place a notebook and pen in front of me. Not that I intend on taking notes, but it looks more official. I barely have time to sit before Annie enters the room ahead of Noel. He's wearing a navy suit, white shirt, and fine-striped aqua tie that brings out the blue of his eyes, and I instantly see what Brookes sees. He's attractive in a polished way that not many ex-cons are. And when he smiles, he transforms into gorgeous.

"Good to see you again, Lizzie," he says, holding out his hand, and I shake it.

"And you must be Max." Noel pumps his hand. "Thanks for this opportunity to interview. I appreciate it."

"No worries, Noel." Max gestures to the seat opposite us. "Please, sit, and we'll get started."

Annie sits on the other side of Max and gives me a thumbs-up sign of approval behind our boss's back. She's confident Noel has the job and I wish I shared her enthusiasm. Though in all honesty Noel appears disarming today, without a hint of agenda in sight, like the vibes I picked up on in my class.

Max steeples his fingers on the desk. "So, Noel, tell us why you're the perfect candidate for the prison liaison officer role."

Noel smiles and once again I'm struck by how handsome he is. "Firstly, I'm a people person. I make it my business to understand what makes people tick and I focus on their strengths. I listen. I learn. I'm open and approachable. I've been that way in my past as a finance manager and during my stint at the correctional facility."

I glance at Max and see he's suitably impressed.

"What about conflict resolution?" Max asks. "You must've seen your fair share in prison?"

I note how Max deliberately says "prison" in comparison to Noel's "correctional facility," as if he was trying to downplay it and Max wants to remind him that he did the crime and had to do the time.

"Diplomacy is key," Noel says, without hesitation. "It's important to know when to be flexible, when to stand your ground, and when to back down. I think conflict is inevitable in life, but it's how we deal with it that makes us grow."

Noel's good, I'll give him that. Even I'm buying into this guileless charm. It makes me second-guess my first reaction to him.

"Will it be a problem for you liaising with prisoners now that you've been out of the institution for four months?" Max asks.

"Not at all." Noel clasps his fingers together and rests his hands in his lap. "While I never take my freedom for granted and am making the most of every day, I haven't forgotten the time I spent in Wilks Inlet Correctional and I'm more than capable of being the go-between for the prisoners and the outside world."

I cast a quick glance at Annie and she's beaming. Her protégé is killing it. And by Max's relaxed posture, he's treating this interview as a formality.

"Annie, why don't you run through the expectations of the role?" Max says, and as she outlines Noel's day-to-day tasks, it gives me time to study him.

He's poised and articulate and asks intelligent questions. Annie's right. He'll be perfect for this job. But while I'm impressed, I can't help but wonder if his answers are too glib, too practiced, like he's playing a part. Or maybe that's just my preconceived bias and I need to give him the benefit of the doubt.

Besides, what's the worst that can happen? If he's lousy at the job, Max will fire him. And if he does anything remotely out of line, ditto. I'm probably worrying for nothing, but regardless of the outcome of this interview, which already seems a foregone conclusion, I want to ask Noel a few questions of my own, without Max and Annie present.

Deep in my musings, I almost miss when Max says, "Do you have anything to ask, Lizzie?"

I shake my head. "I think you and Annie have covered everything."

"In that case, I'd like to thank you for your time today, Noel, and we'll be in touch shortly."

Max stands and we do the same, and after another round of handshakes, we follow Noel out of the building. Max and Annie gesture to me that they're headed to his office, and I hold up a finger that I'll be there in a minute.

But first, I want to do a quick interrogation of my own.

As Noel heads for the car park, I break into a half jog and call out, "Noel, got a minute?"

He stops and turns, and for a moment I swear I glimpse annoyance before his smooth mask slips back into place. "What can I do for you, Lizzie?"

"Sorry to do this out here, but I hate to admit I drifted off for a minute in the interview." I fake a wince. "Late night. But I did have a question to ask that Max and Annie didn't touch on."

He arches a brow. "Oh?"

"This will be a full-time position and the demands of a new job can be challenging. Will it encroach upon your family life?"

The flash of fury in his gaze takes me by surprise before he blinks and I'm once again looking into a serene sea of blue.

"My mother died years ago, and you already know about my brother. I've just started seeing someone and it's going well, and I'm sure she'll be supportive of my new job." He snickers. "Being a prison liaison officer has to be better than doing odd jobs at the grocer where I currently work."

I want to keep him talking to gain insight into what caused that irrational anger a moment ago.

"You don't like it?"

"It pays the rent. And my housemate teed up the job for me, so I'm grateful, because not many businesses hire ex-cons." He shrugs, but there's a hint of bitterness in his tone. "I want to make a fresh start and this job sounds a lot more challenging than my current, that's for sure."

I know Brooke hasn't mentioned me to Noel yet but has Hazel? Then again, Hazel doesn't know I work here, so even if she's mentioned Brooke has a sister called Lizzie, he wouldn't necessarily make the connection.

Maybe I should tell him the truth now? But it's not my place and I don't want Brooke thinking I'm encroaching where I shouldn't.

"You interviewed really well."

"Thanks. I'm grateful Annie sees something in me." His smile appears genuine, but I can't help but feel he's still giving me practiced, rote responses. "And Max seems like a great boss."

"He is."

"How long have you been a psychologist?"

I hesitate, not wanting to reveal too much of my background but knowing I'll have to give him something, especially if we're going to be co-workers.

"I did an arts major in college, then tacked on psychology a few years later. I had an online business for a while that had nothing to do with my degree, but I've always enjoyed art, so when I learned I could combine psychology with art, I was incredibly fortunate to get the job here as an art therapist."

"It must be rewarding."

"It is."

Maybe I'm seeing things, but Noel's staring at me with an intensity that's making me uncomfortable and I get the oddest feeling that he's toying with me.

I make a grand show of looking at my watch. "Anyway, sorry for waylaying you out here, but we need the full picture of candidates before we make a decision."

"Not a problem," he says, his grin a tad smarmy. "I'm sure I'll be seeing you around, *Lizzie*."

His emphasis on my name is unnerving and I feel his stare boring into my back as I walk away, resisting the insane urge to break into a sprint.

TWENTY-NINE

BROOKE

I'm glad Lizzie and I have resolved our differences because she's around more often when she's not at work. And that's a good thing because I'm becoming suspicious of Hazel.

I know I'm prone to paranoia—more than most and with good reason, considering what Alice and Freya did—but I'm missing a few items. Nothing major—my favorite pen, the one with fuchsia sparkles that twinkle as I write; a pair of plastic book earrings; and a small sketchpad that Hope and I doodle in —items that hold sentimental value because Hope gave them to me.

They're not worth stealing for monetary value. Heck, if Hazel wanted to steal from me for money, I've got jewelry in a box on my dresser that's worth a fair bit, so it doesn't make sense.

I hate confrontation, but if I don't ask her, who knows how this may escalate?

I make sure I leave work early so I'm home before five, when she's due to finish today. As I let myself into the house, the tantalizing aromas of chili and freshly baked bread draw me toward the kitchen. Damn, I'm going to hate having to let her go if she's guilty. Hope and I have never eaten so well. Pot roasts, creamy pastas, casseroles, lasagna, fajitas, and spicy chicken korma are just a few of Hazel's culinary repertoire, and I know Hope will miss her homemade chocolate chip cookies and double-choc brownies.

Hazel's wiping down the island bench as I enter the kitchen and she smiles when she catches sight of me.

"Hey, Brooke, you're home early today."

"Yeah, things wrapped up at work, so I made a run for it before they could heap any more urgent tasks on me."

She laughs. "Good for you. I'm almost done here. Hope's writing a book report for English and dinner's warming in the oven."

"It smells amazing."

"Just something I whipped up between cleaning the shower and dusting the den."

The den. Where I kept the pen and the sketchpad.

Dreading this, I take a steadying breath and blow it out. "Hazel, this is awkward, but I have to ask you something."

She stops wiping, but not before I see her hand tremble slightly. Hell, she's guilty, and I'm going to have to fire her.

"What's up?"

"Uh... I can't find a few things of mine and I wonder if you've moved them while cleaning."

A gentler way of leading into it rather than an outright accusation of *Did you steal my stuff?*

She frowns. "I do move items around while I clean but I always replace them. What can't you find?"

"A sparkly pink pen, a pair of dangly book earrings, and a sketchpad. They hold sentimental value more than anything and I can't seem to find them."

Her brow furrows deeper. "Sorry, don't think I've seen them. Is it possible you misplaced them?"

"No."

My response is abrupt and before I can temper it, her eyes widen as realization dawns.

"You think I stole them?"

"I'm just looking for them and—"

"I'm not a thief," she hisses, her expression appalled. "And even if I were, why would I take trinkets?"

"I'm sorry, Hazel, but I had to ask—"

"When did this stuff go missing?"

"They were around earlier in the week, because I used the pen to doodle on the pad while taking a work call, and I wore the earrings two days ago because I was discussing educational supplies with a supermarket in Wilks Inlet, so they went missing yesterday."

"Has it occurred to you I'm not the only one who has access to your house?" She gnaws on her bottom lip, nervous. "Lizzie's been in and out of here."

I bark out a laugh. "Lizzie? Why on earth would she steal from me?"

"I don't know. But I didn't take your stuff."

As her implication sinks in, I hate the tiny inner voice that insists I've trusted my other sister before and look how that turned out.

Freya stole my baby.

"Would you like me to quit? Because I can't work where I'm not trusted." She folds the cleaning cloth and hangs the neat rectangle on the oven door. "And if I can be frank, Brooke, your accusation has hurt me deeply."

I can't honestly believe Lizzie would take those personal items. She knows Hope gave them to me and how much I treasure them. Is this some warped way of her getting back at me for ostracizing her after the Riker incident? Is she toying with me? Or is her motivation something deeper, darker, like old-fashioned jealousy that Hope adores me?

She'd been suitably shocked when she learned Hope's my

biological daughter, so maybe she's envious of our quickly developed bond over the last two years when she's lived with Hope for much longer.

I hate that Hazel has planted these wild suppositions in my head, but I can't ignore them completely. If she didn't take the items—and the jury's still out on that because she may be casting blame to take the heat off herself—then the only other culprit is Lizzie and the relationship I thought is stronger than ever is irrevocably flawed.

"Your silence speaks volumes, so I'll finish up now and—"

"I'm sorry, Hazel. But you can understand I had to ask. Who knows, perhaps in my post-work exhaustion I've misplaced the items."

Something I seriously doubt, but I need to smooth things over with her even if she does leave because she's had complete access to my house, and I don't want her badmouthing me in town. Or worse, to Noel, and I can't believe this is the first time I've thought about how firing her might affect our relationship. She's his housemate and close friend, so I need to tread carefully.

"If you have misplaced them, you need to be careful who you go around accusing," she says, a hitch in her voice, like she's about to cry. "I like working here, Brooke. Hope is an amazing kid, and we get on well. Plus you have a lovely home and I enjoy maintaining it and cooking meals for you. But I'll understand if you have to let me go."

She ends on a stifled sob, and I feel terrible.

"How about you stay on, Hazel, and we see how things go?"

"Meaning as long as nothing else goes missing, I still have a job." She shakes her head. "I know blood is thicker than water, but a word of advice, Brooke? Be careful who you trust."

A shiver runs down my spine at the thought of those closest to me betraying me yet again.

THIRTY

NOEL

Ned and I graduate from Larmville High, in a small town three hours inland from LA and suitably far from Martino Bay. Every time we moved after one of Ned's "indiscretions," Mom made sure it was several hours away from where he'd offended so he wouldn't be tainted by his past. She did so much to protect him when deep down I know he didn't deserve it.

Thankfully, there were no major incidents in our final year of school because Mom read Ned the riot act and said if he screwed up one more time, he'd be kicked out of home.

I'd never seen her so devastated as when we had to leave Martino Bay, and my guilt made me want to confess. But Ned convinced me what would be the point: when she was disappointed enough in one son, why add to her burden?

So I kept silent and in a way it brought Ned and me closer. He admired me for my prank and I was relieved it had the desired outcome: getting us away from Martino Bay before Ned could discover the truth about Freya.

Turns out, that rumor about her being pregnant and going away to have the baby was true, so I'd done the right thing.

Who knows what Ned would've done if he'd found out.

I kept in touch with Damian, the nerdy guy I'd met on my first day at Martino Bay, and he told me about Freya returning to town at the end of senior year with a baby. The entire school was abuzz with the news of her teen pregnancy, but nobody knew the father, though many assumed it was Ned.

If he'd been around, he would've flipped.

But Ned remains blissfully oblivious and eschews college to land a job as a sales rep for a national fast-food company. He travels a lot and I hope that keeps him out of trouble if he doesn't stay in one place long enough. I go to college in LA and get a degree in finance, and I currently work for a bank with branches worldwide. I want to travel, to expand my horizons beyond the States, but I have an irrational fear that if I leave the US, my bond with Ned will suffer, then who knows what he's capable of.

He's never had a steady relationship and I worry about him. Does he still chase unobtainable women? Is it still a game to him? Does he taunt them like he once used to? Has his game-playing escalated?

I know Mom worries too. At Thanksgiving last month, she asked us about our dating lives, and while I'm single by choice—meaning I'm pining for one of my bosses and I can never go there because it would be an HR nightmare—Ned merely laughed, his chuckle so sinister it raised the hairs on my arms.

Mom must've heard something in that laugh too because she reiterated the importance of consent and respect, which Ned snickered at. Later that night, after dinner, I'd quizzed him about significant others, and he reassured me he didn't have his eye on anyone because he was enjoying traveling from town to town too much.

I'm relieved he mainly travels to towns in Southern California and Nevada because I can't stop thinking about what may happen if he returns to Martino Bay and learns Freya has a child.

Then again, Ned's twenty-five now, a man with a steady job, not some obsessive teen fixated on a girl. Perhaps I'm overthinking this and when I return to LA I banish it from my mind. I throw myself into work and look forward to the company's holiday party way too much because who knows what can happen under the mistletoe with my boss.

I'm spending Christmas with Ned and Mom at her place in Shar Forest, a small town about forty minutes from Wilks Inlet. She runs a nursery there and I've never seen her happier. Probably because she doesn't have twins to worry about under her roof anymore.

I have my work holiday party tonight, then I'll drive to her place in a couple of days, on Christmas Eve. I feel in control, like my life is finally working out the way it's meant to, when my phone vibrates on my desk. I'm not usually here at 11 p.m., but I want to finish a stack of loan applications, and I'm surprised someone would be calling so late.

My heart skips a beat when I see Ned's name on the screen.

I know something's wrong before I answer. I can feel it deep in my chest, in that place I've always felt it when my twin has done something bad.

My palm's clammy as I pick up my phone and tap the answer icon. "Hey, Ned. What's up?"

The ensuing silence fills me with dread.

"Ned? You're scaring me."

I hear the faintest sniffle before he says, "Noel, it's Mom."

I freeze, ice trickling through my veins. "Is she okay?"

An inane question because I know she's not. Ned wouldn't sound like this if she were.

"She's dead," he says, his eerie monotone raising my hackles. "You need to come to her place. Now."

I can't breathe as it registers that my sweet mother, who worked so hard to give us everything, who lavished us with love despite our failings, is gone.

"Noel, I'm sorry," Ned murmurs, and I'm sure I'm suffering an auditory hallucination brought on by grief when I hear him whisper, "even though she deserved it."

THIRTY-ONE

LIZZIE

As I park near my bungalow and get out of my car, I see Hazel jogging from the main house with tears streaming down her face.

Concerned, I waylay her before she reaches her car. "Are you okay?"

"Does it look like I'm okay?" She snaps, swiping tears away with the back of her hand, and glaring at me like I'm the cause.

"Anything I can do?"

"No," she mutters, slumping in dejection. "It's annoying when your life is going smoothly, then something happens to upend it."

I'm clueless what's happened but she appears so dejected I can't let her drive like this. "I hear you. Life rarely turns out the way we want it to."

"You got that right," she mutters, shaking her head. "Though from what I can see, you have the perfect life." She flings her arm wide, encompassing our land. "Amazing house, your own bungalow, killer views of the ocean, and close to family. What more could you want?"

Someone to love me, to banish the loneliness that plagues me, pops into my head. Not that I'll share that with Hazel.

"It's hard to judge someone's life looking in from the outside," I say. "We all wear a mask."

"Is that right?" She tilts her head, studying me. "What are you hiding?"

I'm taken aback by her bluntness, and the way she's staring at me, like she knows something I don't. "Nothing."

Her stare bores into me before she gives a laugh devoid of amusement. "Interesting, because according to what you just said, we're all hiding something."

I pause rather than saying, *Just trying to make small talk,* because she's fidgety, on edge, with her fingers plucking absent-mindedly at her handbag.

"Hey, have you seen Brooke's pen, earrings, and sketch-pad?" She eyeballs me and I'm confused by the suspicious glint in her unnerving stare. "They're missing."

Ah, so that's what her funk is about. Brooke must've accused her of stealing stuff. Maybe my gut instincts about Noel should extend to his housemate too.

"I haven't seen them."

"Really? Because I get the feeling you don't like me, Lizzie, and what better way to get rid of me than frame me for stealing?"

What the... Where the hell did that come from? One moment I'm trying to comfort her, the next she's accusing me of stealing. She's crazy and I hold up my hands in placation. "Listen, Hazel, I barely know you, and I wouldn't steal from my sister."

Though it wouldn't be the first time.

She snorts. "Of course you'd deny it. It's convenient that I have full access to the house, and Brooke would assume I'm the only one who would take her stuff."

"I didn't take anything," I insist, heat pooling in my cheeks at the memory of other times I did.

Times when Brooke and Freya were younger, and I hated how Alice treated them the same way she treated me. Me, her own daughter. While Brooke and Freya loved her fairness, I secretly loathed how Alice never played favorites. I should've been her number one. Her priority.

So to get back at Brooke and Freya, I took things.

Trinkets, mostly, stuff they wouldn't miss. A pen here, a hair clip there. I stashed my illegal gains in a shoebox and kept it in the back corner of my closet under a stack of old textbooks. If Alice ever suspected, she didn't say. Besides, Alice already knew Freya coveted everything Brooke had and would've assumed Freya stole Brooke's things if she ever complained. And considering Freya's intense jealousy of Brooke, vice versa.

My petty crimes went undetected, so it's weird Hazel is accusing me now of the very thing I used to do.

"Too bad for you, Brooke didn't fire me, so I'll be around for a while yet." The strange glow in Hazel's eyes is almost maniacal. "And in case you've forgotten, the keys Brooke gave me access the main house *and* the bungalow, so I can always check if you're telling the truth by searching your place."

Before I can respond she pushes past me, and I'm left gaping at her bold threat and unexpected show of strength. I rub my arm where her shoulder bumped it and watch as she gets in her car, revs the engine, and speeds away.

I have no idea what to make of our encounter. I'm not a thief—not anymore. But the memories of taking belongings have resurfaced, along with my resentment toward Alice, who I blame for my kleptomaniac habit.

Turns out, I know now why she didn't play favorites. I'm her niece, just like Brooke and Freya. A fact she should've told me years ago.

That's what hurts the most, that even when I reached adulthood, Alice didn't tell me. Brooke had been the one to reveal our messed-up childhoods and I'll always resent Alice for that.

The devastation when I'd discovered the truth had made me want to lash out at Alice, but we'd all agreed to remain civil for Hope's sake. So I bottled up my resentment and it festered to the point I haven't been able to look at her for the last two years. Her lies made me question my entire childhood and when I think back to the fun times I had with Brooke and Freya, my memories are tainted. I'll never forgive Alice for that.

And I can't help but think if I'd known Brooke was my sister, maybe I could've convinced her to return home earlier and not stay away for a decade. I could've been closer to Freya. Hell, maybe I could've prevented her from jumping off that cliff if she'd trusted me as a sister, but thanks to Alice and her sordid secrets, I'm still stuck in this limbo, wallowing in my hatred of her.

We never had it out, not properly. She thought gifting the main house to Brooke and me would somehow absolve her of her sins.

Nice try.

And now Hazel is accusing me of betraying Brooke. As if I'd do anything heinous to my sister after everything we've been through together.

What Hazel doesn't know is that I'll never let anyone, including her and Alice, get between me and my sister ever again.

THIRTY-TWO

BROOKE

I'm still pondering Hazel's bizarre accusation that Lizzie stole from me when Hope strolls into the kitchen, her expression pensive.

"Hey, sweetheart. Hungry? Because dinner's ready."

"I can eat," she says, tapping the pencil in her hand against her bottom lip. "Then can you help me with something?"

"Sure, as long as it's not math." I screw up my nose. "I'm lousy with numbers."

"That's not what Mom used to say. She said you were brilliant at everything." She cocks her head, studying me, and I quell my disappointment that she still calls Freya "Mom" at times when I'd give anything to hear her call me that. "She didn't talk about you much, which is weird. Especially now that I have to complete a family tree for biology."

"When's the assignment due?"

"Two weeks." She shrugs. "It'll be really helpful if we visit Aunt Alice, so she can help me fill in the gaps."

I subdue a flicker of guilt that we rarely visit anymore when Alice practically raised Hope alongside Freya for the first ten years of her life. But I'm still seething over what Alice did to keep my daughter and me apart and I doubt I'll ever be able to forgive her.

"I'll let Alice know we'll visit this weekend," I say, but Hope's still studying me like she knows I'm hiding something.

"I miss her," she murmurs, and I know it's wrong of me but I'm relieved when she doesn't add, *I miss Mom too.*

"Our lives have changed a lot these past few years. I'm really proud of how you've handled everything."

"That's because I have you. Is it wrong of me to think you're more of a mother to me than Mom ever was?"

My throat tightens with emotion at the nicest thing she's ever said to me. While she knows I'm her biological mother, now's the time to tell her the rest. But how can I do that without painting Alice and Freya in a bad light and further disrupting Hope's world?

I want to tell her what they did to keep us apart, but I can't formulate the words, so I open my arms to her instead and battle tears as she flies into them. I hug her close, my beautiful girl, elated that she thinks I'm more maternal than Freya, but shattered that I've missed out on so much.

Maybe Riker and I have underestimated her and she's ready to hear the entire truth? I think the time has come and I'll call Riker later tonight to discuss it.

When we ease apart, I say, "How about we sit down and complete that family tree together after we visit Alice?"

"Thanks, Brooke." Her smile is tremulous. "After dinner, can you drop me at Sasha's? She's got a new puppy that's adorable from the pics I've seen on her phone."

"Sure, sweetie." It saves me asking Lizzie to look after Hope because I'm going out for a drink with Noel later. "Now let's eat."

Dinner is over quickly as Hope's keen to get to her friend's place, and after I drop her at Sasha's, waving at her mother, who's in the garden alongside the girls frolicking with the Labrador pup, I head to the bar where Noel and I first met.

I hope Hazel hasn't mentioned anything to him about the stealing accusation. Then again, I could see her battling tears when she left my house, and she's friends with Noel, so I assume she would've unburdened herself when she got home.

Noel's waiting at a corner table when I enter the bar and he waves when he sees me. His face lights up as I weave my way through tables toward him and I'm struck anew by his good looks. I haven't seen him since I introduced him to Hope, and after his phone call that night—and his eagerness at being part of the family because I showed faith in him—I've cooled things between us a little. I haven't answered his nightly calls, responding with texts instead about having an early night or being busy with work deadlines. I like Noel and I dislike lying, but I didn't like the way he sounded that night after I introduced him to Hope, and it got my guard up.

Now, with his guileless smile and the way he opens his arms to me, I wonder if I'm worrying about nothing.

"Hey, beautiful. I've missed you." He slants a lingering kiss on my lips before hugging me tight. "I hope you haven't been avoiding me."

He means it as a joke, but as we ease apart I see a glint in his eye that hints at annoyance.

I shake my head. "This new job is kicking my butt. The deadlines are relentless and pop up out of the blue, so I never know when my workload is going to have me up most of the night."

"Sounds tough." He pulls out my chair and I sit, and he scoots his close to me, so our knees are touching. "Speaking about jobs, I've got news."

"Yeah?"

"I've been offered a job as the prison liaison officer at Wilks Inlet. They asked me to interview, and I nailed it."

"Congratulations." Though I can't help but feel a tad nervous he'll be working in close proximity with Lizzie for a variety of reasons—the main one being she doesn't like him and how that might affect my relationship with him—and I hate that I have to fake enthusiasm when I already knew about his news from Lizzie. "What does the job entail?"

He holds up a finger. "I'll fill you in, but first, what are you having to drink?"

"Vodka and lime, please."

I usually get the drinks because I know his finances are tight, but there's a hint of stubborn pride about him tonight that probably comes from landing a new job and he wants to celebrate.

"Be back in a sec." He squeezes my shoulder and as I watch him sidestep patrons on his way to the bar, I can't help but think how bringing up that I questioned Hazel about my missing stuff is going to cause a rift between us.

I'd like to think it wouldn't because Noel and I are solid, but he's known her a lot longer and I'd hate to be the cause of his divided loyalties. I'm enjoying our easy-going relationship and don't want to cause unnecessary angst. But he needs to hear about the Hazel situation from me, not her. Noel's a nice guy. He'll understand. But I need to lead into it gently.

"Thanks," I say, when he returns and hands me the vodka. I down half of it in a few gulps, and he laughs.

"Whoa. Work has definitely got you frazzled."

I shrug, sheepish. "It's exhausting."

"You haven't got family to pick up the slack? I mean, I know you have Hazel to do the housekeeping stuff, but is there anyone else to help you?"

He's leaning forward, his elbows braced on his knees, like he's eager for answers, and I wonder if he already knows about my link to Lizzie and is fishing for information.

But that's crazy. He would outright mention it, surely. And

he hasn't said anything about my run-in with Hazel earlier, which means he doesn't know or he's giving me the opportunity to bring it up. I hope it's the latter.

"Speaking of Hazel, did you see her this evening when she got home?"

"No. Why?"

He's lying. His eyes shift sideways for the briefest moment before refocusing on me and his response was too fast, too glib.

It makes me uneasy. Why would he lie? "Because there was an incident at my place, and she was upset when she left."

His eyes narrow with suspicion. "What happened?"

"I noticed I'm missing a few things. Small stuff, really, that holds sentimental value rather than monetary."

He rears back, his expression appalled. "And you think Hazel stole them?" His lips compress into a thin line. "She's the nicest person I know, and she'd never do something like that. Besides, she loves Hope and enjoys working for you, so she'd never jeopardize her job."

His impassioned outburst is startling, particularly the bit about how much Hazel loves Hope. *Loves?* Hazel is the nanny on occasion, that's it. How can she love Hope?

He drags his hand through his hair and I see it's shaking. My accusation against his housemate has seriously unnerved him and I want to backtrack, to say maybe I've made a mistake, but he's glaring at me like I'm untrustworthy.

As I try to find the right words to smooth over this situation, Noel realizes his outburst has made me go silent because he swipes a hand over his face, and when he lowers it his expression has switched from aghast to contrite. "Sorry. I got a bit carried away there. But Hazel is a good person. You should give her a chance."

"I am. I didn't fire her," I say, and I continue to study him. The tension in his shoulders, his rigid posture, his clenched hands. He's uneasy discussing Hazel and it makes me wonder why.

Are they involved and I've been too blind to see it? I remember when Hazel first told me about Noel, and all the nice things they've said about one another. Are they more than housemates or is having Ned as their common bond so strong their friendship runs deep?

"I'm glad you're giving Hazel a chance. How's Hope?"

It's a normal question, a polite inquiry from someone who's recently met her. But I feel like he's deflecting when all I want to talk about is Hazel.

I'm not a jealous person usually, unlike my sisters, but there's something about this entire interaction, and Noel's defensiveness regarding Hazel, that has me doubting us, and my trust in him.

"Hope's great." I sip my drink, aiming for nonchalant. "What about you? Do have any nieces or nephews?" I pause. "What about Hazel's family? Do you know them well?"

He grits his teeth so hard I hear his jaw click. "Ned didn't have children, and no, I don't know Hazel's family. She dated Ned. I'm just a friend."

I've hit a nerve. His back is so rigid he doesn't realize he's sitting upright. There's something about his relationship with Hazel he doesn't want me knowing.

"And you don't have any cousins?"

"My father died before I was born, and my mother was an only child. When she died"—he stares at his hands clasped in his lap—"it was just Ned and me left. And with him gone too thanks to me..."

He trails off, his eyes clouded by memories I have no right delving into. But I've let this man into my life—and in turn, my daughter's—so I need to make sure his involvement with Hazel won't jeopardize our relationship in any way.

"Did Hazel know your mom?"

His ramrod posture hasn't changed. He's tense, as if he doesn't like discussing Hazel's links to his family. If he didn't want to talk about it from grief, he'd be slumped rather than rigid and his expression would be sad rather than wary.

So I switch tack and probe a little deeper. "It must've been awful to lose your mother. When did it happen?"

He stands so abruptly his chair slams against the wall behind. "I can't talk about this. I'm sorry, Brooke. I'll call you tomorrow."

Noel stalks out of the bar, pushing people out of his way in his haste to leave, and I'm filled with recrimination at letting him into my life too soon.

THIRTY-THREE

NOEL

THEN

I reach Shar Forest by nightfall. Mom lives in a tiny cottage behind the nursery and the place is floodlit, with two police cars parked near the entrance. I pull up beside them and my entire body shakes as I get out of my car.

This can't be happening. My sweet, gentle mother is dead, and Ned had something to do with it.

Only a monster would do something so heinous.

My heart is heavy as I trudge toward the nursery, and before I can enter the side gate, four policemen open it and step out. I don't have to introduce myself. They take one look at my stricken expression and bow their heads slightly.

The eldest, a towering man with a neatly trimmed beard and bushy eyebrows, holds out his hand. "I'm Sergeant Yates. You must be Noel Harwood?"

When I nod, he says, "We're sorry for your loss."

"Thank you," I say, my voice choked with tears. "What happened?"

"Your mother must've tripped over pruning shears and fell.

Unfortunately, when she pitched forward, she fell onto a stake. A freak accident." His gaze is sympathetic. "If it's any consolation, she would've passed quickly."

A freak accident.

Or staged to look that way.

Spots dance before my eyes and I sway, before my knees give out and I sink to the ground, retching on the grass. I can't fathom what's happened. Worse, that my brother may have done this.

One of the policemen helps me to my feet and that's when I see him.

Ned.

Staring at me, his gaze glassy, but his expression a mix of horror and sorrow.

That look stops me in my tracks—surely he can't have murdered our mother. In my shock at hearing the devastating news, I must've imagined I heard him say, *Even though she deserved it.* I tell myself that Ned may border on unhinged at times, but he would never hurt our mother or me. We're family. The only family we have. But that isn't entirely true. There is the father I have always been terrified Ned would take after. And maybe now he has.

Ned gave up asking about our father years ago, but Mom told me the truth not long after my twenty-first birthday after I wouldn't stop badgering her for more information on his life and how he died. She swore me to secrecy because she shared my concerns about Ned and harbored a deep-seated fear that he inherited the worst of our father's DNA.

Our father, the psychopath.

Dray Romez, a charming, sweet talker who wouldn't take no for an answer on our mother's third date. He'd come into the diner where she waitressed part-time every night for two weeks straight until she agreed to go out with him. Her co-workers teased her that he was way out of her league with his movie-star looks—jet-black hair, bright blue eyes, cut-glass jaw—and his suave manners. On their first date, he took her to the most expensive restaurant in town and dazzled her with his gypsy lifestyle. On their second, he took her to an upmarket bar and tried to get her drunk. On their third, he drove to a remote beach and raped her. The next day, he'd left town, probably moving on to the next victim, and our mother hid her shame.

Ned and I were a result of the worst night of her life, but she never showed it. Not once did she resent us. And all through Ned's "slip-ups," she supported him. She lavished us with love, despite the constant reminder we must've been of a night she'd rather forget. Apparently, we look like Dray too, spitting image, so to think Mom must've seen him every day she looked at us... she's amazing. Was amazing. Courtesy of my twin, if he's inherited dear old dad's DNA.

"The scene has been examined and cleared," Sergeant Yates says. "The medical examiner has your mother's body, but we're expecting the cause of death to be accidental from what we've seen."

He glances over his shoulder when he sees me staring at Ned, before turning back and leaning closer. "Looks like your brother is in shock. He discovered your mother's body, then had to make the formal identification."

Sergeant Yates reaches into his pocket and slips me a card. "This is a therapist the boys on the force use for short-term debriefing. He's good, so if you or your brother need to speak to someone, I can highly recommend him."

"Thank you." I take the card and slip it into my jacket, knowing neither of us will use it.

Who knows what a therapist will uncover if Ned lies on his couch?

I hate how the police have deemed my mother's "accidental" death a formality. I want to implore them to investigate further, but I know it won't do any good. According to Mom, the sheriff's department in this town is woefully underfunded, the chief just took early retirement, and they're struggling to find a replacement. She loved regaling me with local gossip during our weekly calls and my heart aches with overwhelming loss.

Ultimately, that's why I hold back and don't say anything to the police. Mom would want me to protect Ned at all costs. It's what she's always done.

"Take care of yourself, son." Sergeant Yates briefly pats my shoulder before moving off with his crew.

My feet are rooted to the spot, and I wait until they drive away before turning back to Ned. He hasn't moved either, and it's like we both know the moment we get close enough, our worlds will change irrevocably.

But standing here won't change anything and staving off the inevitable is foolhardy.

I need to hear the truth from my brother.

I force my legs to move and as I get closer to Ned, I see he's trembling and there are tear stains down his cheeks.

When I reach him, we don't speak. What is there to say? We embrace, and Ned's hug is brief, perfunctory, before he pulls away with a stifled sob.

"How are you holding up?" I ask, earning a scowl.

"How do you think?" He jerks a thumb over his shoulder. "What happened back there..." He shakes his head. "I'll never forget it."

I don't want to ask the next question, I really don't, but I have to.

"What did happen, Ned?"

"Didn't the police tell you?"

"Yeah, but I want to hear your version."

He glances down at his boots, before slowly looking back up, and what I see in his eyes chills me to my soul.

"Do you really want to hear the truth, Noel?"

THIRTY-FOUR

LIZZIE

I'm cleaning up after the end of class the next day when I hear the soft snick of the door closing. I whirl around, to find Noel leaning against it, his smile wide but furtive shadows scudding across his eyes.

My palms are instantly clammy. Classroom doors in the facility are never closed for a reason. No matter how much we like to think our ex-cons are rehabilitated, it pays to be on guard, and that includes never being trapped. Once was bad enough and I still have nightmares about Grant cornering me, the stench of his fetid breath, the maniacal glint in his beady eyes, the heat radiating off his body. During those bad dreams I struggle to breathe and a scream lodges in my throat as he inches closer, and that's when I wake, my chest heaving as I drag oxygen into my lungs, my body drenched in sweat.

That same residual terror after my nightmares claws at me now but I subdue it. I can't allow Noel to see my fear. It will give him the upper hand.

He hasn't moved from the door but that doesn't mean I'm not on high alert. Grant had moved fast when he'd trapped me.

"Hey, Lizzie. Got a minute?"

"Sure, Noel." I'm glad my voice doesn't quiver because I think he'd enjoy it, having me on the back foot. "Though I'm dying for a coffee. Want to chat in the break room?"

For a horrifying moment I think he's not going to budge. His stance is casual—hands thrust in pockets, ankles crossed, leaning against the door—but his neck muscles are rigid, and his grin disappears.

"I'm harmless, Lizzie," he says, dripping with sarcasm, as if he can see right through me, and my gaze darts around the room, wishing I hadn't put away all the sculpting tools or that my handbag, with mace tucked into the outer pocket, isn't beneath my desk in the far corner.

I take a small breath and hope I sound casual. "It's not you, Noel. It's HR policy that we keep classroom doors open at all times, and being your first day, it's understandable you're not up to date on all the tiresome rules yet." I force a laugh. "How's it going, by the way? You're not too overwhelmed?"

He continues to stare at me in that unnerving way he has, like he has X-ray vision, before he finally chuckles. "My head is spinning from all the policies I need to read, but I enjoyed spending one-on-one time with a few of the incoming members. That's what I wanted to talk to you about, one of the guys I met with."

"Great. Let's grab that coffee and chat."

I inadvertently hold my breath as I wait for him to open the door. He takes his time and butterflies slam against my rib cage until he does. I exhale in relief and cross the classroom to grab my handbag, when he says, "Is everything okay, Lizzie? You seem anxious."

"Nothing a good caffeine fix won't cure."

I'm glad he can't see my face when I deliver this flippant response, because fear is making my hands shake as I feel in the front pocket of my bag for the mace.

His silence is unnerving and it's unsafe to have my back

turned from him for too long, so I drag in a few calming breaths before swiveling back to face him. I must've turned too quick and caught him off-guard because his expression is pure malevolence.

Goosebumps scatter across my skin and I swallow my terror. How can Brooke date this guy? Worse, how has she introduced him to Hope?

I've expressed my concerns to Brooke regarding Noel already and she hasn't listened. And even if I mention what's happened today—which is exactly nothing, just a bunch of unease from me—she'll think I'm nuts.

Which means I'll have to do some more investigating on my own regarding Noel.

I know it's irrational, but the first thing that pops into my mind is to follow him home. An outlandish idea fraught with danger, because how will I explain myself if he catches me?

Though we are co-workers now and I can keep a client file on me in case, a ready excuse. Bur what am I hoping to achieve? I can't exactly break into his house. Hazel threatening to search my place for Brooke's misplaced items yesterday had floored me. How would she like it if I threatened her to do the same? Which I could if I lost my mind and broke into their house... Two birds with one stone as the old saying goes...

"Lizzie, you don't look so good," he says, startling me out of my reverie and I silently curse, drifting off.

I make loopy circles at my temple. "I go a little crazy when I'm caffeine depleted."

He laughs, but it's devoid of amusement. "In that case, let's get a coffee pronto."

I don't want to spend any more time than I need to with this guy, but it will look strange if I forgo coffee now after using it as an excuse for my behavior, so we head to the kitchen two doors down from my classroom.

"Who's this client you want to discuss?" I ask. The faster we take care of business, the faster I can leave.

"Derek Burges. He's being released tomorrow and will start here next week. I met with him today and he seems... odd."

Pot, meet kettle, I think, but I keep that gem to myself as I struggle to hide my impatience as I wait for the coffee machine to do its thing. "How so?"

"He didn't make threats directly, but I read between the lines with some of the stuff he said."

Great. Just what I need in my class. Another guy to make me uneasy. "Like?"

"Misogynistic stuff, mostly. And with you being alone in a classroom with this guy." He shrugs. "I thought it best to warn you."

"Thanks, Noel. This is exactly the kind of thing a prison liaison officer does." I'm relieved when the coffee machine light turns to green and I pour myself some into my take-out cup so I can make a quick escape. "Want one?"

He shakes his head. "I'm good. Maybe I should sit in on your class when Derek attends?"

His stare bores into me and once again I'm under the impression he can see all the way down to my soul. It's unnerving. His offer may be genuine but the last thing I want is to spend any more time with this guy than I need to.

"Thanks, but there are safety protocols in place if anyone steps out of line." I take a sip of coffee. "I'll be fine."

"Too bad," he says, not breaking eye contact. "I'd like to spend more time with you, Lizzie."

Hell. Is he coming on to me? I don't think so. His vibe is more creepy than sleazy. Either way, it's time to leave.

"Was there anything else you wanted to discuss, Noel?"

He tilts his head, studying me. "I make you uncomfortable, don't I?"

"Not at all." I will myself not to look at the door, which is open, thank goodness. "I've just got stuff to do."

His upper lip curls in a sneer. "I'm going to make you like me, Lizzie. You'll see."

Swallowing my terror with another gulp of coffee, I stride to the door, cup in one hand, mace in the other, hidden in the outer pocket of my bag, ready if I need it.

Noel is toying with me and loving it. I should've stood my ground and made Max believe my gut reaction. Then again, even with this bizarre exchange now, Noel hasn't tried to physically intimidate me. Though if his taunts escalate... What does he mean by "I'm going to make you like me?"

I suppress a shudder. "Thanks for the update on Derek."

Maybe I'm imagining the sinister undertone to his chuckle. "See you tomorrow."

Not if I have any say in it, and despite my shaky legs as I exit the building, I break into a half jog toward my car.

After my encounter with Noel, I'm too freaked to drive the hour home. My hands are trembling so badly I have trouble gripping the steering wheel. But I can't sit in the car park or hang around town in case he pops up again, and I'm angry all over again that he has this effect on me. I wish I could talk to Brooke and tell her what I really think of him, but I'm not willing to risk my relationship with her and Hope, and that leaves only one other person I can vent my frustration to.

Alice.

I don't want to see her, but I need to confront someone, and if it can't be Noel, then at least I can get some long overdue answers about my past.

Alice will be surprised by this unexpected visit, and she'll probably read too much into it—like I'm forgiving her, which couldn't be further from the truth—but I'm spoiling for a fight, and this is the first time in the last two years that I've felt remotely like confronting her.

She's not expecting me, so her jaw drops in shock when she opens the door to my knock.

"Lizzie, is everything okay? Are Brooke and Hope all right?"

"We're all fine." A lie, because I haven't been fine in a long time, not since I learned my mother is in fact my aunt and she lied to me for decades. "Can I come in?"

"Of course." She holds the door wider and steps back. "You never have to ask. This is as much your home as mine."

It's not, and we both know it. But I don't have the energy to bicker today. I'm still rattled by my encounter with Noel and wanting answers to questions I should've asked Alice a long time ago.

I'm done with shirking the major issues in this family.

"Are you sure everything's okay?" Alice casts me a sideways glance, worry puckering her brow.

"Bad day at work."

She hesitates, before saying, "I know you're very capable, Lizzie, and you love your job, but I worry about you interacting with prisoners on a daily basis."

"Ex-prisoners," I say, my voice shaking, and I grit my teeth against the urge to confide in her like I used to. We had the best mother-daughter relationship. I could talk to her about anything. My fears, my hopes, my dreams. Pity it was all a lie.

She nods, accepting my answer, but her worry hasn't subsided by the concern in her gaze. "Well, I'm here if you ever need to offload, about work or anything else. Would you like a drink—"

"Can we talk?" I head for the living room and sit, waiting until she joins me in the armchair opposite before continuing. "I know this may seem out of the blue but it's long overdue."

I eyeball her, not surprised to see fear in her wavering gaze.

She's always avoided the tough stuff, otherwise I wouldn't have to ask what I'm about to. "Why didn't you ever tell me I was your niece and not your daughter?"

I hear a sharp intake of breath and she presses a hand to her chest, but I'm not backing down this time.

"I mean, you had ample opportunity after I turned eighteen if you didn't want to tell me when I was a kid. So why didn't you?"

She lowers her hand to clasp it with the other, her fingers interlocked so tight the knuckles are standing out. "Because I was afraid."

"Of what?"

"Losing you. Ostracizing all of you." Her mouth twists into a grimace. "Which is ironic, because that's exactly what's happened."

I want to yell, *Whose fault is that?* But I need to keep a leash on my temper, otherwise I'll never get the answers I crave.

"There's more to it than that and you know it." I lean forward, anger making my fingers curl into fists. "You forget, Brooke read your online diary and told me some of it. You were jealous of our mother. Is that why you never told us the truth, that even when you adopted us after her death, in some warped way you really believed we were yours?"

She shakes her head, tears filling her eyes. "Of course not. But no good would've come of me telling you the truth about your mother and me, even when you turned eighteen. Our relationship was complicated, and I didn't want that spilling over onto you girls. I never had a chance to be a mother and considered it the greatest gift that I got to raise the three of you, and selfishly, I loved that you called me Mom. That you came to me first to solve any problems, that you trusted me implicitly."

A tear trickles down her cheek. "For all intents and purposes, I was your mother. So what good could've come of telling you I was your aunt?"

"What good?" I echo, stunned by her selfishness, rage making me tremble. "Because you owed me the truth. Because knowing Brooke was my sister might've brought her home sooner. Because learning that Freya was my sister could've bonded us better and she wouldn't be dead right now!"

She jumps as I yell, but her expression is resigned rather than shocked.

"Nobody could've prevented Freya from doing what she did." She looks away, evasive. "She was troubled from the time she could covet everything Brooke had, and that obsessiveness only intensified as she grew older."

The thing is, I can empathize with Freya. Brooke led a charmed life as a teen. Friends, popularity, grades, she had it all. And as much as I hate to admit it, I was jealous of her also. To the point I stole from her, petty acts of envy that made me feel better because I had a secret the all-seeing Brooke wasn't privy to.

I'm ashamed but annoyed too. Would things have been different for all of us if I'd known Freya and Brooke were my sisters, not my cousins?

"I wish you'd told me the truth all those years ago," I say, tears stinging my eyes. "Though I guess it's futile wishing for things that can't be changed."

Guilt wars with regret in Alice's eyes. "Lizzie, I love you. And I love Brooke and Hope. Trust me when I say, everything I've ever done has been because I love you girls. And never forget, you *are* my daughter in every sense of the word, and it's killing me slowly every day knowing that you hate me."

"I don't hate you," I murmur, some of my anger dissipating now I've finally confronted her. "But I'll never forgive you."

Tears fill her eyes, but they don't sway me. I've been bottling up this resentment toward her for two years and while I feel slightly better after confronting her, it doesn't change facts.

The only mother I've ever known, who in reality is my aunt, lied to me for years.

Logically, I know she didn't have to rescue me from Child Protective Services, because she already had Brooke and Freya to raise. She didn't have to take me on. She didn't have to love me. So while I'm grateful she provided me with a stable home life, I can't forget. Actions have consequences and who knows how different my life, and that of Brooke and Freya, might've been if we'd known the truth from the start.

"I'm sorry, Lizzie," she murmurs, swiping at her eyes, as I stand and fold my arms, unwilling to let go of my resentment all at once. "I miss you so much, my darling girl. You are my rock amid the craziness of this family."

"Maybe you should've thought of that before you lied to me for decades," I mutter, shaking my head as I stride toward the door.

This confrontation has been cathartic and a long time coming, but I'd been honest when I told her that I'll never forgive her. When it comes to my family, I've wised up.

THIRTY-FIVE

BROOKE

Twenty-four hours later, I'm still pondering Noel's bizarre stalk-out from the bar last night. I tried not to let it bother me, but I slept poorly, plagued by insecurities. Are Noel and Hazel involved? Are they more than friends? Am I being unnecessarily paranoid?

Never having an adult relationship means I have no idea if I'm overreacting or if I should take his behavior as a red flag. I'm sure all relationships have ups and downs, and Noel hasn't done anything terribly bad, but having trust issues means I need my boyfriend to be transparent and not freak out when I ask simple questions about his friends and family.

Then again, considering I wouldn't want to talk about Freya if he probed me, maybe I'm expecting too much too soon. Discussing family can be fraught at the best of times with anybody, as most people have skeletons in their proverbial closets. Perhaps I should wait and see how he is the next time we meet and take my cues from him.

Thankfully, Hope kept up a steady stream of conversation on the way home about Sasha's new puppy and didn't notice that I hadn't contributed much beyond the occasional "uh-huh."

I know she'll probably pester me for a pup and while I hate saying no to her, the last thing I need is another thing to look after. And I know teen girls. The puppy phase won't last because entering high school opens up a whole new world of boys and I'll be the one left looking after the dog.

Hope's taking a bath and I'm making an herbal tea when there's a knock on the door, before it opens and Lizzie lets herself in.

"Hey, got a minute?" Her expression is somber as she closes the door. "I want to talk to you about Noel."

I'm about to say, *Not this again*, when I notice her jacket.

More precisely, *my* jacket, the one I'd misplaced last week.

It's distinctive. Charcoal, fitted, with a flare at the hips and pinstriped red edging. I wear it all the time because it goes with black pants, black skirts, a red skirt I love, and a matching charcoal calf-length pencil skirt. Plus it adds panache to the many black dresses I own.

Lizzie coveted it from the moment I bought it. She told me so. Even joked about borrowing it.

So what the hell is she doing wearing it without my permission?

She's nervous, her fingers plucking at the hem. "What's wrong?"

"Why are you wearing my jacket?"

My tone is icy, and she glances down at what she's wearing, bemused, before giving a sheepish laugh.

"I saw it hanging on the back of a dining room chair a few days ago and I had a parole board hearing to sit in on for a potential attendee in the art therapy program, so I borrowed it." She grimaces and shakes her head. "And obviously forgot to return it. Sorry, Brooke."

She shrugs out of it and hangs it over her arm. "I'll get it dry-cleaned and give it back to you."

"I'll do it." I hold out my hand and she gives it to me, an embarrassed blush staining her cheeks.

I don't know what game she's playing. Is this a genuine mistake or is Lizzie taunting me, like Freya used to? Is this her way of showing me she can have anything of mine she wants?

And if so, is Hazel right and Lizzie stole those other things of mine?

"Anyway, I wanted to talk to you about Noel." She screws up her nose. "We had a run-in at work today and—"

"I don't want to hear it." I hold up my hand, because the last thing I need is Lizzie voicing more doubts about Noel when I have a few of my own since last night. "You're bordering on obsessed with him and I'm over it. Fact: I'm dating him. So don't you think I'm capable of judging his character on my own, without your interference?"

Stricken, she pales. "I'm not interfering. I'm just looking out for you."

She appears genuine but seeing her in my jacket, hot on the heels of Hazel implying Lizzie could've stolen my stuff, has my hackles raised.

Only one way to find out if my sister is a thief.

I point to the jacket draped over my arm. "Is there anything else you've *borrowed* and forgotten to return?"

Her guilty gaze flicks away and my heart sinks. Hazel was right. And my sister, the only one I have now, is toying with me.

"Hazel accused me of stealing stuff from you and now you're doing the same?" Disappointment pinches her mouth. "Why on earth would I take your things?"

I wave the jacket at her. "I don't know, Lizzie. Why would you take my things?"

"I already told you, I borrowed that!"

Her face flushes crimson and she jams her hand into her pocket, pulling out a key. "I suppose you want this back? Even though technically this is my house too, and I'm not living in it because you overreacted over something else I did."

Normally, I'd keep my temper in check, but having her harp on about Noel rankles.

"I didn't overreact about you coming onto Riker!" I yell, anger making me shake as I fling the jacket on the table. "Do you know what that was like for me? It was horrendous, having another sister betray me..."

I trail off, my legs giving way as I stumble to the nearest chair and collapse into it.

Because that's at the crux of my beef with Lizzie. Whether she stole from me or didn't, I saw with my own eyes that she doesn't care about me the way I care about her. Seeing her with Riker resurrected memories of Freya flaunting her relationship with Hope, all the while knowing Hope was mine. Two sisters, equally capable of hurting me, and I'm gutted that Lizzie may be more like Freya than I thought.

"I didn't betray you, Brooke. We've already discussed it." When I raise my eyes, I see Lizzie staring at me with pity. "I thought we'd gotten past this. What's really going on here?"

She's always been the smartest of us three girls. I'd been the popular one, who worked hard to get my good grades; Freya, whose intelligence morphed into cunning; and Lizzie, who'd gone to college and made something of herself. She's a psychologist, and right now, she's trying to analyze me.

"Nothing," I mutter, hating that I've brought this up again when Lizzie's right. We've dealt with the Riker issue.

Lizzie shakes her head, sadness bracketing her mouth. "If you can't trust me, we've got a problem."

She pulls out a chair next to me and sits. "Because you and Hope are everything to me. Apart from Alice, you're the only family I've got."

Her sincerity is audible, and I want to hug her, but my gaze lands on the jacket lying on the table where I flung it, and I'm back to doubting.

"And I know you don't want to hear this, but there's something about Noel that's seriously off-putting." She hesitates, before continuing. "You don't pick up on any odd vibes at all?"

"No." I jab my finger at her. "This is getting tiresome."

Her face falls. "Please, Brooke, just hear me out? If not for your sake, then Hope's—"

"My daughter is everything to me, so please don't imply I'm putting her at risk by not taking your constant harping about Noel to heart."

I'm tired of this. I'm finally happy—I'm Hope's mother, I'm on good terms with her father, my new job is going well, I have a new boyfriend, and I thought I'd resolved my problems with Lizzie for the most part—but she won't let this obsession with Noel go.

"Noel is my boyfriend, Lizzie," I snap. "Deal with it."

Stony-faced, Lizzie shakes her head. "I'm always here for you, Brooke. And the same goes for Hope."

She stands and walks toward the back door, her steps wooden, before she pauses and glances over her shoulder. "But I'm not the bad person here and I hope you realize it before it's too late."

With that bizarre warning, she slams the door.

THIRTY-SIX

NOEL

THEN

I sit in Mom's recliner and Ned takes the sofa opposite. We clutch a glass of brandy each, the only alcohol Mom kept in the house. She used it to make fruitcake at Christmas and must've just stocked up because the bottle was full before I sloshed a generous amount into two glasses. I tossed mine back in three gulps and replenished my glass because I know I'm going to need it for whatever Ned is about to divulge to me.

How many times have I heard that old cliché *the truth hurts*? In this case, it's not going to hurt.

It's going to decimate me.

I want to ask my twin what happened, but I know Ned. He'll give me some long-winded, drawn-out version that will amount to an excuse. Because whatever Ned does, it's never his fault. He's been like this his entire life, blaming others for his shortfalls, unable to acknowledge the truth only Mom and I know: that he's damaged in some way, that our father's DNA runs rampant in him, that he's bad to the core.

But never in my worst nightmares have I ever contemplated he'd be capable of harming our mother.

I ask the question that cuts through all the bullshit. The question I want the truth to, all too aware it will gut me.

"Did you kill Mom?"

His look-away glance before he speaks tells me more than his words ever could.

"It was an accident." He stares into his brandy, his fingers clutching the glass tight. "She ran away from me, and she tripped."

He's lying. I've been reading my twin since we were kids and I know when he's evading the truth. After all, he's become an expert at it over the years.

"Why was she running away from you?"

"Because we were arguing, and I lost my temper." He swirls the brandy and continues to stare at it. "I'm not proud of how I spoke to her. She didn't deserve that."

I want to yell, *She didn't deserve a psychopathic son like you*, but I clamp down on my temper because once Ned loses his cool I'll never get the truth out of him.

"You must've scared her pretty bad for her to run from you. Did you threaten her?"

More of that calm brandy swirling that makes my fingers itch with the urge to knock the glass out of his hand. "She got me wound up and I retaliated."

"How?"

If I keep pushing for answers, Ned will eventually crack, and the truth will spill out.

"She's been lying to me for years and she thought I'd never find out." He spits the words, fury contorting his expression. "I can't believe my own mother would lie to me. Would willingly deprive me of what rightfully belongs to me."

I'm lost and he's rambling, but with a little prompting he'll tell me everything. That's the thing about narcissists. It's always about them.

"Mom never hurt either of us deliberately. You're mistaken."

His upper lip curls in a sneer. "Of course you'd take her side. You were always her favorite."

"She never played favorites and you know that."

At last he raises his eyes from staring into the brandy and I almost wish he hadn't. They're glazed with hatred, whether directed at Mom, me, or both of us, I'm unsure.

"What I know, brother dearest, is that even when confronted with the truth I only recently discovered, our mother lied to my face. I saw it in her eyes. She knew and she didn't tell me. So when I picked up a knife to threaten the truth out of her, she ran."

My blood chills at the fanatical gleam in his eyes.

"What did you do?"

"I chased after her, naturally. I swear she loves those stupid fucking plants more than she loves me. But I gave her one last chance to tell me the truth. I'm not a monster."

He must see my horrified expression, because he places the glass on the coffee table between us and holds up his hands like he's got nothing to hide.

"I thought she'd tell me the truth. I thought I meant something to her." He taps his chest. "But turns out, she wanted to take her vile lies to the grave, and I made sure that happened."

And there it is.

The truth.

Ned killed Mom.

Nausea rises and burns my gullet, and I gulp at the brandy like it's water before I puke all over him.

"She ran rather than face me and tell me the truth, so I pushed her onto that stake. It was over, just like that." He snaps his fingers. "Then I planted the pruning shears to make it look like she tripped and I called it in."

In a second his mask switches from evil to devastated. "It was easy playing the grieving son. Those stupid police lapped it up. Never entered their dense heads I might've killed her. And you know the best part?"

I can't answer. I can't speak because my throat continues to tighten with sorrow despite the brandy I'm sipping.

"I'm going to do the same to that bitch Freya for keeping my child from me."

THIRTY-SEVEN

LIZZIE

Brooke's wrong.

I'm not obsessed with Noel.

Though considering the madness I'm perpetuating at the moment, maybe I am.

I hadn't been able to think straight after she accused me of stealing her things and her adamant stance that she doesn't want to hear what I have to say about Noel. Considering she still doubts me, I'm not surprised.

I never should've made a move on Riker. That one momentary lapse in judgment has undermined our entire relationship, a caring, loving, relationship of two sisters who'd discovered the truth two years ago and hadn't looked back.

I'm equal parts mad at myself for doing something so idiotic and furious with her for not believing me when I've implored her to believe several times that I have her best interests at heart.

That's what drove me to do this crazy thing.

If Brooke won't listen to what I have to say regarding Noel, I'll have to show her.

Driving in my current mental state isn't wise, but I feel like I'm running out of options. Noel's behavior toward me today wasn't normal. Any guy who says he'll "make" me like him is delusional, or worse.

That's what I wanted to tell Brooke. Not my usual gut feeling that something isn't right with Noel, but his actual words.

Wearing that jacket had been a mistake because she'd lost all perspective when she'd seen me in it. I had genuinely forgotten to tell her I'd borrowed it, probably because deep down I hoped she wouldn't miss it, like that other stuff I stole from her years ago.

But I need to be smarter because our rocky relationship after the Riker incident had barely recovered before this, and I know it's going to take more than an apology or empty words for her to trust me again.

I pull up outside Noel's place just after ten. It had taken me two seconds to pull up his file from attending art therapy on my phone and learn his address. The red brick cottage with white trimmed windows and matching door is small and nondescript, located a few streets away from the town hall, and thankfully a good twenty minutes from our house on the cliffs.

I park beneath a towering oak several houses away, ensuring my car is cloaked in darkness but giving me a view of the house. Though now I'm here, I have no idea what I'm hoping to find. Sitting in a car spying on a co-worker is certifiable.

That's when the enormity of what I'm doing hits me. If Noel discovers my lunacy, he'll report me to Max, and I could lose my job. Is convincing Brooke to hear me out worth that?

Usually, I'd say hell no. But this isn't a normal circumstance. There's something off about Noel and I need proof to protect my sister and niece.

Fueled by false bravado—and two energy drinks I'd consumed during the drive over—I get out of the car and pull my hoodie up. It's a cold night and I assume not many strollers will be out after ten, but I don't want to be recognized regardless.

Sticking to the shadows on the sidewalk cast by trees on lawns, I walk toward Noel's place, head down, hands in pockets, one of them comforted by the feel of the mace. I may be foolish but I'm not entirely stupid. I need some form of protection if the unthinkable happens and I run into Noel.

I have an excuse ready if that happens: an old friend of my aunt, who lives five minutes away, went for a walk and hasn't returned so my aunt's worried and called me to check on her. I can play up a dementia angle to make it plausible, and hopefully, he'll believe my story—before he wraps his hands around my neck.

That's an exaggeration because I know Noel genuinely killed his brother by accident. There's no way he could've gone through the prison system, being interviewed by countless police and psychologists, without being found out if he did harbor psychopathic tendencies. But I still can't forget that he drove off, leaving his own brother to die. There's something more to what happened, I just know it.

A small part of me is doubting my own professionalism in doing this. I should trust my training as a psychologist and not give in to the whims of a gut instinct, but I've come this far, there's no turning back.

The front of the house is in darkness, but I glimpse light spilling from a side window. I know the moment I set foot on his property I'm officially trespassing, not just stalking, and it's insanity.

Then I remember Brooke's sneer, her hurt, her disbelief, and I steel my resolve. With a quick glance over my shoulder to ensure I'm not being watched, and a scan of the houses opposite that remain in darkness and thankfully don't have CCTV cameras, I sidle along the fence toward that window. I crouch when I reach it, counting to ten to calm my pounding heart, before edging upward.

I see Noel first. He's angry, gesticulating, pacing. Hazel's sitting on the sofa, wrapped in a blanket, her gaze fixed on him. She doesn't look afraid, even when he thumps the wall and makes a fist-sized dent in the plaster.

Spying on these two is irrational and short of doing a physical search of his house, I'm not sure what dirt I expect to find on Noel. And I'm not adding breaking and entering to my dubious behavior when it comes to him.

I'm about to back away when I see Noel pick up his phone and brandish it at Hazel. From this distance, I need to squint to see the photo on it: Brooke and Noel, leaning into each other, wearing identical smitten smiles. Noel's anger fades as he smiles at the photo, presses it to his chest like a romantic sap, before sliding the phone into his pocket.

Maybe I'm wrong. Maybe Brooke's boyfriend is a guy grasping at a second chance? A guy who deserves the benefit of the doubt. A guy with good intentions, and who am I to question them?

Feeling like an idiot, I take a step back and that's when I see Hazel's expression.

She's glaring at Noel's back, brows drawn together in a deep frown, disappointment pinching her mouth. She says something and Noel's head snaps up. His smile has vanished, replaced by a scowl as he gestures at a coffee table I can't see unless I crane my neck.

I can't lip-read what he's saying, but Hazel's shoulders are rigid and anger radiates off her as she picks up something off the table and brandishes it at him. Not just something. It's Brooke's missing items: the sparkly pink pen, a pair of dangly book earrings, and a mini sketchpad.

I *knew* she'd stolen Brooke's stuff, but why is she showing

Noel? Does he know his housemate took Brooke's things, and if so, is he complicit? Are they both messing with her?

If so, I'm right about him too, and he's not as upstanding as he likes everyone to believe.

Hazel flings Brooke's things away and starts gesticulating wildly, and Noel shakes his head and stomps out of the room. I wish I could take a photo of the items but can't risk the flash on my phone going off and alerting them to my presence.

There's something odd about Noel and Hazel's relationship. Though by Noel's tender reaction to that photo of him and Brooke, maybe he isn't the one Brooke needs to be wary of?

How well does she really know her housekeeper?

THIRTY-EIGHT

BROOKE

After another lousy sleep courtesy of Lizzie's visit last night, I drink copious coffees to get me through the day. I'm working from home and trying to focus on an upcoming sales pitch to a new chain of supermarkets, but the constant hum of activity from Hazel—vacuuming, cleaning the windows, cooking—distracts me. I could close the den door, but after my things went missing, I can't help but want to keep an eye on her when I can.

Which is crazy, because I hired her to do all the things I can't when I'm at work, including care for Hope, so what use is a housekeeper I don't trust?

I press the pads of my fingers to my eyes, wishing my brain fog would clear, and when I open them Hazel's in the doorway, staring at me.

"Would you like me to clean in here or shall I leave the den until tomorrow?"

Her tone is polite but flat, and nothing like the previous chirpiness—before I practically accused her of stealing.

"Tomorrow is fine, thanks Hazel." I glance at my watch,

surprised to see it's four. "You can finish up. Riker should be dropping Hope off any second."

"Okay."

But she doesn't move. Instead, she shifts her weight from side to side, and fiddles with the mop in her hands. "I hope you don't think I'm overstepping, Brooke, but can I ask you something about you and Noel?"

My relationship with Noel has nothing to do with her, so yeah, she's overstepping. But she introduced us and she's his friend. At least, I hope that's all she is.

"Sure."

"I've known Noel a long time. He's a good guy and he deserves to be happy after all he's been through." Her gaze fixes at a point over my shoulder as she continues to absentmindedly twirl the mop. "I guess I just want to know if you're serious about him. Because if you aren't, it's probably best you end it now."

Wow. She has some nerve. Then again, she's known him a lot longer than me and has a right to be protective. Unless my suspicions about her having feelings for him is correct and this is some warped mind game she's playing to scare me off.

Now I'm sounding like Lizzie and her far-fetched theories, and the thought alone annoys me. I'm trying my best to get a handle on my trust issues and playing into conspiracy theories isn't conducive to moving forward with my life.

"I understand Noel's your friend, Hazel, but honestly? Our relationship isn't any of your business."

Predictably, she bristles. "Actually, it is because I saw how wracked with guilt Noel was after Ned died. How it still haunts him to this day. How he'll probably never get over it and the last thing he needs when he's getting his life back on track is someone who's toying with his heart."

Her caring should be endearing. Instead, I find her bossiness abrasive, so I try to catch her off-guard.

"Are you sure you don't have feelings for Noel?"

She rears back like I've poked her in the eye and drops the mop. "Don't be ridiculous. We're friends, that's it."

She's lying. Her gaze is evasive and an incriminating blush steals into her cheeks. Great, it looks like Hazel has feelings beyond friendship for my boyfriend. Just what I need, another woman coveting what's mine. Been there, done that, and was deprived of the first decade of my daughter's life because of it.

For an insane second, I wonder, *Is it me?* What is it about me that inspires jealousy and covetousness in women closest to me? I'm a nice person. I do right by others. I don't flaunt what I have.

A tiny voice inside whispers, *Maybe you choose the wrong men?* But I refuse to let Hazel's crush on her dead boyfriend's brother undermine what I have with Noel or make me second-guess him. We're happy and I won't let her, or anyone else, mess with that.

"If you say so, Hazel."

I'm deliberately flippant, wanting to goad her into a reaction or worse, for me, a confession. But her lips compress into a mutinous line, and she shakes her head.

"If it's all right with you, I think I'll take tomorrow off."

I bite back my first retort, *Don't come back*, because that's childish and petulant. And I don't want to get Noel offside by firing his overly protective bestie.

"That's fine, Hazel." I smile, hoping to smooth things over. "I think it's great we can have these frank discussions. Especially as I'm dating Noel and you and I will cross paths socially."

Some of the earlier fight drains out of her and she nods, squatting to pick up the mop. "I know I sounded like a fierce mama bear protecting her cub earlier, but Noel really has been through a lot, and I don't want to see my friend hurt."

"Noted," I say, with a nod.

The look she shoots me—part resentment, part envy—reinforces my earlier inkling that she has real feelings for Noel, before she lifts her free hand in a wave and walks away.

Leaving me with a hankering to interrogate my boyfriend about his friendship with Hazel, knowing I'll have to tread carefully considering how things ended between us the last time I tried to ask him about those closest to him.

I meet Noel on the clifftop about two miles from my house. The views across the Pacific are spectacular, and the winding coastline with its jagged promontories curves on either side of us. Seagulls soar and dive, plucking fish from the shimmering ocean, their cries mingling with the rhythmic, pounding waves against the rocks below. The gusty winds up here chill me to the bone but never fail to clear my head and give me the perfect excuse to snuggle into him.

"I'm glad you called," he says, wrapping his arm around my shoulder tighter. "I wanted to apologize for overreacting the other night when you asked about my family."

He grimaces. "Losing my mother, then Ned, in quick succession, is a sore point with me, and to be honest, I don't think I'll ever get over it."

He glances down at me. "I'm not a head case, but the guilt is relentless. And I don't think I'll ever get past it. So I guess I'm screwed up." He taps his temple. "Up here. I hope that doesn't scare you?"

On the contrary. His vulnerability is heartwarming and his ability to open up following our last minor disagreement means I'm falling for him even more.

"You don't scare me, Noel Harwood." I press a soft kiss to his lips. "Besides, we're all screwed up."

"Yeah?" He rubs his nose against mine. "What's messed you up?"

Where do I start? The part where my aunt told me my baby died at birth, only to return home a decade later to discover she'd given my child to my sister to raise. Then for that sister to tumble to her death not far from here, and I discover my cousin is in fact my sister too.

So many twisted secrets in my family... so many reasons to mistrust.

Maybe it's time to break the cycle?

"My sister died on these cliffs," I say, trying not to remember the day Freya tumbled to her death, the fear of her trying to kill me, the horror mingled with relief when she went over the edge. "She jumped."

He holds me at arm's length, concern darkening his eyes to indigo. "I'm so sorry, Brooke. That must've been awful."

"You don't know the half of it," I mutter, lowering my gaze to stare at the second button on his shirt. "We had a complicated relationship, and her death unleashed a host of problems."

We fall silent and after a few moments when I wonder if I've revealed too much, he says, "Hey, look at me." He places a finger under my chin and tilts it up. "If anyone knows how complicated a sibling relationship can be, it's me. Ned and I were nothing alike. Physically, yeah, we were identical, but that's where the similarities ended."

His thumb brushes my bottom lip. "We can't choose our families, but we can choose how we deal with the fallout when things go wrong. And I just wanted you to know how Ned's death messed with my head, so there are no secrets between us."

Our gazes lock, before mine slides away to the cliff edge, remembering. Freya and me locked in a tussle a few miles away, Freya trying to shove me over the cliff, her feet slipping, her pitching over, and Riker there, saying he'd tried to save her but she'd already tipped over. We told everyone she jumped rather than admit the truth: my sister tried to kill me and had died in a freak accident open to interpretation.

I love Noel revealing so much to me, but some secrets—like most of mine—are meant to remain hidden.

Needing to change the subject and lighten the mood, I smile. "Want to know another secret?"

His eyebrows arch. "Absolutely."

"I think I have feelings for you." I frame his face in my hands. "I hope that doesn't scare you."

"Are you kidding?" He lets out a whoop that reverberates off the cliffs. "That's the best news I've heard in forever."

He kisses me and I melt, clinging to him, reveling in the feel of his arms around me and his skillful lips rendering me mindless.

Screw Lizzie and her obsession with maligning Noel.

He's the guy for me.

I just know it.

THIRTY-NINE

LIZZIE

Since stalking Noel at his house two nights ago, I've barely slept. I can't get that weird interaction between him and Hazel out of my mind. I've replayed it over and over, trying to figure out the dynamic between them. Are they involved? Have they had a fling in the past? Did Noel do the dirty on his twin? But if that's the case, did he run over Ned deliberately?

It's an outlandish thought because I'm sleep-deprived and spiraling, so I get out of bed at five, shower and get dressed, and hit the road. There's a diner halfway between Martino Bay and Wilks Inlet that's frequented by truck drivers mostly, but they serve the best coffee and pancakes, according to several of the ex-cons who've done my art classes, and I can do with both the caffeine and sugar hit.

The first streaks of mauve and sienna crest the horizon as I pull into the diner's car park, the neon BERT'S sign flashing intermittently. There are five trucks parked parallel and a few cars besides mine, fellow early-birds or insomniacs. Bert's exterior is weathered, the retro wooden façade of cream and forest green blending with the trees surrounding it, soft lighting spilling from the windows and hinting at warmth inside.

I wrap my jacket a little tighter around me, the crisp morning air a tad colder than normal for this time of year, as I push the heavy glass door and enter. The inside of the diner is exactly how I imagined it: vinyl booths upholstered in red, Formica tables, vintage posters of surfers adorning the walls, and a jukebox in the corner.

I inhale, savoring the heady aroma of sizzling bacon and freshly brewed coffee, and my stomach rumbles. A fifty-some-thing woman with russet hair swept into a topknot smiles at me from behind the counter and I cross the diner, spying a few old timers in lumberjack coats seated in several booths, and three middle-aged guys perched on stools at the counter. They glance up from their plates in unison and give a perfunctory nod, before returning to their all-American breakfasts—eggs on toast with bacon, sausage, and hash browns on the side.

"What'll it be, love?" The server behind the counter points to the blackboard perched over a long rectangular window open to the kitchen. "These are today's specials, or I can get you a menu."

I glance at the chalked specials—cinnamon French toast; breakfast burrito filled with scrambled eggs, peppers, onion, and chorizo; and a Bert's Omelet, stuffed with tomato, cheese, and avocado—and my mouth waters.

The woman laughs. "Can't decide, huh?"

"Is it that obvious?" I smile. "I had a hankering for a pancake stack until I read all those delights."

"Here." She hands me a menu and points to the fifth item from the top. "Bert makes the fluffiest buttermilk pancakes, topped with banana, coconut, and maple syrup."

Her finger slides to the next item. "But my personal recom-mendation is the Bert's Taco. He makes the corn tortillas himself, then fills then with scrambled eggs, shredded lettuce, black beans, and the tangiest tomato salsa." She kisses her fingertips. "Perfection."

"You're not making my decision any easier." My stomach grumbles again and this time, it's audible.

The woman, whose name badge states she's MAGGIE, laughs. "Don't take too long to decide. I think you're hungry."

I chuckle and take a seat at the counter. "Actually, I think I'll stick with the pancakes, otherwise I might be tempted to stay here all day and I won't make it to work."

"Where do you work?"

"I run art therapy classes in the annex adjacent to the Wilks Inlet Correctional Facility."

Maggie appears impressed as she pours me a coffee. "That's an excellent program. A lot of the men stop by here after they're released, and I hear nothing but good things."

"That's great. We gather feedback from participants once they've completed the three-month program and it's mostly positive."

Maggie pats my arm. "It's a good thing you're doing over there. Many are too judgmental, and some ex-cons have a hard time adjusting to life on the outside again."

She jerks a thumb over her shoulder. "Bert has employed quite a few here, just to get them back on their feet before they move on."

"Bert sounds like a nice man."

"He better be. Otherwise, my taste in men is questionable." She winks. "I had the sense to put a ring on him years ago. You married?"

I shake my head, the ever-present loneliness clawing at me. "But never say never, right?"

"That's the spirit." She taps the menu in front of me. "Anyway, I need to refill coffees, so you have a quick peruse of this and I'll be back to take your order in a moment."

I smile my thanks and run a quick eye down the first few offerings, wondering if I should stick with the pancakes or try another favorite, eggs Benedict. There's a granola parfait that sounds good too, yogurt layered with house-made granola, locally sourced berries, and honey. But I need something substantial, so when Maggie returns, I order the pancakes, with a side of crispy bacon, and a coffee.

I'm about to scroll through my phone while I wait when the door opens and the last man I expect or want to see strolls in, his gaze fixed on me. I stiffen and resist the urge to rub my arms where goose bumps have sprung up.

Noel lives in Martino Bay and works in Wilks Inlet like me, so there's nothing untoward about him stopping halfway for breakfast, like I am. Though he doesn't start until eleven, so he's up mighty early to make the hour trip.

Plus there's the way he's staring at me, part smirk, part leer, that suggests he's here for one reason only.

He followed me.

I hadn't noticed any car lights tailing me. Then again, I've had two sleepless nights and am bleary-eyed, so I mightn't have noticed. I trust my gut when it comes to Noel, but maybe my guilt at stalking him is making me more paranoid than usual. He could have many reasons for stopping here: he's an early-bird and wants to get a head start on job tasks for the day, one of his fellow inmates might be getting released today and he wants to smooth his friend's transition into the outside world, he's joined a gym near work. All perfectly logical explanations, except for the way he's staring at me. Too intense. Too knowing.

Nerves join hunger in making my stomach gripe, and I force a smile as he approaches, refusing to show how much his presence intimidates me. "Hey, Noel. Fancy seeing you here."

"My first time. You?"

"Same."

We lapse into an awkward silence as I silently pray he doesn't sit on the empty stool next to me.

"Do anything interesting the last few nights?" He asks, his

penetrating gaze boring into me, like he knows exactly what I did: stalk him.

"No. You?"

He shakes his head. "I lead a quiet life these days. Best to slip under the radar after what I've been through."

A twinge of sympathy makes me relax a little. "How's everything going?"

"Okay, I guess," he says. "Though I get the feeling that no matter what I do, some people are always going to treat me like an ex-con."

He smirks and the feeling I had earlier, that he knows what I did, intensifies. But before I can say anything, he continues. "Take you, for instance."

I swallow, hoping my voice doesn't come out squeaky. "Me?"

"Yeah, you. You have this way of looking at me that, I'll be completely honest, makes me very uncomfortable."

I could say the same thing, but I keep my face devoid of emotion, and give him a snippet of the truth. Anything to get rid of him.

"It's nothing personal, Noel. But you're right, I don't trust people easily and it takes me a while to warm up to co-workers."

I hope he notes my emphasis on the last word because that's all we are. I can't think of him anywhere near Brooke and Hope, and I'm intent on telling Brooke what I saw at his house so she'll come to her senses and dump him. It's incomprehensible that I may be forced to spend time with him as Brooke's boyfriend in the foreseeable future. No way. I won't.

"I'm suspicious of people too." He pauses and his lips curl into a sneer. "It's why I make good use of hidden cameras. They tell me more about a person than words ever could."

Fear courses through me and heat flushes my cheeks.

He must've seen me at his place and now he's toying with me.

So his presence here isn't a coincidence and he's goading me into... what? Confessing? He'll be waiting a long time because I can't show this guy fear. As long as he's Brooke's boyfriend—and has access to Hope—I have to play nice.

Besides, if he has recorded footage of me sneaking around his house and peering into his window, I'm screwed. What will happen to me professionally if he shows it to Max? Or worse, reports me to the police?

I'd done the wrong thing creeping around his place. I'm smarter than that, but when it comes to my family, I'm a tad irrational. With Alice out of the picture, Brooke, Hope, and I only have each other to rely on. And if Brooke's blinded by this guy's smarminess, I need to be the one to step up.

Not that anyone else will buy my rationale. They'll think I'm crazy.

"Here you go, love." Maggie places my breakfast in front of me and I could've hugged her for her impeccable timing. "I'll refill your coffee in a second."

She casts Noel a narrow-eyed glare, suspicious that some stranger is hassling me, and I shoot her a grateful smile. She must see something in my eyes because she gives me a little nod and mouths something I don't understand but interpret to mean when she returns to top up my coffee she'll be hanging around.

Noel doesn't take kindly to the interruption and glares at her retreating back. "I'll leave you to your breakfast."

Not that I want him to stay, but I ask, "You're not having anything?"

"No, I'll grab a coffee at that café near the annex." He leans in closer, and I grit my teeth against the urge to pull away. "Maybe we can continue our chat at work later?"

Like hell.

"I'm super busy prepping for a new class today but I'll probably see you around."

For all Noel's fake niceness around others, like Annie and

Max and I presume Brooke, he doesn't like me. Animosity radiates off him—I swear it's almost palpable—or maybe it's my overt suspicion he doesn't like, that he has everyone fooled but me.

"Hide all you want, Lizzie. I'll find you."

With a wink that makes my skin pebble again, he lopes out the door, and the breath I've been holding rushes out.

I need to be smarter when it comes to Noel and not show him how much he bothers me.

And I need to tell Brooke about Hazel stealing her stuff and Noel knowing about it, sooner rather than later.

FORTY

NOEL

THEN

My heart stops.

Ned knows the truth and, just like anticipated, he's gone crazy.

I know what he's going to ask next.

"Did you know?" He stands so he's towering over me. "Did you know about Freya and the baby?"

What I say next is going to make or break us. More precisely, he'll break me in two if he thinks I'm part of the cover-up conspiracy to keep him from Freya.

Thankfully, I must have some of Dad's deceptive DNA too because I muster my best blank expression.

"Freya from our high school days at Martino Bay?" My eyebrows rise in mock surprise. "How the hell would I know about her and a baby? And what's that got to do with you?"

He studies my face so intently, looking for the slightest tell I'm lying, but thankfully, Ned's been so wrapped up in himself for years that he hasn't paid enough attention to me to know when I'm not telling the truth.

"You really are a clueless idiot." He shrugs, and sits, and I release the breath I've been inadvertently holding. "I drove through Martino Bay two days ago for work. Saw Freya and a girl about eight coming out of the supermarket. Freya was holding her hand, so I assume it's her kid. But that gets me thinking..." Ned taps his temple. "Freya told me I was the only guy she'd ever been with, then she left town, and now I start to wonder if maybe she was pregnant with my kid. So I go into the supermarket and I don't even have to ask questions, because I overhear two of the cashiers talking about how Freya's come a long way from being the teen with an illegitimate kid who had to leave school to being a respected nurse in the community raising her daughter, and I knew, I just knew, that kid is mine and Freya kept it from me."

"That's a lot to take in, Ned. Are you sure you're not looking for connections that aren't there?"

"Don't treat me like an idiot," he yells, transforming from calm to irrational in a second. "I wanted to confront Freya immediately, but I needed to confirm the truth first, so that's why I asked Mom. And I saw it on her face. She knew the truth, so she kept me from my child deliberately, like I'm some kind of aberration."

His eyes narrow and he pins me with a stare so chilling I wonder if I've got the strength to overpower him if he attacks me.

"Were you in on it? Did Mom ask you to stage that prank so I'd get expelled and we'd have to leave town?"

I knew he'd eventually make the connection but I'm ready for it. I have to be, because one slip-up now will mean the end of me, and then who will protect Freya and her child from this madman?

"Are you serious? I knew you liked Bonnie. You'd been trailing after her, so I wanted to be supportive and show you I wasn't the nerd you thought I was, so I snuck that photo." I shake my head, feigning hurt. "I had no intention of getting caught, but because I was the goody-goody you labeled me as, I screwed up. Besides, Freya had already left town by then. How was I to know she was pregnant with your kid if you didn't know?"

My long-winded explanation mollifies him and I'm weak from relief, grateful I'm sitting down.

"Well, Mom knew. And she's known all these years, which is impossible to comprehend." He presses his fingertips to his temples. "I can't believe I have a kid and she didn't tell me. As for Freya..."

He lowers his hands to his sides, where they curl into fists. "I thought we were kindred spirits. Soulmates."

His grin is maniacal. "Turns out, I was wrong, and she's going to pay."

"Calm down, Ned. You don't even know if her kid is yours. She could've lied to you about being a virgin. She could've—"

"Are you calling me gullible, bro?"

"I'm just pointing out you can't confront her half-cocked. And you certainly can't do anything foolish, because if it turns out that girl is your child, you'll be locked away and won't be able to see her."

My logic is confusing him, because he's blinking rapidly, his gaze darting around the room.

"Just think this through, okay?" My tone is calm, placating, but inside I'm reeling. If Ned murdered Mom in a fit of rage, I hate to think what he's going to do to Freya when he confronts her. "Take some time to—"

"Shut the hell up."

He leaps to his feet again and starts pacing, so I try again.

"Ned, you've been through a lot, and seeing Mom like that must've really affected you. Why don't you wait until the morning—"

"Stop telling me what to do." He pauses and his glower is

formidable. "I'm going to Martino Bay to see Freya now and you can't stop me."

Ned's wrong.

Because I'll do whatever it takes to stop him from committing another murder.

FORTY-ONE

LIZZIE

I'm leaving the diner when I realize that in my sleepy haze this morning I left several crates of new art supplies at home and I need them for today. Thankfully, it's barely six-forty-five so I have plenty of time to return home, pack my car, and head to work. Maggie refilled my coffee cup twice, so the caffeine has kicked in, and the sublime pancakes have stopped the gnawing in my gut, so I'm more awake now. Which is good and bad, because I can't stop thinking about Noel showing up at the diner to hint that he filmed me at his place.

It's a worry, but I have to stay strong and get some proof that will prove to Brooke I'm right about him. That's why I didn't say anything to her yesterday. I didn't want to rush in and get her more offside before I had tangible evidence. I mull a few ideas on the half-hour drive home and all I can think that might remotely work is getting him to finish the conversation we started at the diner and recording him on my phone.

Once I get proof, I can tell her about what I saw at his house —Hazel stole her things—because I've had time to think about it for over twenty-four hours and if I barge into the main house this early in the morning and tell her, she'll want to know how I came by the information, and confessing I stalked her boyfriend won't endear me to her. I need to be smarter about this, and getting tangible proof of Noel and Hazel's collusion, or whatever they're up to, is the only way Brooke will believe me.

It doesn't take me long to pack my car when I get home and I'm slamming the trunk shut when Hazel arrives. It's the perfect opportunity to push her buttons a little and see what, if anything, she reveals after what I saw two nights ago.

Her expression of disappointment when she saw Noel mooning over that photo of him and Brooke together, followed by their argument, implies she may have transferred her feelings for Ned onto his brother. Is that why she stole Brooke's things? To mess with her? Out of jealousy? I've seen what another woman was capable of when she envied Brooke, and Freya's many indiscretions were awful. I know I'm leaping to conclusions, but what is Hazel capable of doing if she's jealous of Brooke and thinks she stands in her way of happiness?

Is that why she took the housekeeping job here? Though the timing is off. She introduced Brooke to Noel after she started work. Perhaps she didn't think much of having drinks with her boss and housemate, never expecting them to hit it off, and now that Noel and Brooke are dating, Hazel is insanely jealous because of a secret crush?

Whatever her rationale, I can put my psychological training to good use, ask a few pointed questions, and carefully watch her reactions. Not that Brooke will pay much attention if I warn her against Hazel—she's ignored my misgivings about Noel—but I can't sit back and do nothing, not if my family is in danger.

The thing is, Brooke may listen to my reservations about Hazel, considering some of her stuff has already gone missing. If I can present her with new information, something concrete to cast a disparaging light on Hazel, Brooke might finally take notice that those she's allowed into her life recently might not be good for her or Hope.

I wish I could confront Hazel about the items she stole from Brooke but that will mean revealing how I know, and that's not going to end well for me. But there are other ways to rattle Hazel and I can probe for information without antagonizing her, which is exactly what will happen if I reveal I have proof of her thieving ways.

I raise my hand in a wave. Hazel doesn't return it and is sullen as she gets out of her car.

"Hey, Hazel, how are you?"

"Fine," she mutters, thrusting her hands into her jacket pockets and hunching her shoulders against the wind.

I fake a yawn. "I stayed up way too late last night reading that new spy novel everyone's talking about. Did you get up to anything exciting?"

"No. Noel and I stayed in. Watched some TV."

I've led into my question gently. "He's lucky to have someone like you around to offer him a place to stay."

She likes my praise because her rigid shoulders relax a little. "Noel's a good guy, so I was pleased to help him out when he was released."

"Is he still moving out?"

Her lips thin. "No, the rental he applied for had a lot of people after it and he didn't get it."

"Too bad. Though it's nice to have someone to come home too, huh?"

Her eyes narrow with suspicion and I quickly add, "That's what I miss most living in the bungalow rather than the main house. It can get lonely sometimes, but I do value my independence."

Thankfully, my quick thinking placates her, and she nods. "Yeah, it's nice to have him there."

I glance over my shoulder and lean in, like I'm about to impart a secret. "Please don't think I'm prying, but in my last year at college I had a male housemate and while we were friends, I ended up having the biggest crush on him, and it was the pits watching him date while I wished he'd realize how I felt." I pause and give a sheepish laugh. "Have you ever thought about Noel in that way?"

There's a flash of understanding in her eyes. "He's dating Brooke."

Not a refusal, so that means she does have feelings and Brooke is potentially standing in her way of happiness.

"Crushes are hard." I grimace. "But you never know, huh? Friendship can sometimes develop into more."

"I wish," she murmurs, her narrow-eyed gaze focused on the main house, as if she's wishing she had superhuman powers and could make it explode with a single glance.

I'm right. Everything she's said, the way she's staring at the house, indicates she has feelings for Noel and is potentially jealous of Brooke. And while I don't have concrete proof—other than seeing with my own eyes the evidence that Hazel stole Brooke's stuff—I have enough to forewarn Brooke.

Belatedly realizing what she's admitted, Hazel blinks several times and refocuses. "Anyway, I better start work. Have a good day, Lizzie."

"Thanks. You too."

I almost feel bad for her as she trudges toward the house. Unrequited love can make the best of us do crazy things.

But Hazel won't do anything to Brooke with Hope around and that means I'll wait until I can get Brooke alone tonight and talk to my sister.

When I arrive at work, I see Noel in the car park. He's staring at a piece of paper in his hand and muttering under his breath, before he balls it up and shoves it into his pocket, kicks his car tire, and slams his palms against the trunk.

He hasn't seen me, which is probably a good thing, because I get the feeling this is a side of Noel he doesn't want anyone to see. After spying on him a few nights ago and witnessing his obvious feelings for Brooke, I'd been willing to cut him some slack. But after our run-in at the diner early this morning, and whatever's in that letter that has angered him to the point he's physically furious, vindicates my initial impression: he wears a mask most of the time.

If Brooke could see him like this, maybe she'd believe me when I say I'm not trying to come between them because I'm jealous—or want Noel for myself, as she wrongfully assumed.

If she could see him like this...

"That's what cameras on smartphones were invented for," I mutter, sliding my phone out of my bag and swiping left to bring up the camera function. I'm about to hit the "record" button when Noel stops thumping the trunk of his car and looks straight at me.

Hell.

I surreptitiously slide my phone back into my bag, hoping he didn't catch sight of it. He won't react well to me recording him.

"Hey, Lizzie," he calls out and waves, and as he gets closer, I'm relieved to see his usual affable mask in place: wide smile, crinkly eyes, calm expression, at complete odds with the way he'd looked when he'd confronted me at the diner.

But the speed in which he switched his demeanor is off-putting and proves what I already know.

This man isn't to be trusted.

"Bad news?" I ask, hoping my unease doesn't show.

He scowls. "Something like that."

"Not the best way to start a morning, huh?"

"You got that right. How's Brooke?"

For the second time this morning, he blindsides me. First by implying he saw me at his house via hidden cameras, and now this. He knows about me and Brooke, that we're related. Why hasn't he said something before? Is this yet another sign of his game-playing?

"She's fine."

"That's good. We had a lovely stroll along the clifftops last night. A beautiful spot, but dangerous." He shakes his head, but his eyes don't leave mine, like he's hoping for a reaction. "You never know when one wrong step can send you plunging to your death."

A chill sweeps through me. Is that a threat? Is it more proof he knows I was spying on him and he's trying to scare me?

If so, it's working, but before I can muster an appropriate response, he continues. "Brooke has already lost one sister on those cliffs. You better take care, Lizzie."

That's when I see the gleam of victory in his eyes.

He's known my connection to Brooke all along and has been toying with me.

And I'm more convinced than ever he saw me stalking him.

I should come straight out and ask what game he's playing, but from what I saw a few minutes ago, Noel has a temper, and I don't want to risk his ire when I'm alone. I want to catch him out but I'm not an idiot.

Besides, I won't give him the satisfaction of knowing he's under my skin. "I hate the blustery wind on those cliffs, so I avoid them at all costs, but thanks for the heads-up." I force a smile, hating that his taunting has got to me and wanting to return the favor. "Was that note that got you riled up from Hazel?"

I've scored an unexpected direct hit as he clenches his jaw.

"What makes you say that?"

"I left some supplies at home, so after breakfast at the diner, I went back and was packing my car when she arrived. We had a nice chat. She said some interesting things."

"Like what?" he snaps, clenching his jaw so tight I'm surprised it doesn't crack.

Yeah, there's something off about his relationship with Hazel, and maybe it's not one-sided? After my chat with her, Hazel's crush is obvious, but what's Noel's story?

"Girl stuff." I chuckle and his eyes narrow slightly. "You know her better than me, being housemates and all."

He nods but he's on edge. "Actually, the note's from Brooke. She must've slipped it into my jacket last night after our walk, when we got a drink at the cigar bar."

Interesting. What's so important that Brooke had to write it rather than text or call? And why is Noel so furious about it?

"Not trouble in paradise, I hope?" Which is exactly what I hope.

"Not at all. We're solid." His bland smile is back in place. "Though maybe you can put in a good word for me regardless?"

Brooke doesn't want to hear the words I have to say about this guy, but I keep my expression neutral. "It's not my place."

"*It's not my place,*" he mimics, his friendly mask slipping again, a glimmer of anger in his unnerving stare.

In that moment, I'm all too aware we're alone in the car park and I fervently wish that the rest of the staff would arrive.

I've dealt with far more dangerous ex-prisoners in my art classes. Men who've been convicted of crimes far worse than Noel accidentally running over his brother. But none of those men gave me the vibes Noel does, like he's one step away from losing it and anyone in his firing line will end up collateral damage.

I have to placate him. "Your relationship with Brooke is none of my business, so it's best I keep out of it. Though I wish you'd mentioned sooner that you knew we're related. I was worried about blurring professional lines with us working together and you dating my sister."

His chuckle is sinister and his switch from making chitchat

to playing mind games is startling. "Listen, Lizzie, I have nothing against you. But I have a major problem with liars, and I think Brooke has been lying to me."

He ignores what I've said about him knowing about me and Brooke, seemingly intent on dragging me into whatever problem he has with her. "That note she slipped into my pocket is proof she's been lying to me."

His jaw juts, his neck muscles bunch, and he's vibrating with anger. Hell, what did Brooke write in that note? If he's overreacting like this, I'm genuinely scared for her.

"Noel, I'm sorry to hear you're having problems with Brooke." I choose my words carefully, not wanting to antagonize him, buying time for my co-workers to arrive. Because if he's furious with Brooke, I don't want that anger spilling over onto me. "But we don't interfere in each other's lives, so I think it's best you have this conversation with her."

Over the phone, preferably, and that's what I'll be telling her as soon as I get inside. She may not want to hear what I have to say but from this encounter, it's imperative she listens to my concerns about Noel.

"Hazel said you were a doormat." His upper lip curls in a derisive sneer. "She also said you're on the outs with Brooke and she knows why."

He leans in and I grit my teeth against the urge to take a step back. No way in hell I'll show him how terrified I am. "You're a thief."

I stiffen and curl my fingers into my palms so tightly my fingernails bite. I want to fling his bizarre accusation back in his face, because he knows I didn't take Brooke's things, Hazel did. So this is more of his weird games, taunting me for some inane reason known only to himself.

I bite my tongue to stop from blurting I know he's full of crap, because in the mood he's in, only a fool would fire back, no matter how much I want to.

Instead, I settle for a sedate, "Her accusations are unwarranted, and quite frankly, it's unsavory and unprofessional that you're bringing this up." I edge back a fraction, wishing I hadn't engaged him in conversation in the first place. "We're co-workers now, so let's stick to discussing work from now on, okay?"

His lips peel back in the type of grin seen only in horror films. "In case you didn't get the memo, Lizzie, we can discuss anything I want to, because I'm dating your sister, and there's nothing you can do about it. Martino Bay was my home once and it's time I reclaimed my life."

He stalks away, toward the main building, but I stay rooted to the spot, fear making me shake.

Does Brooke have any idea that the guy she's allowed into our lives has the potential to tear our family apart?

FORTY-TWO

BROOKE

The teachers at Hope's school have a curriculum-planning day scheduled, so she's home today, and I'm working from home today too. After her day off, Hazel's back and acting like I never confronted her about stealing my stuff. She's sorting the garage, which means Riker, Hope, and I will have privacy as we finalize her family tree project. I thought it best Riker be here, because while Hope knows the truth about us being her parents, I have a feeling completing the assignment might raise questions Riker and I should answer together.

I'm ready to tackle anything that comes our way because I'm still floating from my date with Noel last night, and how we opened up to each other. Our relationship is developing nicely, despite the unwarranted interference from Lizzie, and I'd been so buzzed about our deepening connection on the clifftops that I'd slipped him a corny note when he'd gone to the bar to order our drinks later.

I haven't heard from him yet, which means he hasn't read it. I just hope he doesn't think it's too much too soon when he does. Then again, he might not wear the same jacket for weeks and it'll be a nice surprise because I'm sure our relationship would've deepened by then.

I'm grinning as I scroll through the selfies we snapped last night on my phone, when I hear Riker's motorbike pull up.

Hope looks up from her phone where she's been chatting with friends online. "Riker's here again?" She smiles, looking more like her father every day. "Cool. He can help us with my family tree project."

"Absolutely. The faster we get it done, the faster we can have whatever you want for lunch. My treat."

Her eyes narrow slightly. "What's going on?"

She's smart like her dad too.

"Nothing," I say, grateful when Riker knocks before letting himself in.

"Hey, Riker." She stands to hug him, and their bond warms my heart.

"Hey, kid." He points to her phone. "Aren't you supposed to be doing homework on your day off?"

"Yeah, though Aunt Alice is probably the one who can help me most with it, but Brooke hasn't taken me to see her in ages." Hope's glare is accusatory. "I'm pretty sure they had a fight because she's lived here forever and moved out after Freya died, and we hardly see her anymore."

Riker ignores that minefield and says, "How much have you completed of your family tree?"

"Not much." Hope flips open her sketchbook to show us, and my heart turns over when I see Riker and me linked by lines above Hope. We've lost so much time as her parents and I'm more determined than ever to make sure my daughter knows how much she's loved. Freya and Lizzie are there as her aunts, with Alice above, but she's done nothing beyond that.

"Hope, you know families can be complicated." I reach for her hand and squeeze it. "We love you. We're always here for you. No matter what."

"O-kay..." She shakes her head, worry clouding her eyes. "You're freaking me out. Did our family do something?"

What didn't they do?

Riker eyeballs me and I see my doubts reflecting in his fraught gaze. But we've made this decision, we have to see it through. It's never going to get any easier and the longer we keep Hope in the dark, the more I fear she'll resent us for it.

"I'm going to tell you everything, sweetie, and if you have questions at any time just ask."

She remains silent and I swallow, dread tightening my throat. Riker sees my discomfort and, dependable as always, says, "You know Brooke and I are your parents, but we've waited until now to tell you the rest because you're growing up so fast and we want to treat you like the responsible young adult we know you are."

He's said the perfect thing, because like most tweens and teens, she longs to be an adult, and giving her ownership of responsibility empowers her like nothing else.

"Thanks, Riker," she says, flashing him a small smile, and I shoot him a grateful glance.

"What's going on?" Hope looks at me, more curious now than worried.

Here goes nothing. "There's a reason Alice moved out and we don't see her much anymore. Remember I told you I wanted to give my baby up for adoption when I was a teen?"

She nods. "But you decided to give me to Aunt Alice and Freya to raise instead because you couldn't cope."

I stifle a grimace. "That's not entirely true. When I gave birth, Alice told me my baby, a boy, died, and that shattered me. Because deep down I didn't want to give my baby away. I couldn't cope with the sadness, so I spent the next ten years of my life moving from place to place."

Her nose crinkles in confusion. "I don't understand."

"Alice lied to me. As you know, my baby didn't die, and it

wasn't a boy. It's you. She gave you to Freya to raise. I was devastated when I discovered the truth, because if I'd known my baby lived, I would've returned here and raised you myself. And I know Aunt Alice thought she was doing the right thing at the time because of her complicated family history, but it's very difficult for me to forgive her for what she did."

Tears swim in Hope's eyes as she stares at me, wide-eyed. "She deliberately kept me from you?"

"Yes, sweetie." I take a deep breath and blow it out. "I'm finding it difficult to forgive her but I'm working on it because she's the only mother I have. But I know you've got questions about why we're estranged, so Riker and I thought you should know the truth."

Hope's gaze swings toward him, and he says, "I know this all sounds crazy, but it doesn't change facts. Brooke and I love you and we think it's cool we get to be your parents." He rests his hand in the middle of her back and makes soothing circles. "I've adored you since we first met, and I know Brooke fell for you just as quickly." He blinks rapidly but I see the sheen of tears. "We're crazy about you, kid."

"We love you so much," I add, grateful she hasn't yanked her hand out of mine. "Do you want to ask us anything?"

"No," she whispers, a second before her face crumples and she bursts into tears.

We embrace in a group hug, Riker and I joining in the tear-fest. We sob together, but amid the pain, there's a hint of something better for the future, for all of us.

Our daughter finally knows everything. My relief is huge.

When we stop crying and ease away, Hope says, "Is it okay if I go to my room? I'm not mad or anything, I just want to process."

"Sure, sweetie, take your time. We'll be here when you're ready."

"Thanks." She stands and wraps her arms around her

middle. "Thanks for telling me everything. And I love you guys too."

She runs to her room, while I resist the urge to follow her.

"That went better than expected," I say, when her bedroom door closes.

"Yeah." Riker dabs at his eyes with the hem of his shirt. "She's mature for her age."

"She takes after her wise parents."

We share a smile, but a small part of me knows this is just the start. Hope will have questions. I gave her an abbreviated version of our crazy past and when she asks the hard stuff, I'll need to be ready.

FORTY-THREE

NOEL

THEN

Ned's irrational, storming around Mom's house in search of his keys.

I can't believe he killed her. I'm filled with loathing and sadness because my family as I know it is gone.

I'll never forgive him for this. My brother is dead to me. From now on, he's on his own.

I'll keep his secret because Mom would want me to. She always protected him, always asked me to look out for him, and I know she'd be disappointed in me if I abandoned him now, no matter how much he deserves it.

Besides, I have a feeling it won't take long for Ned to fall foul of the law. Because while he won't be prosecuted for Mom's murder, I won't hold back when I warn Freya and encourage her to take out a restraining order. Plus if law enforcement starts digging into Ned's past few years, I'm sure they'll be able to tie crimes against women in various towns with his timeline of visiting those towns.

All it's going to take is pointing them in the right direction and they'll do the rest. I, for one, will breathe easier when my twin is incarcerated.

"Where the fuck are my keys?" he yells, storming back into the living room. "Have you seen them?"

Like I'd tell him even if I had.

I try one last time to talk sense into him.

"Ned, you can't confront Freya. Not in this frame of mind."

He stops and stares at me, his eyes eerily blank. "Why? Because you think I'll physically harm her?" He barks out a chilling laugh. "Been there, done that, bro. That's why I thought she left initially." He snaps his fingers. "But turns out, she was pregnant with my kid and did a runner so I'd never know."

He's insane. Certifiably.

"What do you mean you physically harmed her?"

He rolls his eyes, like assaulting a woman is nothing, and my hands automatically curl into fists. I abhor violence of any kind, but to think he might've hurt Freya... it's abominable.

"It was nothing. I just shoved her, but she went apeshit." He makes circles at his temple. "Full cray-cray. Not that it mattered, because we were infatuated with each other." He intertwines his fingers. "Like this. Before she left me without a backward glance."

He mutters, "Bitch," and I hate to think what he'll do when he gets to Martino Bay.

"You need to leave her alone, Ned. Take some time to calm down. Think things through. Then if you still want to see her, give her forewarning and a chance to explain—"

"Shut your mouth!" he shouts, his eyes bulging in his reddened face. "Stop telling me what to do. Why don't you get in your car and head back to where you came from?"

I'm not going anywhere, but before I can tell him, he stills, like a calming blanket has been thrown over him, before bolting for the back door.

I have no idea what he's up to now, but I follow. He's

running toward the front of the house. Toward my car, more precisely. And in that second, I know what he's doing. If he can't find his keys, he thinks he'll take my car.

But he can't because I have the keys. I pat my front pocket where I usually keep them.

To find it empty.

The gravity of the situation hits me as I realize I must've been so distraught over Mom when I arrived that I might've left the keys in the car.

The car Ned is about to get into.

"Ned, wait." I run after him, seeing the moment he locates the keys, because he grins and gives me a jaunty wave like he's going on a joyride.

I reach the car as he starts the engine. "Please, stop. Or let me come with you."

"No can do, bro. You're too weak to witness what I have in mind for Freya."

He revs the engine and in a panic I dash behind the car and start thumping on the trunk. Foolhardy, maybe, but I trust in our twin bond. We've been through a lot, and I've always had his back.

Ned won't hurt me.

I thump on the trunk again and lean forward to look through the back window. Our eyes meet as he glances in the rearview mirror, and what I see sends a tremor of terror through me.

Ned is past the point of no return, and in the next moment I feel the impact of the bumper against my shins as he puts the car into reverse and floors it.

FORTY-FOUR

LIZZIE

Thankfully, Max arrives not long after Noel stalks away following our bizarre encounter and I cite a family emergency I must attend to.

Max is a great boss and doesn't hesitate in giving me the time off and I run to my car, calling Brooke in the process. I need to warn her about Noel's frame of mind.

Noel divulging to me that he once lived in Martino Bay changes everything. I forgot that snippet from his prison file and that I meant to ask Alice about a possible connection to our family. I hope she might know more and that's where I'm headed now.

I'm desperately hoping Alice remembers Noel and can give me more information.

When Brooke doesn't answer I try calling again, but it's the same result, and I experience a moment of panic before remembering Noel's at work and isn't anywhere near my sister, so I leave a message on my second try.

"Hey, Brooke, it's me. I don't want to scare you, but I just had a run-in with Noel at work. He was acting nuts, rambling about you lying to him after reading a note you gave him. He's pretty mad. Then he mentioned he once lived in Martino Bay and wants to reclaim his life there. Did you know? Anyway, I'm on my way to Alice's now to see if she remembers him back in the day. I'll let you know what I find out." I pause, and add, "Love you," because I have a bad feeling about all of this.

I'm at Alice's in under ten minutes, and not for the first time I wonder if she moved to Wilks Inlet because I work in the same town, and she hoped that would encourage me to visit more often. As if. She's the last person I want to turn to at a time like this, but I need answers, pronto, and I'm slightly relieved to have her close when I pull into her drive and see her weeding.

Her face lights up when she sees me, until I get out of the car, and she catches a glimpse of my expression.

"What's wrong, Lizzie?"

"I need to ask you something. It's important."

"Okay." Alice shucks off her gardening gloves and points to the top step of the porch, where we sit. "What's on your mind?"

"Do you know a Noel Harwood?"

If I'd been worried before, my sense of foreboding increases as Alice's expression instantly morphs to one of fear.

"Why are you asking?"

"I'll explain everything, but first, tell me what you know."

She nods, but I notice her fingers digging into the denim of her jeans, like she needs an anchor. "The Harwood twins, Noel and Ned, moved to Martino Bay when Freya was seventeen. I met their mother, Julia, in the supermarket a few weeks after they'd arrived. Lovely woman. When I introduced myself, she said how wonderful it was that Ned and Freya had struck up a friendship already. I played along, even though Freya hadn't said anything to me."

I want Alice to get to the point about Noel but rushing her won't do any good. She appears lost in the past and reciting from memory.

"Freya changed over the next few weeks, and I attributed it

to a boy. She mentioned new twins at the school, Noel and Ned, and she lit up while talking about them. I was glad she'd made new friends. But I was concerned too because Freya could be obsessive about people and things, and she seemed too caught up with these boys. But Brooke was my priority at the time due to her boyfriend's death, so I shelved my concern, until the night I witnessed that boy do something horrific…"

My heart skips a beat. "What did you see?"

"I heard Freya sneak out. Brooke was already in bed asleep for the first time in weeks, after I slipped an antihistamine into her soup." She holds up a hand. "Don't judge me. I was desperately worried about her, and she needed to rest. Anyway, when I heard Freya climb out her bedroom window, I followed in my car. I stayed a fair way back with the headlights off, so she didn't see me, and that's when I saw a young girl stagger out of the forest on the edge of town. Her dress was torn, she had bruises around her neck, and she was sobbing. I pulled over and helped her in."

Alice shakes her head, sadness clouding her eyes. "That's when I saw Ned or Noel stroll out of the forest like he didn't have a care in the world, and into a house two doors down. He was grinning, before pursing his lips, so I can only assume he was whistling, which indicated a chilling lack of remorse." Her breath hitches and she swallows. "I didn't want him anywhere near Freya, but the girl needed medical attention. She wouldn't say much at first, but she recognized me as Freya's aunt, and on the way to the hospital she warned me that Freya should stay away from Ned because he'd just raped her, and he'd boasted about doing it to four other girls at his last school."

Nausea makes me clammy. If Ned's capable of that, how much of his tainted blood runs in Noel's veins?

"I dropped the girl at the ER, then hightailed it back to that house to drag Freya out by the hair if I had to. But I didn't need to, because as I neared the house, I saw Ned manhandle Freya, then he shoved her, and she bolted..." Alice trails off, her lips pinched. "I tried to question her about the twins, but she clammed up, and not long after I discovered Brooke was pregnant and we moved away. By the time we came back seven months later, the twins and Julia had gone."

"And that's it?"

Alice grimaces. "There's more. About four and a half years ago, I had a call from Julia completely out of the blue. I'm assuming Ned had our landline number from the old days. She sounded upset and said that Ned had discovered Freya had a child and was rambling about it being his and how he intended on taking that child. I told her that was impossible, because only I knew that Hope wasn't Freya's biological child, so I asked for her address. Ned was with her, so I hoped I could talk sense into him. But by the time I arrived..." She presses the pads of her fingers to her eyes before continuing. "Julia wasn't there, and I saw Ned lying dead in the driveway, so I came home. No use me getting involved."

Alice blanches and I see her hands tremble before she tucks them into her pockets. "Because of the situation with Freya and Hope..." she whispers, her pallor startling as she takes a deep breath before continuing. "Because I took Brooke's baby and gave Hope to Freya to raise, I didn't want the police coming around, looking into me, digging into my family and home life, which might've happened if I'd been the one to report the body, so that's why I left and returned home."

I'm incredulous. How many more secrets and twisted lies has Alice been hiding? To think she'd left Ned to die, just like Noel. I'd judged him for it, for his sheer callousness, so to discover that the woman who raised me did the same thing... I'm disgusted.

"Then I heard on the news about Noel being part of a hit-and-run involving his brother, so that was that." Her voice is tremulous, and her eyes are begging for forgiveness.

If only it were that simple.

"I'm working with Noel. He's the new prison liaison officer, but he's also dating Brooke," I blurt, anxiety tightening my throat. "I've picked up a weird vibe off him from the start, but she's smitten."

I want to tell her what I saw at Noel's place, but bringing Hazel into this will only complicate matters, not to mention having Alice question my methods in how far I'll go to protect my family.

So I keep my explanation simple and confined to today. "I think he followed me this morning, when I stopped at Bert's diner early for breakfast. Then I had a run-in with him at work about an hour ago. He's acting crazy." I make circles at my temple. "Something about Brooke writing him a note and lying to him."

"That's odd." Alice's brow furrows but she doesn't seem terribly concerned. "I do know Ned was an awful boy who assaulted girls, and if he hadn't died, he would've probably grown into someone much worse. But Noel never put a foot wrong, so perhaps you're overreacting?"

Alice lays a placating hand on my arm. "The Shomack women pay too much attention to our gut reactions, but we've been known to be wrong."

Alice's cautious tone with a hint of condescension makes it clear that she doesn't believe a word I'm saying, and I inwardly cringe as I imagine her finding out I stalked Noel at his house. She'll think I'm taking things too far, but Alice isn't the only one who's done crazy things in the name of family. I'm willing to do whatever it takes to protect my sister.

I shrug, trying to appear like Alice has eased my fears. "Ever since I found out Brooke is my sister, I guess I worry about losing her."

"Because you lost Freya," she murmurs, her eyes filled with understanding. "Makes sense. Maybe you're being overprotective with Brooke because this is the first man she's dated?"

"Maybe."

I deliberately sound offhand so she'll think I'll drop my concerns about Noel, but I know there's more to him than meets the eye and I'm going to make sure Brooke knows it. Though I guess I should be grateful Brooke's dating Noel, the good twin, and not Ned.

But twins share matching DNA and if anyone knows how good and bad traits run in a family, I do, so perhaps I'm justified in obsessing over Noel and what he's potentially capable of.

FORTY-FIVE

BROOKE

"How are you holding up, sweetheart?"

I glance sideways at Hope in the passenger seat in time to see her roll her eyes. "That's the fifth time you've asked me since we got in the car. I'm fine."

That's what she says, but my beautiful girl's eyes are red-rimmed and her skin blotchy, so I know she's been crying ever since Riker and I delivered the news an hour ago. He left after Hope holed herself in her room and I said I'd keep him informed.

Coincidentally, I'd just listened to Lizzie's bizarre voice message when Hope came out of her room, asking if I could take her to Alice's house so she could hear her version of events. I'd only been too happy to comply—happy that Hope now knows I didn't give her up willingly—so I'd jumped in the car and headed to Alice's. It's only the third time I've visited since she moved out two years ago, because I can't abide being near her since I learned the truth.

She stole my baby and gave Hope to my sister to raise. It's diabolical, despite her rationale, and the only reason I've been anywhere near her since I discovered the truth is because of

Hope. She loves Alice, who raised her alongside Freya, and my daughter's life has spiraled out of control the last few years, without adding an enforced estrangement.

During our previous visits, I'd go for a walk while Hope catches up with Alice. They usually bake together like they used to, and I have to force myself to eat the brownies and cupcakes Hope returns with because every mouthful is tainted by Alice's treachery.

This visit, like the others, is for Hope's benefit. She wants to talk to Alice about what I've just revealed, and while I can't forgive or forget what my aunt did to me, I know she has Hope's best interests at heart, and she'll be gentle with her.

As I turn into the drive, I hope Lizzie is still here so I can grill her about her confrontation with Noel and what has her in such a funk.

As for that tidbit about Noel living in Martino Bay, he already told me. But him acting crazy about my note... that doesn't make sense. Nope, Lizzie is mistaken. And I hate to admit it, but the way she sounded on the phone, irrational and highly strung, reminds me of Freya and the warped way she used to toy with me.

Logically, I know Lizzie isn't as unhinged as Freya once was, delighting in torturing me, but I can't shake the feeling there's something seriously wrong with her.

Lizzie and I have always been close but maybe our recent estrangement changed things for her? Is she still holding a grudge, despite our apparent reconciliation, and taunting me the way Freya used to?

As we near the house, I see Lizzie and Alice outside. Their expressions are somber as I pull up near the carport.

"They don't look happy to see us," Hope murmurs, and my heart aches for how much this poor girl has had to endure because of our family.

"I think something's happened that has nothing to do with

us, sweetie." I reach across and squeeze her hand. "Why don't you wait in the car, and I'll go see what's going on?"

Her face falls, but I add, "This may not be the best time for you to speak with Alice, but I promise I'll make a time with her right now if it's not, and we'll come back later, okay?"

"Okay."

I open the driver's door as Hope says, "Brooke, I feel really bad because I've been blaming you for giving me up and it wasn't your fault."

Tears burn the back of my eyes for all the time we've lost. "Don't feel bad, honey. I wanted to tell you everything at the start, but you'd just lost the only mom you've ever known and you needed time to grieve."

She screws up her nose. "It's wrong I called Freya Mom for so many years when she wasn't. I know I should be super mad at her and Aunt Alice, but they were really nice to me and I'm just too tired to take it all in, to be honest. But I feel bad for you, because you must've been really sad when you learned I'm your daughter and they hid that from you."

My amazing girl is incredibly insightful, and I do her the courtesy of giving her the truth. "I was beyond sad, sweetie. It gutted me that I missed out on the first decade of your life. And while the last two years have been tough because we lost Freya, it's also been an incredible gift to me, being able to support you and love you and be a mother to you." I blink the threatening tears away because she needs to hear this. "I love you, Hope. From the moment we met, I felt a connection and I'm so proud of how you've handled the hardships thrown your way. And I'm looking forward to being your mom for many years to come."

Tears fill her eyes, and she sniffles. "I think you better go see Lizzie and Aunt Alice before we start bawling."

"Good idea." I lean across and press a kiss to her cheek before getting out of the car, dashing my hand across my eyes.

As I approach Lizzie and Alice, I see something serious has happened.

"Is Hope okay?" Alice asks, glancing over my shoulder then back at me. "Are you?"

"Riker and I told her everything."

Alice's eyes widen and I add, "Yeah, she now knows the part you played in keeping her from me and she wants clarification from you. But by your expressions I can tell something's wrong, so I told her we'd save her questions for another time."

"That's why you missed my calls," Lizzie says, and I nod.

"I got your message. What's all this about Noel having a meltdown over my note?"

Before Lizzie can respond, Alice says, "There's nothing to worry about. Lizzie got a little freaked when Noel mentioned living in Martino Bay, which I'm sure you know?"

I nod, my gaze swinging between them, because I have a feeling there's more to this. "Yeah, of course I know. He told me at the start."

"Well, he never mentioned it to me, even though I knew about it from his prison file, but he also dropped a little bombshell that he knows we're related," Lizzie says, in that censorious tone she gets whenever she discusses Noel. "Don't you think it's weird he's waited until now to mention it?"

"Lizzie, stop." Alice shoots her a warning glance and Lizzie's lips compress. "Your sister is being overprotective. Long story short, Ned and Noel moved to Martino Bay for a short while around the time you lost Eli, Brooke. Ned was obsessed with Freya and vice versa," Alice says. "Ned raped a girl, and I witnessed him manhandle your sister, so when you told me you were pregnant in that same week, moving away to LA was the perfect solution for all of us. Then just over four years ago, the twins' mother reached out to me, with serious concerns for Freya because Ned thought she'd had his child."

My mouth drops open. "Why on earth would he think that?"

"Who knows," Alice says, "but you have nothing to worry about, Brooke. Noel is nothing like Ned. He helped Freya with an algebra test once and was so sweet and polite. And he helped me carry groceries to the car that time I hurt my wrist. A lovely boy." She pauses, genuine curiosity in her eyes. "How serious is it between you two?"

Heat creeps into my cheeks. "He's great. I really like him."

"So why did he freak out over that note?" Lizzie asks, unwilling to let this go.

While I don't need Alice's stamp of approval regarding Noel, it's nice to hear nonetheless. But Lizzie's obsession with Noel is beyond tiresome, and while what I wrote to Noel is private, if I can shut her up, I'll do whatever it takes.

"I already told him I have feelings for him last night, so I basically said the same in the note. I wrote, 'I'm falling in love with you.' That's it." I glare at Lizzie. "Are you sure he was freaking out over my note and not something else?"

She shakes her head. "He said the note is proof you'd lied to him."

"But I didn't lie. And he already knows how I feel because I told him. Unless..."

No, it's crazy, but did Hazel interfere? I can't forget her distraught expression and the way she dropped the mop when I asked her if she had feelings for Noel, followed by her curt refusal belied by her blush during our last conversation. Her odd behaviour when questioned merely reinforced my gut reaction that she has a crush on Noel or is reading more into their relationship than is healthy. And if so, how far is she willing to go to sabotage us? Did she find my note and swap it out? But that doesn't make sense because surely Noel would recognize her handwriting? Then again, nobody writes anything these days. We text.

Though once my suspicions take root, I can't dislodge them.

"What are you thinking?" Lizzie's watching me, her brows grooved.

"This might sound crazy, but do you think there's a possibility Hazel swapped notes to mess with my relationship? I've been wondering if she has feelings for him and—"

"Yes, that's entirely possible," Lizzie says, her conviction startling. "I've been wondering the same thing myself, about her being into him." She blushes and I have no idea why. "I asked her this morning and she didn't deny it."

I'm annoyed by Lizzie's interference, but she's backed up what I already suspect about Hazel. I need to confront her.

Now.

"Lizzie, can you do me a favor and take Hope home? I'm going to call Noel and sort this out, then I'm going to call Hazel and get her to meet me in town to confront her and see if I'm jumping to conclusions or if she's messing with me."

"That sounds wise, dear." Alice tut-tuts. "You don't need anyone interfering in your relationship."

I don't miss the glance Alice shoots Lizzie. But I'll deal with my overprotective sister another day.

"You're right. He means too much to me." Thanks to Hazel's game-playing, if my suspicions are correct, I need to tell him that in person. "I'll see you at home later, okay?"

"Okay," Lizzie says, but her expression isn't reassuring. "Just be careful. I don't trust... her."

She doesn't trust Noel either, that much is clear, but I say, "I'll be careful."

I have to be. I have a daughter to raise and the last of our sordid family secrets are finally out in the open. Life's about to get a whole lot better and I won't have anyone ruining it.

FORTY-SIX

NED

NOW

I've always hated that old cliché *The apple doesn't fall far from the tree*.

We are not our parents.

Sure, we inherit their DNA but who we become is entirely on us. At least, that's what I believe. Nurture over nature. What we're exposed to shapes us far beyond our genetic makeup.

Which means I know who to blame for the way I've turned out.

The one person who lied to me. The one person I trusted the most in this world. The one person who should've had my back.

My twin, Noel.

He knew about Freya, her kid being mine, all of it, and he kept it from me. For years.

Noel deserved to die. And I guess fate took care of Freya too, so I didn't have to.

But I'm impatient to reclaim my life, the life I should've had without Noel's interference. Screw him. And screw anyone who stands in my way.

Like Brooke.

For years, I hid too much. I resented. I hated. I festered. I remained silent and became who I swore I'd never be.

A monster.

I hide it well. I function like a normal human being. I fake feelings like happiness and love. I care about the environment. I pay my taxes.

But I walk among everyone and the fact they don't see me, the real me? That's all on them.

Everyone sees me as inherently good. More fool them.

Because what I'm about to do?

They won't see me coming.

I've been so patient since I got out of prison. I've had to be because I knew if I rushed headlong into forging a relationship with my daughter, I would've failed.

She wouldn't come away with me. She would be scared. She might even be terrified of me, and that's no way to start a father-daughter bond.

My plan is smarter.

Get close to the carer to get close to my daughter.

Besides, being with Brooke hasn't been a hardship. She's easy on the eyes, nice body, good conversationalist. I'm guessing that's why Hazel's been getting angsty. She thinks I'm too close to Brooke, that I'm falling under her spell a little.

As if.

There's only one reason I started dating Brooke.

To gain access to my daughter, to build a rapport with Hope, so that when I take her, she won't put up a fight.

But I'm getting tired of waiting and now Brooke's lied to me. That note proves it. She's been toying with me all along and I won't be outplayed.

She has no idea what I'm capable of, how hard I've had to rein in my impulses and not decimate her.

But after reading that note, my patience has run out.

That's what I'd been angry about this morning when that nosy cow Lizzie had seen me. I'd just got off the phone with Hazel, because I'd read the note and we'd had a massive argument. She wants us to slow things down and not do anything rash, whereas I want to move our timeline up.

I want to take Hope and make a run for it.

The sooner the better.

Though I can't get Hazel offside. I need her. Hope trusts her and with Hazel along for our little family reunion, Hope won't freak out as much as she would with just the two of us.

It's been a drag, having to fake interest in Hazel since I got out. We'd never officially dated before I went to prison, but I slept with her once and she took that as a vow and trailed around after me ever since. It annoyed the crap out of me but turns out she's been handy, because the moment I learned Brooke needed a housekeeper, I had an in to get close to my daughter. And Hazel being Hazel—obsessed with me, willing to do anything to be with me—she thought my idea was genius.

I'll keep her around long enough for Hope to trust me.

Then I'll get rid of her like the others.

Noel wasn't the first person I killed, but he's the one I regret the most. He always had my back, but when it mattered most, he let me down and I couldn't let him stop me from seeing my daughter.

Being caught hadn't been in my plans though. It had been sheer bad luck that Noel's car had a faulty taillight and a highway patrolman had pulled me over in the relentless rain that started not long after I sped away from Mom's. I'd been on the verge of doing something completely reckless, like murder a policeman, when he asked me for my license, and I saw Noel's wallet in the console.

It had come to me in an instant.

If I had to be arrested for the murder of my brother, why not make it look like an accident and become the "good" twin?

Everyone loved Noel. Revered Noel. They'd believe him if he accidentally ran over his brother and left the scene in a dazed panic.

They'd throw the book at me, and if law enforcement started delving into my past—cities I'd been to, women who'd been violated there, and worse—no, I couldn't have that.

So I became my brother.

Brilliant and diabolical, my plan worked.

I got a four-year sentence where I channeled Noel. I was the model prisoner, kept my head down, obeyed the guards, did my rehab.

And I counted down the days until I'd be reunited with my daughter.

Hazel had been the one to tell me Freya had died two years ago. Jumped off a cliff. Too bad. I would've liked to watch her face as I shoved her off it. But in a way, it made access to Hope simpler, because her aunt Brooke would be an easy target. Hazel had watched her, tailed her, and informed me of her every move.

So that when we put our plan into play, the rest fell into place.

Hazel and I insinuating our way into Brooke's and Hope's lives has been easier than anticipated. Lizzie has been annoyingly suspicious, and I've contemplated getting rid of her several times. Who knows, I might have a little fun before I leave town?

But that's crazy talk because I can't jeopardize my future with my daughter.

The goal is within reach and my timeline has moved up.

I'll be taking my daughter on a little trip.

Today.

FORTY-SEVEN

BROOKE

I call Noel twice on the way back to Martino Bay, but he doesn't answer. Not a big deal, considering he's at work and probably busy or in a meeting with a newly released prisoner, but a sliver of unease gnaws at me because I want to talk to him and discover firsthand if anything's wrong or if Lizzie is exaggerating about his reaction to my note.

I didn't need Alice vouching for Noel, but it's nice to hear her memories of him are positive, and once I sort out this mess with Hazel, I'm more determined than ever to move forward with my relationship with Noel. Our strengthened relationship if he returns my vow of love.

Thoughts of Noel alleviate my tension for this upcoming meeting a little, and I'm smiling as I park near the café where I'm meeting Hazel. I heard her mention to Hope last week that The Jade Frog is her favorite and she was happy to meet me here when I texted her before I left Alice's.

The trendy vegan café isn't really my scene, though the aroma of brewing fair-trade coffee is tempting as I push open the wrought iron gate that resembles a frog on a lily pad. Riker's so talented with his metal sculpting and would do a much better job of crafting an accurate depiction of a contemplative frog that I'm tempted to mention it to the staff, but they're bustling around serving patrons inside and outside.

Large bifold doors are open and the outside patio area boasts beige wooden walls covered in seascapes from local artists and a plethora of hanging plants. The menu is scrawled in calligraphy on a blackboard, the predominant item being bowls of various description and most featuring avocado, nuts, and vegetables. The listed lattes are made with nut milks and organic coffee beans, and the only thing that catches my eyes is a turmeric ginger cappuccino, but I'll wait until Hazel arrives to order. Then again, hopefully I won't be here too long, so maybe I'll hold off on the cappuccino.

I choose an outside table, public enough that I hope she won't make a scene when I interrogate her. Or worse, have to fire her. Not that I want to, but I may have to. I can't have someone undermining my relationship with Noel. He's become too important to me. After last night, I trust him. He doesn't have feelings for Hazel, but that doesn't mean she's not crushing on him. And if she did switch notes as I suspect, whatever she wrote that he thinks came from me... it must be bad.

But I'm not jumping to conclusions. I'll lead into my questions gently and hope my suspicions are wrong. I like Hazel, I trust her. I wouldn't have let her into my house, into our lives, otherwise. Though the irony isn't lost on me. I've been taking things slow with Noel because of my trust issues, but maybe he's not the one I should've been wary of.

Though I wonder, if Hazel does have feelings for Noel, why did she introduce us? Unless she's so deluded that she thinks Noel is hers and he'd never fall for anyone else. I mean, my feelings for him came out of the blue at a time I least expected it, it might've been the same for him. He's virtually said as much. In which case, it must be tough for Hazel to sit back and watch the man she wants fall for me.

And if her resentment toward me is festering, she must've stolen my stuff in petty revenge, probably to mess with my head. I hate to think how much further she might've taken her vendetta if she hadn't seen my note and realized how strong my feelings for Noel are?

There's a line to order coffee at the outside window of the café and I'm looking at a cute couple bickering over whether a matcha latte or cacao cappuccino is better when a shadow looms over me from behind and I spin around quickly, to find Hazel glowering at me.

"Hey, Brooke. Why did you want to meet here rather than at home?"

I bite back my first snappish response, *It's my home, not yours*, and force a tight smile and gesture to the chair opposite. "I was in town, and this couldn't wait. Would you like a coffee?"

Confused, she glances at the line at the café window then back at me before she sits. "No. I'm fine. What's going on?"

"Did you see Noel this morning before he left for work?"

A faint crimson flushes her cheeks at the mere mention of his name and my heart sinks. If I'm right, and she's messing with me and my relationship, I'll have to let her go, meaning an end to a spotless house and amazing homecooked meals. And a possible cause of contention between Noel and me when I fire his bestie.

"No. Why?"

"He's not returning my calls and Lizzie says he was in a bad mood at work."

"Lizzie?" She sneers, her animosity palpable. "I wouldn't listen to anything she says. She's nuts."

Annoyed by her bravado, I say, "My sister isn't crazy."

She snorts. "For argument's sake, let's say cray-cray is right and Noel is in a mood. What's that got to do with me?"

I don't want to outright accuse her yet, so I need to push her buttons, get her to confess. "I left a note for Noel last night. Have you seen it?"

Genuine confusion clouds her eyes, making me wonder if I'm wrong about her. "No. Is it important?"

"Yes, actually. But he mentioned to Lizzie that I lied in it, which is impossible, because I know what I wrote."

"How would I know what you wrote..." She trails off and her eyes narrow as she figures out what I'm implying. "You think I did something to your precious note?"

"Look, Hazel, I may be wrong but—"

"You are wrong," she says, her tone lethal. "And I'm sick of your bullshit. You're as crazy as your sister." Her hands curl into fists and she thumps the table, making me jump. "You need to stay the hell away from Noel. He's too good for you."

Considering her twisted expression and malevolent glare, I'm not the crazy one, and I need to end our association ASAP. I'm just glad I discovered her madness before she could get closer to Hope than she already has.

"I'd like to thank you for your hard work, Hazel, but I'm afraid I have to let you go." I reach for a little white lie to prevent her blowing up completely. "I have family moving back in, so we won't need a housekeeper or nanny any longer."

Her silence is unnerving, her expression a scarily quick transition from rage to blank, so I continue, "I appreciate all you've done for us. Can I have my keys back please?"

She blinks once, twice, before the nonchalant mask cracks, and she radiates loathing again. "Family moving in, huh?" She snickers. "You're a liar."

"Hazel, this doesn't have to be unpleasant—"

"Do you know what it's been like for me, watching the man I've loved forever pretend to like you?"

Hell. I'm right, Lizzie too. She has a thing for Noel and is treating me like the enemy.

"It must be difficult for you, Hazel, having feelings for a man who loves someone else. But Noel and I are happy—"

"You're such a moron." Her laugh is maniacal. "Even when I stole your pathetic things because I saw how much they meant to you and I hated how you fawned over my man, you kept me on. Are you that stupid you can't see what we've been doing?"

She's unhinged and I wish I'd seen it sooner. Losing the man she loves has made her snap and I need to placate, at least until she hands over my keys.

"Hazel, let's keep this civil. Return my things and my keys, and I won't press charges. Noel and I can help you move, find a new place, perhaps in another town?"

She smirks and her glare is pure malevolence. "Stop calling him that."

Confused, I try again. "Listen, Noel and I—"

"Don't you get it? Ned instigated me working for you. He's been pulling strings from the beginning, and you've been too dumb to notice. I did whatever I could to help him because that's what true love is. I've been loyal to Ned forever and we're going to be together, one big happy family."

She called him Ned.

Is she more delusional than I thought? Has she transferred her love for Ned onto Noel, mistaking his gratitude toward her as something more?

"It's Noel—"

"It's Ned." She shakes her head. "Hope is his daughter, and once we take her with us, we're going to be the family I've always wanted."

My blood freezes at the extent of her lunacy.

"Hope isn't Ned's daughter. She's mine. Mine and Riker's."

"More lies." Spittle flies from her lips as anger contorts her usually calm features. "Say what you like, it's irrelevant. Ned's always one step ahead of everyone and you're no exception."

I'm done with this. Conversing with a woman I seriously

misjudged is a waste of time. She's blindly loyal to a man who's dead and her memories born from grief have warped all sense of reality.

"The keys, Hazel." I keep my tone steady and hold out my hand.

She snickers as she rummages in her handbag before flinging the keys at my face and I catch them before they take out an eye. "Take your precious keys."

She stands, towering over me, but I refuse to be intimidated, and stare her down. Her grin is chilling as she leans down to say, "I'm sure you already know that I've had those keys a while now, Brooke, and I could've copied them any time I wanted."

I shiver as she walks away and the doubts I've been suppressing during our exchange surface and make me wonder.

Is there any truth to the possibility she's right and Ned is the guy I've fallen for?

But according to Alice, Ned's a monster. A rapist. How can a man like that hide his true self from me?

No, Hazel's lost all perspective and has taken her love for Ned and transferred it onto Noel.

I can't contemplate the other probability: that I've let a madman into my family.

But on the off-chance Hazel is right, and she might've copied my house keys, I need to call Lizzie and warn her to lock all the doors and be alert.

Lizzie doesn't answer my first call. Or my second. My heart pounds as I call Hope. She always has her phone glued to her hand. But when my daughter doesn't answer, I know the unthinkable may have happened.

A lunatic is at my house and the ones I love are in grave danger.

FORTY-EIGHT

LIZZIE

For the entire drive home from Alice's, I put on a brave face for Hope. The poor kid is obviously reeling from the news about what Alice and Freya did to keep her from her real mother all those years ago, and thankfully, she doesn't pepper me with questions. She's stoically silent and I don't start a conversation. I'm too busy thinking about what Alice said.

Ned was a rapist according to Alice, and violent toward women, and Noel is nothing like his twin. But I can't dismiss the vibes I've picked up from Noel—the taunts, like he's toying with me, the general uneasiness I've felt every time he's near me —right from the beginning.

If Noel has one tenth of his twin's DNA, he's not as amazing as Brooke thinks and I wonder what a guy like that is capable of?

Considering the number of ex-prisoners I've worked with, I believe in rehabilitation because it's what I do. But there are more than a few who are incapable of change and reoffend, so in Noel's case, is he just biding his time? Is Brooke oblivious to the real Noel, a man more like his brother than we've given him credit for?

Hope's silent as we reach the house, and when I turn off the engine, she faces me. "Can I tell you something and you'll promise not to freak?"

My heart sinks. If Hope wants to ask me more about our convoluted family tree, I don't think it's my place to tell her. If Brooke's only just revealed everything to her earlier, it's natural Hope will have questions and while I'm glad she wants to confide in me, I'm also worried.

"Sure, honey. You can trust me."

She nods and chews on her bottom lip. "I wanted to tell Brooke but didn't want to mess with her new relationship."

Uh-oh. My instincts are on high alert now. Has Noel done something untoward? Has he reached out to Hope behind Brooke's back? If so, it's further proof her boyfriend is not who she thinks he is, and with a little luck, this may be the final nail in Noel's proverbial coffin and Brooke will dump him.

"Tell me, sweetie. What happened?"

Hope takes a deep breath and blows it out before continuing. "It's about Hazel."

I try to hide my surprise, as I was sure this had to be about Noel. "What about Hazel?"

"I really like her and she's been cool to talk to since she started working here, but then yesterday..." She gnaws on her bottom lip again and fear ricochets through me. If Hazel laid a finger on this precious girl, I'll kill her.

Willing my voice to stay calm, I prompt, "Yesterday?"

"She kept looking at me funny. And every time she was around me, she had her phone in her hand and was taking photos." Hope screws up her nose. "When I asked her about it, she said she was taking photos of the way the furniture was arranged because she wanted to do a big spring clean and had to move stuff back the way it was when she finished, but..."

Hope's eyes lock on me, beseeching me to understand and trust that she's not exaggerating. "There's no furniture to move at the island bench, or the dining table where I was doing home-work, or on the couch when I was watching TV, so I know she was taking photos of me."

My mind leaps to all kinds of conclusions: Hazel's as weird as Noel and is becoming obsessed with her charge; Hazel's obsessed with Brooke and, not content with stealing her things, she's latching on to Hope; or if what Alice said is correct, and Noel thinks Hope is his niece, maybe Hazel's cosying up to Noel by presenting him with photos?

None of my suppositions are good but I can't let Hope see my fear. She's been through enough today, learning the truth about Alice and Freya.

"I can see she made you uncomfortable, honey, so I'm glad you confided in me." I hold my hand out to her, relieved when she takes it. "I'm here for you. Always. Would you like me to talk to Hazel?"

She hesitates, before nodding. "Though maybe I'll tell Brooke later today and she can talk to Hazel?"

Brooke's talking to Hazel right now and, with a little luck, is firing her, before I have to tell Brooke that Hazel stole her things. I've been so fixated on Noel hiding something that I haven't looked into Hazel enough, and once I get Hope settled inside, I plan on doing a little online investigating into the weird housekeeper.

"That sounds like a good idea. Brooke needs to know." I squeeze her hand. "Thanks for trusting me."

Her smile is wan. "You're a pretty cool aunt."

"I can handle being cool." I make a peace sign that indicates I'm decidedly uncool and I'm relieved to hear a faint chuckle. "You hungry?"

I want to cheer her up and there's nothing like something sugary to do that.

"I can eat, maybe," she says, with a diffident shrug.

"I can work with maybe." We get out of the car, and as I

unlock the back door and we enter the kitchen, I say, "I feel like blueberry pancakes."

It's Hope's favorite and she could definitely do with some comfort food today, so she might be tempted.

"No thanks," she says softly, way too subdued, and I want to envelop her in a big squishy hug.

"Then how about—"

"She said no." Noel's tone is flat and I freeze as I hear a foot-fall behind me. "You should listen better."

"Who let you in?" Hope's wide-eyed as she glares at Noel over my shoulder, sounding stronger than a moment ago.

"I let myself in." Noel moves in front of me and dangles a set of keys on his finger. "Thanks to Hazel."

Damn, so they are working together to undermine Brooke. Though to what end? Does he have genuine feelings and Hazel is trying to undercut Brooke or is this all about Hope, who he thinks is his niece?

Whatever his rationale, the fact that Hazel gave him keys to Brooke's house, and he's used them, speaks volumes. His intentions aren't good.

I want to scream. Rant. Do something. But terror is coursing through me and all I can think is I need to do whatever I can to protect Hope.

"She shouldn't have given you our keys." Hope folds her arms and glares at him. "Brooke needs to fire her."

"I don't care about Hazel or Brooke," he snaps, and Hope visibly recoils. "We'll leave them behind when we go."

We.

Is he here to kidnap Hope?

Alice mentioned Ned's and Noel's mother reaching out to her four years ago with concerns for Freya because Ned thought she'd had his child. Does Noel think the same and he wants to take his niece in some warped retaliation against Brooke because Freya's no longer around to blame for keeping them apart?

My breathing is shallow, but enough oxygen gets to my brain that I can finally subdue my fear and think straight.

"Noel, whatever you think is going on in your relationship with Brooke, you're mistaken—"

"Shut the fuck up!" He yells, and we both jump. "But you're right. Noel was mistaken about a lot of things, which is why I'm much smarter than him."

The blood drains from my head and I sway a little as realization crashes over me.

No. This can't be happening. The truth is too horrendous to contemplate. Because if what I just heard is correct...

Our worst nightmare is coming true.

My sister hasn't been dating the good twin.

She's fallen for Ned.

Which means Hope and I are in grave danger.

"You switched places with your brother after you killed him."

It's a statement, not a question, because from what Alice told me, this man is capable of anything. He's a psychopath and there's no way he could've run over Noel accidentally. I knew that a good man couldn't have run his own brother over and fled the scene, and I was right—I just had the wrong brother. He's violent and remorseless, so the longer I can keep his attention on me and off Hope, the better. With a little luck I can signal to her with my eyes to make a run for it.

He slow-claps. "Well done. You're the first person to figure it out."

Which means he probably won't let me live because I'm a threat to him.

"But in case you didn't know, Freya had my kid." He points at Hope and his grin is chilling. "Meet your real daddy, Hope."

Damn, he's just confirmed what his mother told Alice. He's not just a psychopath, he's delusional. Then again, according to Alice, Noel and Ned left town by the time Freya came back with Hope, meaning if he found out about her existence and the timeline fit, he's jumped to the conclusion Alice and Freya wanted everyone to think. That Hope is Freya's child. As if Alice hasn't caused enough damage with her lies, perpetuating her deception has resulted in this madman putting Hope's life—all our lives—at risk.

"She's not yours," I say, infusing a calm I don't feel into my voice. "Freya never had a kid. Brooke got pregnant, our aunt moved the girls to LA, but because of a warped family history, Alice told Brooke her baby died at birth, but gave the girl to Freya to raise."

"You're lying!" he roars, sweeping crockery off the benchtop and sending it crashing to the floor. "Stop trying to twist the narrative."

"She's not lying," Hope says, her eyes wide with fear. "Brooke told me the truth not long after Freya died. My dad is Riker, not you."

"That wannabe hippie?" Ned snorts. "No way. She must've known I'd come for you eventually and she made up that bullshit."

He sneers at me, any hint of civility gone, rage darkening his eyes to midnight. "And you both believed her. How stupid are you?"

I bite back my first response, *Not as stupid as you*, because that will only anger him more and he's unstable enough.

"Look, Ned, why don't you wait for Brooke to get home, then we can discuss this rationally—"

"I'm done waiting." He advances toward Hope, who shrinks away from him. "We're leaving now, Hope. Time for some daddy-daughter bonding time."

Spots dance before my eyes as terror grips me. I need to stop him. But the frying pan on the stove is across the kitchen and I have to pass Ned to get it. Same with the block of knives.

I try a different tack.

"If you're hellbent on doing this, she needs to pack." I know Hope's smart enough to escape if I give her the opportunity. "You can't take a young girl on the road without personal belongings."

Ned hesitates, his eyes narrowing as he ponders my suggestion. "No. Stop delaying." He takes a step toward Hope and she shrinks back. "We go. Now."

I've dealt with narcissists like Ned before, ex-cons who think the world revolves around them, a world that owes them. So I need to play this smart and pander to him.

"You're a smart guy, Ned. Not many people I know would've got away with the whole twin-swap thing, but you've fooled everyone for years."

He practically puffs up with pride before my eyes, his shoulders squaring, his expression smug. Idiot.

So I continue. "And a smart guy would know that a young girl going on a trip needs stuff. A change of clothes at least. Toiletries. Essentials." I shrug, pretending like I'm not a quivering mess inside. "The last thing you'd want to do is have to make regular stops to pick up emergency supplies."

I hold my breath, watching his eyes shift from wary to cockiness.

I've got him.

"Fine," he snaps. "But don't try anything funny because you have no idea what I'm capable of."

Sadly, I do, and my heart aches when Hope blanches, her eyes terrified as they lock on me. I give a reassuring nod, knowing I'll have to play the next few minutes very carefully if she's to have any chance of escaping.

To emphasize his threat, he grabs a knife from the block and brandishes it, and I swallow a scream as Hope whimpers.

"Hurry up," he yells, and we both jump. "Get your stuff and let's go."

As I move toward Hope, he says, "Stop. We all go together."

It's what I expected, but for my plan to work, I need for him to enter the room with me and leave Hope near the door so she can make a break for it when I create a diversion.

I hate to think what he'll do to me with that knife, but I have to take the risk.

I have to protect Hope.

Ned follows me into Hope's bedroom, and I draw him toward the dresser in the corner, leaving Hope behind us. It's a small victory, exactly what I wanted him to do, but my plan has so many flaws I pray this works.

"Just use your small backpack, honey," I say, pointing to the purple one she uses on weekends because it's near the door. "I'll get you a few things."

Thankfully, Ned stays near me, rolling the knife between his thumb and forefinger, enjoying my fear, if his smug grin is anything to go by. Prick.

I open the top drawer of the dresser and choose a clean pair of jeans and a sweatshirt, relieved that Hope hasn't moved far from the door. I want to yell at her to run but I need to time this right, so I place the clothes on top of the dresser and pick up a small makeup bag, taking my time to fill it with a brush, sunscreen, and lip balm.

My body is angled away from Hope, but I'm facing the mirror, waiting for the moment our gazes lock. For the last few moments, her eyes have been downcast, so I clear my throat and, thankfully, she looks up.

I mouth "run" and her eyes widen. She's got the message. However, before she can take a step, Ned grabs my hair and yanks me back.

I scream as he brings his face close to mine, his cheeks flushed an angry puce.

"I told you not to mess with me." His spittle sprays me and terror turns my legs to jelly. "You've been a pain in my ass from the start, always glancing at me sideways, snooping around my house at night." His leer is terrifying. "Even following you to that diner didn't deter you and I shouldn't have waited this long to get rid of you."

It means little that I've been right about him from the beginning as my legs crumple and he releases my hair. I try to dodge and shove past him, but he's too quick, too strong.

His fist connects with the side of my head, and the last thing I see before everything turns black is tears streaming down Hope's face.

FORTY-NINE

ALICE

I've made so many mistakes in my lifetime.

Coveting my sister's husband.

Loving him more than her.

Lying to Lizzie that I was her mother.

Pretending I didn't see Freya's madness and how badly she envied Brooke.

Taking Brooke's baby and giving Hope to Freya to raise as hers.

And more, some too dark to contemplate.

But every single bad thing I've done has been to protect my family,and despite my earlier bravado, I'm worried. Brooke telling Hope the truth changes everything and despite me deserving their wrath, I love these girls too much to stay away.

I drive to Brooke's to see how Hope's doing. She must have a million questions, and I know Brooke said now isn't the time, but that precious girl doesn't deserve any of this and if I can ease her confusion in any way, I want to do it.

However, when I arrive, I see something so shocking I pull over behind Lizzie's bungalow.

Noel has a length of rope wound over his arm and a roll of

duct tape dangling from his hand. But that's not what shocks me.

He's whistling, wearing the same smug expression I've seen before, over a decade ago, when Ned strolled out of those woods after raping Freya's friend.

Which means Brooke hasn't been dating Noel.

She's in love with a fiend.

But how could Ned be back from the dead... unless Noel was the twin who was killed that day?

In that moment, I have no doubt that Ned killed his brother and switched identities. A man capable of rape without remorse is capable of anything and killing a sibling he envied would be a mere blip on his conscience.

The irony isn't lost on me that I once wanted to do the same to Diana, my sister. But I relented at the last moment because I couldn't go through with it.

Ned, on the other hand...

I get out of my car and skirt the trees, watching what he's doing. He opens his trunk and dumps the rope and duct tape inside, and I hate to think what he's used that for. I have no weapon, but if he lays one finger on Lizzie and Hope, I'll kill him with my bare hands.

He starts his car, then heads inside, which makes no sense. Unless he's opened the trunk because he wants to deposit a body in there and the car's running for a quick escape.

I'm chilled to the bone as I creep closer. If I grab his keys, it will delay his departure, and if I can take him by surprise, knock him out with something, then call the police, we may have a chance at surviving this ordeal.

I gasp as Ned backs out of the front door, dragging something. More precisely, someone. It's Hope. He's bound and gagged her.

Bile rises in my throat, but I swallow it down. I have to make a move—now. But before I can do anything I see Lizzie slipping out the back door. There's a huge bruise on the side of her face and my heart clenches.

That monster hurt her.

She's crouching and scuttling toward the car, and I know she's had the same idea I have. Grab the keys, delay his departure. I assume my smart girl has called the police and they're on their way, so the longer we stall Ned the better.

She ducks behind the driver's door. Ned's too busy trying to subdue a wriggling Hope that he doesn't see Lizzie slip into the driver's seat, her manically determined expression reminding me of how I'd once been, willing to do anything to protect my girls.

Stunned, I realize what she's planning.

Lizzie isn't taking the car keys.

She's going to finish him.

FIFTY

LIZZIE

Ned's blow stuns me and I must've blacked out, because when I come to on the floor of Hope's bedroom, the house is eerily silent, and that's when my horror at what's happened morphs into panic.

He's taken Hope.

My head spins as I get up off the floor and I stagger a little, bracing myself against the wall. I don't trust Ned, so although the house is quiet, I stick my head around the corner of Hope's bedroom to see if he's lurking. He's not, but neither is Hope around, and that means he might've already left with her.

Fear makes me stumble as I sprint to the kitchen and see the back door wide open. I run toward it, seeing something that makes me duck out of sight.

Ned is hefting Hope on his shoulder like an animal carcass, and I swallow the feral growl that rumbles in my throat.

This madman, this demon who I was right about all along, is abducting my niece and there's no way in hell I'll let him get away with it.

I'll kill him before that happens.

The car is running, the driver's door wide open less than five feet from me, and I know I only have seconds to save Hope.

It comes to me in a flash, what I must do. It's outlandish. Ridiculous. Crazy. But I've spent my life protecting this precious girl and I'm not about to stop now.

Taking a deep breath, I crouch and make a run for it, skirting around the car, and dive into the driver's seat.

It breaks my heart when I hear a thud as he dumps Hope unceremoniously into the trunk.

That's my signal.

I slide the gearshift into reverse, waiting for the moment he slams the trunk shut. I jump when he does and watch him in the rearview mirror as he pushes on the trunk to make sure it's closed.

In that moment, I take my foot off the brake and floor the accelerator.

The thud of the bumper hitting him is oddly satisfying, but it isn't enough. I have to make sure he doesn't survive.

Because no way in hell will I do jail time for this psychopath if he survives and testifies to what I did. A jury will believe him too. They'll think I targeted him from the start. Max and Annie know I had misgivings about him from the first time we met in class. And Ned will have video footage of me stalking him at his home. Hazel will testify on his behalf, implying I'm mad. Then this, me running him over deliberately. And considering how he's been able to fool everybody for years, he'll make a convincing witness to my "insanity" if he chooses to spin it that way.

No, he can't live to tell anyone about this.

I won't give up my life for his.

I put the car in park and open the door, terrified of what I may see but needing to ensure I've done this right. I slink toward the trunk and my stomach falls when his head rolls slowly toward me and he has the audacity to grin.

My lungs seize and I can't breathe, but I don't have time to hesitate.

I'll never forget this moment when I make a conscious decision to end another person's life.

This will haunt me.

But I have to finish what I started.

This monster will never stop tormenting our family. Even if nobody believes what he says about me and he's convicted of his past crimes along with kidnapping Hope, he'll get out of jail eventually and he'll come hunting us.

I get back into the car, and do what any loving, protective aunt would do.

I put the car into gear and this time when I run over him, I make sure to get the job done.

FIFTY-ONE

BROOKE

When I'm not able to get hold of Lizzie or Hope on the phone, I speed the entire way home. Something isn't right, and if what Hazel said is true, my family is in serious danger.

And it could be all my fault, for bringing Noel into our lives. For that stupid letter. For all of it.

Will my daughter suffer for my mistakes?

Thinking about what could be happening to my girl renders me breathless. Nothing can happen to Hope. Not when we finally have a chance at being a real family.

As I turn into the driveway, I see Alice's car parked behind Lizzie's bungalow. Maybe Lizzie and Hope have been busy with Alice and that's why they didn't answer my calls?

A voice at the back of my mind whispers, *And maybe they never need to know what I did...*

But as I get closer to the main house, my heart stalls.

There's a body lying in the drive.

Lizzie and Alice are standing over it.

I screech to a halt, fling my door open, and run toward them, my heart in my throat the entire time. Until I get closer and see it's Noel, and my steps slow. Sorrow clutches my chest as I register his eyes are wide open, staring, unseeing. The man I've fallen for is dead. Yet another person I love gone too soon.

Tears pool and I dash them away with the back of my hand, aware I don't have time to grieve until I find out if Hope's okay.

My eyes meet Lizzie's and I know, deep in my gut, that whatever she did, it was to protect us.

"That's Ned, not Noel. He was taking Hope." A lone tear tracks down her cheek. "I couldn't let that happen."

"Thank you." I squeeze her arm, relieved and grateful that my sister did whatever she could to save my daughter. Gratitude and relief overwhelm me, and I can barely speak past the lump in my throat. "He can never hurt us again."

"Yes."

I only just hear her add, "I made sure of it."

"Where's Hope? Is she okay?"

Alice says, "She's in the trunk. He bound and gagged her."

Nausea swamps me at the thought of my poor girl being confined and abducted, and I move toward the trunk. However, Ned's body—I still can't comprehend I'm in love with a monster who fooled me totally—is in the way and if I pop the trunk now, Hope will have to step over him.

My daughter has been through enough and I don't want her to see Ned's corpse let alone have to be anywhere near it when she gets out of the trunk, but there'll be a police investigation and if I move the car, I'm tampering with evidence. Then again, if I don't move the car, there might be evidence to convict my sister of a crime she committed to save us.

As much as every maternal instinct is urging me to get Hope out of that trunk as soon as possible, it's a no brainer. Lizzie saved my daughter by doing the unthinkable. I need to save her.

"I'll move the car away from here and get Hope out," I say.

Our eyes meet again, and she knows what I'm doing.

I'm protecting her.

But in reality, I'm protecting Hope and me. The family I made, not the one I've been born into. Because while I care about Lizzie and Alice, it's Hope I love.

She is worth doing anything for.

Lizzie gives a brief nod and winces. She rubs the side of her head, where she's sporting a huge lump. "I've called the police. They'll be here any moment. I told them he knocked me out because he was going to abduct my niece, but when I regained consciousness, I ran outside to see him put Hope in the trunk, so I jumped behind the wheel to drive away, but in my panic, I accidentally reversed over him."

"That's what I saw too," Alice says, her voice tremulous. But there's a determined glint in her eyes, one I've seen many times growing up, when our protective aunt would warn us against the "wrong type of boy" or stand up to mean teachers. "I arrived in time to see Lizzie trying to save Ned by performing CPR, saying 'I didn't mean to do it, it was an accident' over and over."

I know that's not how it happened, but having Alice corroborate Lizzie's story will go some way in her favor when the police investigate.

And if they're right, and Ned has a record of criminal behavior, I'm hoping they'll see what happened as a blessing in disguise: one less psychopath to rehabilitate in a clogged prison system.

That's when the enormity of what we've potentially escaped hits me and a wave of anger obliterates any lingering ounce of sorrow.

The man I fell for was capable of horrendous crimes. How far would he have gone to get what he wanted, namely Hope?

A kernel of hatred unfurls deep inside and I embrace it. I need to cling to it, need to use it to help me forget how foolish I've been in trusting the wrong person yet again. What does that say about me? About my judgment?

How will I be a good mother if I can't identify threats against my daughter?

"Thank you for backing me up," Lizzie murmurs, shooting Alice a grateful smile, and she nods, determination squaring her shoulders. Despite all the bad our aunt has done, she's standing by us now, when we need her most.

"I'll get Hope out."

Lizzie nods. "The keys are in the ignition."

I move the car around the side of the house, out of sight of the body, and pop the trunk, nausea rising when I see the sheer terror in my daughter's eyes.

"It's just me, baby girl. You're safe now." My hands tremble as I carefully peel the duct tape from her mouth, loosen the rope knots binding her wrists and ankles, and help her out of the trunk.

When she's standing, she bursts into tears and launches herself at me. "Thanks for saving me, Mom."

Every muscle in my body stills and my heart expands.

It's the first time she's called me Mom.

As we hug each other tight and cry until we have nothing left, I'm grateful for the good to come out of the bad.

My daughter finally sees me as her mother.

All the pain of the past, all the lies, all the unnecessary deaths, need to be forgotten.

Because we finally, *finally*, have a future.

I can never let her find out that I put our lives at risk by reaching out to Noel when I returned to Martino Bay two years ago and discovered Freya had a child.

At the time, I'd seen an article in an online newsfeed about Noel Harwood being jailed for the manslaughter of his twin, and I remembered Freya mooning over Noel—or so she'd said, probably to throw me off, because in her warped mind she might've thought I'd make a play for him, despite me grieving for Eli at the time.

Who knows what went through my sister's head, but for some reason she told me she liked Noel—maybe because he was the good Harwood and she didn't want Aunt Alice forbidding her to see Ned, the evil twin—so when I saw that article, a light-bulb went off.

Freya had hidden her child's paternity. Understandable, as I found out a few weeks later, considering Riker and I are Hope's biological parents. But at the time I thought, what if I could do the right thing and reunite a father with a child he didn't know about?

I sent a letter to Noel in prison, never in my wildest dreams imagining I'd contacted Ned and put our entire family at risk.

I'd kept the sender anonymous with no return address but mentioned Noel might like to contact Freya Shomack in Martino Bay about her child, and had given Hope's age, assuming Noel would be smart enough to figure out the dates and the possibility of Hope being his.

Turns out, I was way off with my supposition, but hadn't given that letter a second thought, because if Noel ever showed up, I'd tell him the truth.

I thought he was the good twin.

But when Noel and I started dating, he never mentioned Freya. Even when I introduced him to Hope, he showed no signs of knowing of her existence, so I assumed the letter I sent two years ago before I learned the truth had got lost or waylaid in the prison system.

Little did I know I'd set off a chain reaction by reaching out to a monster.

While Ned already assumed Hope was his according to what his mother told Alice, I'd unwittingly confirmed his delusion by sending that letter.

I'll never forgive myself.

After what Lizzie said, that my note had caused Noel to have a meltdown, and Hazel outlining his plan to me earlier, it clicked. It wasn't my declaration of feelings that set him off. He must have recognized my handwriting. Because it was Ned who received my note in prison, and he had been playing me all along. Cozying up to me to get closer to Hope. And I'm angry all over again at how stupid, how trusting, I've been. I'm humiliated, a gullible idiot who put my family at risk. Worse, I'd ignored Lizzie's misgivings because I trusted the wrong person.

But I can't wallow in guilt. I have a daughter to raise. We've been given another chance and I have every intention of making it count.

I'll never let anyone find out what I did. What's one more secret in this family?

FIFTY-TWO

LIZZIE

As I pull into Alice's drive on the outskirts of Wilks Inlet, I see her silhouetted in the window. She's watching, waiting, and some of the tension holding me rigid eases. Of all the people to understand what I'm going through, she might.

It's been two days since I killed Ned, two days of police interviews, two days of trying to justify what I did, albeit to myself. Remorse floods me at the oddest of times, like when I'm drying my hair after a shower, or fixing pancakes for Hope. But then I remember what Ned was capable of, what he would've subjected my niece to if I'd let him escape, and I feel better.

Justifying my actions may eventually let me sleep at night and that's why I'm here. To tie up another loose end that's been bugging me. Alice came through for me in a big way, despite how I've treated her the last few years. The least I can do is thank her.

With a heavy sigh I park near the front door, and it opens before I'm out of the car. Alice looks well, with her gray-streaked brown hair pulled back in a low ponytail, foundation covering the wrinkles, and a new pink sweater I haven't seen before ending mid-thigh over jeans.

I clamp down on the urge to run to her for a hug as I used to —Alice gave the best hugs when I needed them growing up— and walk toward her, my steps sedate and steady, at complete odds with the nervous churning of my gut.

As I reach the porch and trudge up the steps, Alice beams and opens her arms. "It's so good to see you, my darling girl."

I smile and embrace her for a moment before stepping back, clamping down on the urge to cling to her and blubber. "How are you, Alice?"

Her face falls like it always does when I call her by her name and not "Mom" like I used to. Despite everything that's happened the last forty-eight hours, it's still too soon to revert to our previous relationship, before she lied to me about everything.

"I'm well, sweetheart, all things considered. You?"

"Can't complain."

She doesn't buy my flippant response, her scrutiny intense before she turns away and heads inside. I follow her into the house, the familiar aroma of stewed apples and chocolate chip cookies bringing tears to my eyes. She's baked foods I loved as a child—apple pie, cookies, red velvet cake, brownies—comfort food at a time I need comforting the most.

"Are you hungry?"

"Maybe later. I'd love a cup of chamomile tea though."

She nods, understanding the significance as she bustles into the kitchen and I follow her. "The perfect calming soother. I'll make us some."

In my teens, when I'd stress over homework, she started an evening ritual of brewing a pot of chamomile tea in a quaint teapot I gifted her one Mother's Day, dimming the lights in the dining room, where my stuff was strewn across the table, and sitting with me while we sipped tea, ensuring I took a break. I'd learned to value those times with her when she'd let me talk if I wanted, or we'd sit in companionable silence, sipping tea like old ladies.

I've deliberately blanked out memories like this the last two years, not willing to let Alice's good undermine the bad. I made a conscious decision to hate her, but now, I don't have the energy anymore. Maybe it's time to let the past rest.

"How's Hope? Brooke?" she asks.

"They're good. Exhausted, like I am from the interrogations, but Brooke isn't letting Hope out of her sight at home and Hope's starting to push back, which means she's getting stronger every day."

"That poor girl is so resilient after what she went through..." Alice pours boiling water into a teapot and places it in the middle of the table, alongside the brownies, which are tempting despite the churning in my gut for what we have to discuss. "She's lucky to have a quick-thinking aunt like you."

Her eyes are wide and shimmering with unshed tears and I blink back mine as my throat clogs. "How are you really, Lizzie? I know you. You're a wonderful, caring girl, and what you did must be weighing heavily on your conscience."

"I'm okay," I whisper, making a mockery of my rote response, when I burst into tears, the sobs I've been keeping at bay for two days bubbling up in a torrent.

"My sweet girl," she murmurs, cradling me in her arms, stroking my back in long, soothing sweeps. "It's okay. You did what any good Shomack woman would do. You protected what's ours. You saved Hope and that's all that matters."

Alice has always had a calmness about her that's contagious and my sobs peter out, leaving me feeling cleansed.

"But I'm a killer," I say, as she releases me to sit on the chair next to me. "And I think what upsets me most about that is this strange invincible feeling that won't go away. Like I'm capable of anything now. Is that wrong?"

Her eyes are kind as she shakes her head. "Of course not.

You're a strong woman who did what had to be done. Embrace that power. Nurture that confidence. It's liberating."

I mull Alice's words. She's right. I'm done being at the mercy of men like Grant and Ned. No one will ever hurt me, or the people I love, again.

"Thanks, Alice. For everything." For the first time in two years, I reach for her hand and hold it between mine, like I used to. "Thank you for backing me up with the police." My voice hitches. "For lying for me. I know we're family, but I haven't treated you as such for a while now and—"

"You don't have to say anything other than that, sweet girl. We're family. And that's what family does. We back each other. We support each other. Always." She squeezes my hand before slipping it out of mine and picking up the teapot to pour. "I love you and I hope we can work toward re-establishing a closer relationship."

I can't make any promises, but I nod. "I'd like that."

Because if there's one thing the last forty-eight hours has taught me, it's how I'll do anything to be a part of our family.

EPILOGUE
ALICE

The investigation into Ned's death is brief.

Once they hear the sham Ned perpetuated in assuming his dead brother's identity, Lizzie and Hope's account of his kidnapping plot, and my corroboration of Lizzie's story about her running over Ned accidentally, they're inclined to believe us. As a bonus, Hazel crumbled under police interrogation and reiterated Ned's plot to take his daughter and was charged with being an accessory.

It didn't hurt that once they started investigating Ned, they uncovered rapes and assaults in several states. Not to mention what he did to his twin, because they know now Ned's unhinged and that running over his brother couldn't have been an accident.

What the police don't know won't hurt them.

Because Ned didn't murder his brother.

I did.

I feel bad about it now, realizing I killed the wrong brother.

Because that night at Julia's, after Ned drove off, I thought it was him lying on the ground and I wanted to complete the job.

To ensure he never came after Freya and Hope, as his mother told me was his intention.

I had to protect my girls, so I drove over him. Aiming for the neck. Knowing that crushing vital arteries and nerves would ensure no chance of survival.

I'd seen it on TV years ago, on a crime drama, the perfect way to run over someone with the intent to kill but make it look like an accident. Thankfully, it had started pouring just after I arrived and the torrential rain didn't ease for hours, washing away the evidence of two different cars and varying tire track marks. I don't believe in karma, but I took that as a sign I'd done the right thing.

I feel bad for poor Noel, because from all accounts the young man I remembered had grown into a good guy. And who knows, if he'd lived, he could've testified against his brother and put him away for a long time.

But Ned would've been released eventually, and with him convinced Hope was his daughter, he wouldn't have stopped harassing my family. And if he'd succeeded in taking Hope, then done a paternity test and discovered she wasn't his, who knows what he would've done to her?

Ned was sick and he deserved to pay.

Do I feel remorse for killing the wrong twin first time around? Yes, but thankfully, Lizzie finally did the right thing and eliminated Ned.

My family is safe.

Now, three months since Ned's death, Hope and Brooke are closer than ever. Hope is thirteen now and the most resilient teen I know. She adores Riker too and I'm glad he has a chance to parent her alongside Brooke.

My niece is doing okay but she blames herself for bringing Ned into the fold. She's craving a relationship, and I hope she'll let love in when it eventuates. Brooke's a good person and deserves the best life has to offer; especially after I took so much from her.

Lizzie and I are making slow progress, but progress nonetheless. I've moved back to the family home I bought decades ago in Martino Bay, though not into the main house. Lizzie's still in one of the bungalows and I'm in the other, but I love it because I'm close to all my girls again.

We're one big happy family.

I intend to keep it that way.

Nothing or nobody threatens what's mine.

Because if they do, they'll pay the price.

A LETTER FROM NICOLA

Dear reader,

I want to say a huge thank you for choosing to read *My Sister's Boyfriend*. If you enjoyed it and want to keep up to date with my latest psychological thriller releases with Bookouture, just sign up at the following link. Your email address will never be shared and you can unsubscribe at any time.

www.bookouture.com/nicola-marsh

Some stories appear out of nowhere and that's exactly what happened with this one. When I wrote *My Sister's Husband*, it poured from my imagination to the page in 18 days. Readers loved the story and it's still a personal favorite.

But at the time, I never anticipated revisiting the characters. Fast-forward four years later, and Brooke, Lizzie, and Alice demanded they had more to tell, and this time, the words flowed just as fast. I wrote *My Sister's Boyfriend* in 17 days!

The twists and turns in their lives captured my imagination and I hope they capture yours.

Don't you love it when characters won't let you go?

I hope you loved *My Sister's Boyfriend*, and if you did, I would be very grateful if you could write a review. I'd love to hear what you think, and it makes such a difference helping new readers to discover one of my books for the first time.

One of the perks of this job is hearing from satisfied readers —you can find me on social media or my website.

Thanks,

Nicola

www.nicolamarsh.com

facebook.com/NicolaMarshAuthor
x.com/NicolaMarsh
instagram.com/nicolamarshauthor

ACKNOWLEDGMENTS

Writing is a solitary occupation, one that I love, but this book wouldn't make it into readers' hands without the help of many. My immense thanks to the following:

Jennifer Hunt, editor extraordinaire, for her encouragement when I reached out with "What if I wrote a sequel to *My Sister's Husband*?" Jen, your excitement for this story from the start when you read my synopsis has been great. Let's hope this one flies like the first. Love working with you.

Sinead O'Connor, your line edits were fabulous and helped me add layers to this story that made it stronger in the end. Great job!

Ian Hodder, for your excellent copy edits.

Elaini Caruso, for your eagle-eye proofreading skills.

Jen Shannon, for her proof production.

Jess Readett, Noelle Holten, Kim Nash, and the entire team at Bookouture, for the way you promote and champion my books.

Sandy Barker, our chat during a writers' lunch at The Harlow late last year sparked my imagination on the train ride home and this story was born as a result. I can't thank you enough for your brainstorming. Enjoy your travels around the world while writing your next fab story.

Heidi Catherine, we sat next to each other at the writers' lunch where the idea for this story came to life and I had a ball chatting all things publishing with you. Who knows where this crazy journey will take us?

Erica Made, your enthusiasm for books and publishing is unparalleled and I love our chats when I pop into Robinsons Bookshop.

Soraya Lane and Natalie Anderson, my writing buddies, we don't get to talk as often these days because deadlines and life gets in the way, but I know you're only an email away.

My folks, Millie and Ollie, for not giving me a sister like the crazy ones in my psychological thrillers!

My incredible boys, love you so much.

The librarians, the booktokers, the bookstagrammers, and book bloggers, thanks for promoting my work.

And for every single reader who picks up one of my books, takes the time to read, and leave a review, I appreciate you. Without your word-of-mouth recommendations, I couldn't keep doing this amazing job I love.

Until next time, happy reading!

PUBLISHING TEAM

Turning a manuscript into a book requires the efforts of many people. The publishing team at Bookouture would like to acknowledge everyone who contributed to this publication.

Audio
Alba Proko
Sinead O'Connor
Melissa Tran

Commercial
Lauren Morrissette
Hannah Richmond
Imogen Allport

Data and analysis
Mark Alder
Mohamed Bussuri

Editorial
Jennifer Hunt
Sinead O'Connor

Copyeditor
Ian Hodder

Printed in Great Britain
by Amazon

48915556R00152